Tasting Barcelona

JUNE PATRICK

FLORENCE & REYNOLDS

First Printing 2023

Florence & Reynolds Publishing

For Thomas and Zephyr. My adventure team for life.

Chapter One

The hum of the airplane engine served as the backdrop to my burgeoning excitement. Barcelona was just a red-eye flight away. The words "You've got the assignment" kept replaying in my mind like a looped film reel. After years of nudging Joanne, my senior editor, she had finally conceded that the eclectic and global food scene of Barcelona was mine to cover for *Travel Luxe & Leisure,* the exceedingly popular travel magazine-turned-website I wrote for in Manhattan. Spanish food, and Catalan food, in particular, deserved global attention. And I intended to give it just that.

I tried to contain my excitement about spending an entire glorious week in Barcelona. I had visited once right after high school with a tattered backpack and a money belt full of crumpled Euros and had fallen head over sneakers for Gaudí and Picasso and lazy strolls through winding cobblestone corridors. Back then, I was a penniless backpacker whose dining experience was largely vicarious—staring longingly at trendy restaurants from the outside while nibbling on a market *pa amb tomàqu*et and a wedge of cheese.

Times had most definitely changed. Now, I was traveling

on my company's dime and had some extra cash of my own. Don't get me wrong, being a food critic isn't exactly a gold mine, even in New York. I hate to break it to the aspiring Carrie Bradshaws of the world, but the glamorous life of journalism doesn't pay in Manolos. However, I managed to supplement my income inadequacy by creating my own brand with a popular blog and a large following on Instagram and TikTok. My personality and dry humor have given me a unique edge in a field known for acerbic commentary.

My following was steadily growing, and my reputation was undoubtedly blossoming. Sure, I was a tough critic, but it's a tough world out there. There's a lot of great food, no shortage of intriguing restaurant concepts, and plenty of creative designs. To stand out, you have to consistently bring your A-game. Being a critic isn't necessarily about how much you love the restaurants or their food. There are a lot of places I genuinely enjoyed, but if you throw around five-star reviews like confetti, you lose credibility, so you have to be discerning. I'm not intentionally harsh in my reviews, but brutal honesty is just something the industry has come to expect from me.

The magazine had entirely transitioned to a digital format last year except for quarterly special editions, reflective of changing reader habits. Print was a dinosaur, even when I'd first entered journalism a decade ago. People had warned me it was a dying field when I'd idealistically decided to major in it. But I had politely disagreed. It wasn't dying—it had simply evolved. When I first started, my niche had been to cover lifestyle topics—wine, food, fashion, and travel—because the world has enough gloom. Why add to it?

Then, I found my true calling in food.

At the end of the day, I love what I do. I adore food, restaurants, and good wine. I love the chaos of professional kitchens and chef's over-inflated egos—honestly, I pretty much think about food 24/7. To counterbalance this calorie-laden love affair, I jog about six miles daily. It's worth every step.

My phone pinged.

How excited are you? A text from Jas, a fellow writer at *Travel Luxe & Leisure*, popped up.

Pretty much over the moon, I texted back. I was fortunate enough to cover restaurants all around the U.S. and even a few internationally, but this was a major assignment for anyone.

Everyone is so jealous, she replied.

As they should be, I shot back with a wink emoji.

It would be a shame if you ate some bad paella your first day, and I had to fly out and replace you. Wink emoji.

I sent back a laugh emoji and hoped she wasn't actually sending me food poisoning vibes.

With an expanding international presence and increasing website popularity (we'd hit eight million total visits last month—the executives were popping the good stuff, I imagine), the magazine had been debating whether or not they should have people on the ground reviewing up-and-coming culinary hotspots in Europe. Getting the budget approved for this was a stretch, but my editor Joanne convinced the board there was something about having a well-known American writer speaking to the American audience that people would find more endearing.

I set down my phone and leaned back in my airline seat. I sipped down the dregs of my first glass of cava and sighed with contentment as I daydreamed about my first bite of paella—hopefully not poisoned. I heard the unmistakable sounds of the approaching food cart. Ahh, but first things first—the in-flight meal. My stomach grumbled in anticipation of the little microwaved dinner.

A flight attendant in a neat blue uniform and neck scarf, her dark hair pinned back, rolled the cart toward me. Her English came through a strong Spanish accent.

"Chicken or beef, señora?"

Embracing the spirit of the trip ahead, I tried out my rusty Spanish, "*Pollo, por favor.*"

She offered me a tight, polite smile. "*Muy bien.*" She pulled a meal tray from her cart and set it down in front of me.

"*Vino tino o blanco?*"

"Oh, um. *Tinto*. Por favor."

She nodded again and set a mini bottle of red wine and a plastic cup on the tray.

I unwrapped the foil to reveal a chicken breast and an assortment of colorful—slightly soggy—vegetables. It was accompanied by a bread roll and tomato paste, and a small chocolate pastry. I might have been in economy, but I felt as swanky as first class. I ventured a glance through the first-class curtain a few rows up and spied the attendant refilling champagne glasses with reckless abandon. Next time.

I refocused on my meal. I pulled out my phone and hit the record button. "The chicken," I began, talking more to myself than any potential online audience, "is... a valiant effort for 30,000 feet. The vegetables seem to be playing hide and seek — mostly hiding. And the dessert... Let's just say it's... optimistically flaky."

A chuckle from my left interrupted my musings. Turning, I met the amused eyes of my seatmate, a middle-aged man with ruddy cheeks and a thick mop of salt and sand hair.

"Feedback for the chef?" He was definitely American, sporting a Denver Broncos sweatshirt.

I blushed slightly. Sometimes I forgot I didn't live in this world alone.

"Sorry. I'm a food blogger. I'm just playing around." I set my phone down and felt my cheeks flush.

"A live performance," he said with a wide grin.

"Well, it's not an official review, but we'll see what this chicken does for me," I said teasing.

"I don't call myself a critic of much, but I do like food. Are you traveling for work?"

I felt my vibrations rise even confirming I was. "I am actually. I'm doing a piece on the Barcelona food scene for *Travel Luxe & Leisure*. It's this online magazine."

"No kidding! My wife—well, ex-wife now, I guess. She loves that magazine. Used to always have a print copy lying around. She always had a dream about traveling the world, eating food. If she was talking to me, I'd tell her I met you. She'd love your job."

His words were delivered with a grin that told me he wasn't too broken up about the whole thing.

I smiled. "Small world. What brings you to Barcelona?"

He let out a heavy sigh. "I'm retiring and decided to have one last hurrah before settling down in Florida. Figured I'd see some of the world while I still can. I'm Mark Cando, by the way." He extended a rough hand.

"Vera Stone."

"So what exactly you gonna write about?" Mark asked.

I sipped my wine—a surprisingly easy palate table red— and nodded. "Specifically, I'm looking at a few new concepts opening—innovative players that are shaking up the old guard."

"Sounds like you're living the dream."

My cheeks warmed. "It really is my dream assignment. I count myself among the lucky."

Mark smiled. "That's great. I love hearing about your people livin' their dreams." I smiled at the sentiment. Was thirty-two young? I went back and forth on the idea. As I watched my friends escape to the suburbs with shiny new husbands and squishy babies, trading subway passes for SUVs and cocktail parties for bouncy-house birthdays, I definitely felt age creeping up on me. But sometimes I looked at my editor, Joanne, late 40s, thriving career and the energy of a teenager, and I felt like a puppy on training wheels.

"Thanks, Mark. I hope you enjoy your retirement."

He shook his head and chuckled. "It's the thing we dream about, and the one day it's on you, and you think, hell, I got old fast. Enjoy your life, Vera. It goes by real fast."

I smiled and leaned back. I had every intention of it.

Chapter Two

"This is as far as I can go," the taxi driver said in slow, clipped English. Distracted, I looked up and out the window to see we were on a busy street connected to a series of narrow corridors.

"Oh? Is this where the hotel is?" I asked, scanning for an address among the indecipherable signs.

He offered an apprehensive smile and shook his head. "I'm afraid not. You'll need to walk a bit. See that alleyway? Follow it, make two right turns, and you'll find the hotel on the third corner."

I listened carefully, committing his directions to memory. The last thing I wanted was to look like a clueless tourist on day one. Um, *hello*, I was a sophisticated international food writer now.

"Thank you. Gracias," I said, paying the fare with my credit card before stepping out and pulling my suitcase behind me, trying not to let the cobblestones cause too much damage to the upscale pebble leather. My designer travel bag signaled how far I'd come from my backpacking days—it was actually a gift for receiving the *Golden Jet* award last year. Assignments had taken me to some pretty swank places—I'd been so fortunate—but navigating Spain's ancient uneven streets with my notebook in hand felt like I'd finally arrived.

I dragged my suitcase up the slight incline—grateful that I opted for my trusty broken-in Manhattan-approved sneakers. Finally, the historic hotel came into view. I knew that "historic" often meant "lacking modern amenities," but I'd read this one had been renovated, complete with air conditioning —a must in Europe's scorching summers. And even though we were about to technically step into fall, the sun was still blazing.

As I entered the lobby, a medley of aromas greeted me— rich spices, fermentation, warm pastries, cinnamon, and honey. My senses were instantly overwhelmed, and I felt the saliva pooling. Soft guitar music streamed overhead. The gentle babble of a fountain sang along from an old mosaic wall.

A woman in a simple black sheath dress rushed around the corner to greet me. "*Bienvenida a Casa Gòtic.*" A cascade of black hair was secured back with a tie, and she had long false lashes over wide brown eyes. Her name tag read Sandra.

"*Buenos dias. Um, yo tengo una reservación,*" I stumbled out.

She smiled understandingly. "Si. The name?"

"Vera Stone," I replied, handing over my passport.

With a few clicks-clacks of long false nails, she entered my information into the computer. "Yes, I see you here. Ahh, for the full week! How marvelous."

"I know it's a bit early, but I was hoping my room might be available."

She nodded. "Si, si. No one was there last night, so you can check in now."

I sighed with relief. The idea of killing time until the afternoon had been wearing on me.

"Are you here for work or holiday?" Sandra asked, rapidly typing into her computer.

"Work, actually. I'm a writer. I'm here covering your local food scene," I said, perhaps sharing too much, but with pride.

She paused, perhaps translating my words into Spanish, then smiled. "Our food scene is definitely up-and-coming."

"I'd argue it has already arrived," I countered.

She laughed lightly. "Si. So many good things to eat here. You must try *Pintxos Celia*. And *El Rincón de la Abuela*. Both are here in Barri Gòtic. Just up the street. Local favorites."

"Thank you, I will," I said, committing the names to memory.

"OK, here is your passport back, and here is our standard waiver. No smoking, no loud noises after 11. The usual, si?"

I jotted down my signature. She completed my check-in and handed me a copy of the contract outlining the hotel's policies. "Spanish breakfast is served until nine in the morning, and we offer afternoon wine. Feel free to join the other guests. Here's your key." She handed me an old-fashioned skeleton key. "You're on the fifth floor, with a view of the Gothic Quarter and a private terrace. It's small but quite charming, perfect for enjoying an evening glass of wine. Thankfully, the heat has finally let up—we nearly melted this summer. Oh, before I forget—" She reached for a cup and poured me a glass of vibrant red sangria from a large jar on the counter. Then, she handed me a small jar of olives. "We pickle these in-house. Compliments of Casa Gòtic."

"Thank you. This is perfect," I said. I slipped the olives into my handbag.

She beamed. "You can either take the stairs there at the end of the hall. Or take the lift. I am Sandra if you need anything at all."

"Gracias, Sandra."

I picked up my bag and headed toward the lift at the back

of the lobby, with ornate ironwork nodding to a bygone era. Pressing the button, I waited for what felt like an eternity for the tiny elevator to descend. The sound of clinking and rumbling filled the air as it landed on the ground floor with a thump, followed by a soft ding. The door opened to reveal a small interior gate. With some effort balancing my precious sangria and bags, I pushed the gate aside and stepped into the confining space.

An immediate sense of claustrophobia enveloped me—the elevator was scarcely large enough for both me and my suitcase, its faded velvet lining feeling almost oppressive. I pressed the button for the fifth floor and waited as the gate, and then the door, slowly closed, sealing off the airy lobby behind me. With an abrupt jolt, the elevator began its ascent. I closed my eyes and breathed. I'd been terrified of elevators ever since being trapped in a Manhattan high-rise car with an irate stock broker for nearly three hours last year in the dead of summer. I was trying to overcome my fear, but this tiny carriage wasn't doing me any favors. I closed my eyes and breathed as it painstakingly crawled up each floor.

The lift chimed, finally reaching the fifth floor with a slight jolt. A soft light illuminated the space as the door opened, and I exhaled a breath I hadn't realized I was holding. Small, confined spaces were definitely not my favorite.

Stepping into the hallway, I heaved a sigh of relief and felt a sense of accomplishment for having survived the elevator ride. So far, the trip was off to a stellar start.

I found my room at the end of the hall and slipped the ancient key in, feeling like I was entering a secret room. The little suite was small, yes, but elegantly furnished with antique pieces that oozed history. A gold-framed mirror on the wall caught my eye, reflecting the ornate chandelier hanging from the ceiling. An aged, red Persian rug covered the creaky wooden floor, lending a warm touch to the room.

And the view—Sandra wasn't lying, it was breathtaking. Large windows framed not only Barcelona's historic Gothic Quarter but also a panoramic sight of the ocean, all the way to the distant, shadowy hills. Ships glided across the sparkling water, and terracotta rooftops created a vivid, romantic landscape below me. I allowed myself a long moment to sip sangria and stare out into the horizon, pretending that this was my everyday life.

I began unpacking, placing my limited wardrobe on hangers in the compact armoire and storing other items in cleverly hidden drawers beneath the windowsill. As someone who hated to check bags on flights, I'd learned to be a light packer—a couple of key pieces that folded nicely, didn't wrinkle, and could be mixed and matched. A pair of trusty walking shoes and, for this trip, one pair of evening-appropriate heels.

The bathroom, though one of the smallest I'd ever seen, was surprisingly efficient. A clever array of built-in shelves housed toiletries, and the shower, despite its petite size, featured an ingeniously designed rainfall showerhead. I checked my reflection and shuddered at the travel-weary reflection. My carefully constructed "messy" bun now looked more like a dark brown bird's nest that angry crows had picked apart. My blood-shot blue eyes had a lovely black-eye effect from smudge-proof mascara that had been tested to the limit over the past twenty-four hours, and all of my foundation had rubbed off on an airplane pillow hours ago. But who cares—I WAS IN BARCELONA!

I washed my face and brushed the fur from my teeth, then went back out into the little sitting area. I pulled out my leather-bound notebook—the one with the vintage metal clasp I'd picked up from an artisan shop in Soho, the one I adored and carried everywhere. It was my third refill of pages since I'd purchased it. Every thought about food and work went into this journal. I set it on the antique mahogany bedside table, its polished surface gleaming in the soft light, and gave it a good-luck tap.

Here I was, living my dream assignment. I had to pinch myself to believe it. I popped a couple of the house-pickled olives into my mouth, savoring the mix of brine and smooth texture. Could I call down for another glass of that incredible sangria? I was elated but also tinged with a slight panic. A lot rode on this assignment—both personally and professionally. My usual doubts crept in—was I an imposter? Did they make a mistake in choosing me for this story?

Shaking off the negative thoughts, I took a deep breath, glancing once more at the extraordinary view. No, this assignment was mine, and I was going to kill it.

I stepped out onto my terrace and surveyed the tableau below.

Barcelona absolutely brimmed with life below. I glanced down at the narrow lanes, wide pedestrian-friendly boulevards with bustling market halls. In the distance, I could see the horizon of an elegant modern uptown area and then, on the other side, a long beach promenade peppered with tiny people and restaurants. Certain aspects of this cosmopolitan corner of Spain instantly wrapped my memories in a warm embrace— the Gaudí architecture, the bustling markets, and the omnipresent FC Barcelona paraphernalia.

However, other elements seemed grander and more vivid than even my nostalgia could recall.

Barcelona has always been renowned for its rich culinary tradition, but in recent years, the city had evolved into a gastronomic playground catering to every palate. From the simple delights of street food to the opulent luxury of Michelin-starred restaurants, the city had become a global mecca for foodies, and I couldn't wait to dive in.

Officially, I was reviewing only three restaurants, but I was determined to sample as many as possible. After all, I needed a broad basis for comparison, didn't I? I could spend a lifetime here and barely scratch the surface of what this vibrant city had to offer.

My stomach rumbled, and a sudden wave of hunger-induced nausea came over me. First thing—I needed something to eat immediately. Between terrible airport food, too many mini-cocktails overnight, and the jetlag, I suddenly had a pounding headache to go with the stomach complaints. I filled up my water bottle and chugged the entire thing. Then I freshened my makeup, slid on some deodorant, and pulled my black hair back up into a messy top knot. I grabbed my notebook and day bag and went out in search of my first victim—I mean restaurant.

Chapter Three

Jetlag was absolutely awful. It didn't matter how seasoned of a traveler you were, or how well you planned it all out, you were always just going to feel wretched for at least a day following your arrival. And mine was definitely kicking in with a vengeance as exhaustion and hunger conspired with time zones to ruin me. With a groggy head, I shakily followed my Google Maps directions through the old town until I came across El Rincón de la Abuela, one of the places Sandra had recommended.

I had Googled it and read that while it wasn't anything terribly unique, the reviews online had promised authentic Spanish comfort food. Apparently, it had been slinging up traditional Spanish omelets for thirty years, and that was exactly what I was in the mood for after my long journey.

From the outside, the restaurant was unassuming—a worn, wooden door barely hanging onto its hinges, framed by walls adorned with weathered tiles in floral designs. Yet, as I pushed the door open, the atmosphere seized me with immediate warmth.

But glancing around and witnessing the unfolding chaos, I

decided to give him the benefit of the doubt. Everybody has bad days, I suppose.

I scanned the menu and was delighted to find classic Spanish favorites listed—Patatas Bravas. Arroz Espanola. And of course, paella, just to name a few. I mentally calculated what dishes I was going to savor, then scanned the small wine list and picked out a mid-range glass. And then I waited. And waited. And waited some more. After what felt like an hour, but was probably fifteen minutes, I was finally greeted by a panicked-looking waiter.

"Do you know what you want?" he asked rapidly in English. I guessed I stood out as not being a local.

"Yes, I think so. But I had a few questions. Could you—" He shook his head before I could finish asking my questions.

"Sorry, I don't have time for that. Do you know what you want or not?"

I blinked. Was he really going to be so rude? But the look on his face told me that, yes, he was, and I could get on board or not. I chose to get on board because my insatiable hunger dictated.

"Okay, fine. I'll go with the Gambas al Ajillo and the Vegetable Tortilla. And a glass of Crianza." I slid the menu toward him.

He didn't even acknowledge my order before rushing off.

Well, that was a whole new level of rudeness, even for Europe.

Another server rushed my wine over and at least offered me a smile as she set it down.

I had nearly drained my glass before my dishes arrived. The portions were generous, and the smells were delicious. But when I bit into them, there was something lackluster. The shrimp were a bit rubbery, the potatoes in the tortilla were a little mushy. It felt like they had been sitting out under a heat lamp, growing soggy and stale. I could taste the potential, but they had missed the mark on execution—or they really had been sitting under a warmer while I drank on an empty stomach. I debated saying something but, looking around, realized that it would get me a whole lot of nowhere. So, I haphazardly shoveled the food into my mouth and drained the last few drops of my wine. Finally feeling satiated and somewhat more relaxed, I considered ordering a second glass and perhaps something from the *dulce* menu. I waited for my waiter to return, but after a few minutes, I finally waved my hand in the air to flag him down. The look he shot me was pure vitriol.

Exasperated, he asked, "Si?"

"I get that you're busy," I said. "But there's no need to be rude. I just wanted to order a second glass of wine. Do you do second glasses of wine?" I felt my irritation mounting as he basically glared at me.

"American *turista*," he muttered.

I perked up. "What was that?"

He shook his head. "Nada. More wine, si. You're just always very demanding."

I leaned back, completely offended. "I see. I'm so sorry to have disrupted you with my business and American money."

My exhaustion was fueling my anger, but seriously, he needed to be beaten over the head with the customer service handbook.

My words seemed to register in his expression, but he said nothing more. He returned quickly with my glass of wine and my check. I dropped the appropriate euros onto the tray, finished my wine, and headed back out into the Barcelona night. Maybe it was the jet lag or my overall sour mood, but I was freakishly upset by the interaction. I ate in restaurants all the time, like *all the time*, and I had never been treated so rudely. And it wasn't just because people knew who I was. Most places understood the basic concept of a customer.

I pulled out my phone, snapped a photo of the restaurant,

and then typed out a post on my Instagram: "The Importance of Customer Service."

"How was it?"

I looked up to see an impeccably put-together, statuesque blonde woman standing beside me, eyes lingering on the restaurant's facade. Her oxblood dress was well-tailored, skimming a tall, trim frame. She sported classic beige pumps and a very expensive-looking but discreet leather tote bag. I did not miss the glittering platinum and diamond Rolex on her thin wrist. Goals, Vera. Goals.

"Hmm?" I said dumbly, distracted by her perfection.

"The restaurant. Did you eat here? I read it's a local favorite, and I was curious if it was good?" She had a crisp German accent.

"Oh. Yes. I did. And it was…Well, to be quite honest, I've had much better. Both in service and food."

She pursed her lips—painted the exact reddish shade of her dress. "Mmm. That's too bad. I had high expectations. *Wie das so ist.*"

She said nothing more as she meandered down the street. I turned back to my phone and hit "Post."

Chapter Four

Rafa looked around at his creation. Everything was exactly how he had envisioned it when he first dreamed up this dream a decade ago, sketching out concepts on bar napkins. Back then, he had been just an ambitious culinary student, glued to epicurean websites and travel shows. He practiced day in and day out. He hosted dinner parties just to try out new recipes on his friends. He even cooked Sunday dinners for his mom, who, with extraordinary culinary talent of her own, gracefully humored him. Now, here he was, finally in his very own restaurant in the heart of Barcelona, the city of his birth. The city of his soul.

The clink of dishes rattled in the background as the kitchen staff practiced the recipes. The front-of-the-house staff was reviewing table set-ups and menus with his front-of-the-house manager, Juan. Saffron and paprika permeated the air with a smokey perfume.

He had painstakingly gone over every detail, tasted every ingredient, and personally shopped for ingredients at the farmers' market. It hadn't been easy. Barcelona's food scene had exploded in the last decade, and competition was fierce. Finding investors had been a challenge. What made him special, after all? What made any artist special, really? Because that's what he was, at least in his own mind. A chef was an artist. Sure, they had reputations for being arrogant and lost in their own worlds, but like any painter, writer, or musician, they were dedicated to their craft. The way flavors blended together. Different aromas. Slight variations in an herb or spice. The pairing of food with certain wines or even non-alcoholic beverages. There was a delicate dance to it all, a very fine art form. He also loved the imperfections. You could do your best to replicate a recipe over and over, like a chain restaurant, but you could also let your creativity fly and see what happens. Sometimes those were the best dishes, the ones created when he just went with his gut. Sometimes they were also the biggest disasters, but that was the fun of life, wasn't it?

He'd finally found the right backers who saw his vision and believed in him. His team believed in him. Most days, *he* believed in him. But now he had the daunting task of actually delivering.

Now came the tricky part. As the eve of the grand opening approached, he was terrified that no one would actually show up. He had hired a local publicity firm to generate some buzz —that stupid word his general manager, Lorna, wouldn't stop saying. Their budget was limited, and the cash he did have, he'd rather see turned into quality ingredients and not Facebook ads. But, while he knew they had good backing, most restaurants failed. And even those that were successful struggled to turn a profit within the first few years. If he was honest with himself, he knew that most restaurants, if they wanted a chance of survival, needed a small miracle. He'd bet his entire life's savings on receiving that miracle. If it failed—he wasn't sure what he would do.

"Hallo, boss!" Lorna burst into the room like a flash of

light. She sported a black linen jumpsuit with chunky red boots. Her bleached blonde bob was held back with a bright red headband, revealing eclectic earrings that looked like they were made from mosaic tiles. Hailing from some little town near London, she'd come to Barcelona to attend university and never left. She was funky, edgy, and creative, but also had a good business sense that kept Rafa grounded. And she had an uncanny ability to stay positive when they were in the weeds. Something his broody artist brain desperately needed for balance. When she'd applied for the job two years ago—during the absolute start-up phase—he'd practically tried to talk her out of taking the job, going on about the chaos and stress sure to ensue in the coming years. She had just grinned and asked about holiday compensation.

She was the perfect partner to help him open the next trendy place in *Barri Gòtic*, Barcelona's historic Gothic Quarter, and what he considered the pulsing heart of his city.

"Hola, Lorna," Rafa said, noticing something in her eyes. "*Que paso?*"

She set her oversized bag down and exhaled sharply. "Okay, so don't freak out. This is either a really good thing or a completely terrifying thing. Probably a bit of both." She spoke quickly, a sign she was nervous.

"Okay. What is it, then? Don't keep me in suspense."

She took a deep breath. "Fine. There's this really famous food blogger coming to Barcelona."

Rafa almost laughed, thinking she had to be joking. Bloggers were on every corner in Barcelona.

"So?"

"No, listen," she hurried on. "I know what you're thinking: 'Who cares? Just another food blogger with an Instagram.' But she's not like that. She's a senior writer for *Travel Luxe & Leisure*. It's this online magazine with a crazy fan base."

"Si, I know it. Of course, I know of it."

"Right. Ok, so this particular writer, she's good. Really good. Also, super harsh. She's one of those reviewers who can make or break a restaurant."

"Ok—"

"And Mari, our publicist, told me she's put Santos California on the list for her feature of new and innovative Barcelona concepts."

Rafa felt his heart rate escalate. This was, as Lorna put it, either a miracle or a disaster.

"Well, *mierda*," Rafa said.

"Yeah, mierda," Lorna agreed with a laugh. "But, if she writes a glowing review of Santos California for *TLL*? Can you even imagine?"

"Yeah, but if she hates it, we're screwed," Rafa said.

"Always looking on the bright side," Lorna said, rolling her eyes.

Rafa picked up a random polishing rag and began mindlessly polishing a wine glass. "How does she even know about us?"

Lorna shrugged. "Mari is the best, I told you. You still refuse to believe how much buzz there is about this place right now."

"*Buzzzz*," Rafa said like a bumblebee.

Lora simultaneously shook her head. And rolled her eyes. "Rafa—I don't know what to do with you sometimes."

"Love me unconditionally. I am quite broken."

"Don't I know it. Barcelona is the hottest Western food scene right now, and this girl—Vera is her name—posted on her blog that she's excited to finally get the assignment. And that she'd be coming *here.*"

Rafa ran his hands through his sweaty hair. This added a whole new layer of heart-attack potential.

"If the pressure to be perfect wasn't on before, it certainly is now," Rafa said.

Lorna offered him a reassuring smile. "It's going to be okay, Rafa. This place is amazing. You are so talented, the food is genius, the atmosphere is wonderful, and the location is perfect. What could go wrong?"

"Do you really want me to answer that? Because I can make you a list." Right then, all the potential disasters raced through his mind.

Lorna let out a clipped laugh. "Relax. Just do what you do best, and you'll impress her."

Rafa pretended to hate her down-to-earth calm, but it was admittedly usually just what he needed. For all his surliness and anxiety, Lorna was a counter bubble of positivity, creativity, and joy.

"Si, si. You take care of the operations, and I'll take care of the food," Rafa said.

"That's the deal we have, isn't it?"

Rafa took a deep breath and nodded, his mind already racing with the possibilities of what this reviewer could do for his restaurant. A glowing review from *TLL* could bring in a tidal wave of new customers, all eager to try out his new concept that not everyone was pleased about. The traditionalists got twitchy when you started messing with traditional recipes. But he couldn't let himself get too caught up in that possibility. As Lorna said, he had to just focus on the food, on making sure that every dish that left his kitchen was a masterpiece in its own right.

He grabbed his notebook and pen, flipping through the pages until he found the paella recipe he had been working on for the past week. It was a dish he was particularly proud of, one that he had put his heart and soul into. He had tested and tweaked the recipe until it was perfect, and he knew that it had the potential to be a showstopper. It was an outside-the-box take on the classic with *pulpo* and he wasn't sure he'd been ready to try it out, but now he thought it was a sign.

"*Vale*," he said, determination in his voice. "Let's get to work."

Chapter Five

Absolutely wrecked from almost twenty-four hours of global travel and no sleep, I passed out for a glorious twelve hours my first night. I woke rested, rejuvenated, and absolutely famished. I mean, I was pretty much always famished, but this felt a little extra—maybe my body's preparation for the culinary adventure before me.

After a Spanish breakfast in my hotel, which is basically just espresso, fresh orange juice and some *pa amb tomàquet*, I set out to explore. Wandering through the labyrinthine streets of the Barri Gòtic, memories rush at me. Eighteen with a battered backpack and a used guidebook. Freshly graduated from high school in Nowhere Special upstate New York with dreams of world travel. I waved at my past self through time.

"You made it, Vera," I smiled at myself in a shop window. Then I smiled wider when I saw the display of *napolitana de chocolate,* otherwise known as a chocolate croissant. I'll take two, please.

Licking my fingers of the chocolaty, flaky pastries, I found myself standing in front of the bustling Mercat de la Boqueria, or simply La Boqueria as locals called it. Perfect. I remembered being here as a starry-eyed backpacker, drooling over the delicacies, strange and familiar, and I'd been dreaming of returning ever since. Even with its popularity, it still felt like a beating heart of Barcelona—a canvas of colors and textures.

The market's atmosphere was an intoxicating blend of aromas—freshly ground coffee mingled with the sweet tang of ripe oranges and strawberries. The briny smell of fresh seafood clashed and combined with the earthy musk of newly harvested vegetables. There was a raw, yet invitingly fragrant undertone of herbs—rosemary, thyme, and saffron—that wafted through the air, as if a choir of spices had erupted in a joyous hymn.

I strolled each corridor, marveling at the plethora of wares. Not just food, but colorful silk scarves and woven baskets. Incense and candles and pottery. I stopped to smell a hand-dipped candle oozing amber and cinnamon.

A cacophony of sounds enveloped me. The rhythmic chopping of knives against wooden cutting boards served as a base layer, accompanied by the syncopated harmony of haggling in passionate, guttural Spanish, which I only half-understood. An old woman, her face etched with wrinkles like the rings of an ancient tree, sang a haunting melody from a small corner stage. Her voice blended with the modern laughter and shouts of vendors trying to hawk their wares. I closed my eyes and leaned into the music—a ghostly flamenco lullaby that transported me to a different world.

I passed stalls loaded with pyramids of fresh fruit, a vibrant rainbow of colors catching the sunlight filtering through the market's canvas roof. Strawberries the size of small plums blushed deep red, gleaming canary yellow lemons, and dewy purple grapes. I couldn't resist—the allure was too magnetic. I bought a small basket of cherries and savored each juicy bite as I strolled.

"*Senorita! Pan fresco!*" A vendor shouted as I passed a bakery stall. The yeasty smell of warm bread assaulted me. I stopped in my tracks. Maybe I needed more bread like a hole in the head...but maybe I just *needed* more bread.

"Buenos dias," I said, eyeing the mountain of bread before me.

"Which do you like? I give you two for one because you are so beautiful."

I laughed at how cheesy he was but he just grinned a crooked smile as though he knew very well how he appeared. "How could I resist?" I said. "Give me your favorites."

He nodded with immense satisfaction and eyed his display. He plucked up a long baguette-style loaf. "You must have a classic Pan de barra. And I think..." he tapped his finger against his round chin, thinking. Then he selected a crusty round loaf dusted with flour. "Si. And Pan Gallego."

He wrapped the two loaves in brown paper and passed them to me. "Three Euro, por favor."

I almost wanted to laugh at the reasonable sum for fresh artisan bread. I handed over the bills with thanks.

As soon as I was around the bend, I tore off a chunk and popped it into my mouth. I closed my eyes in ecstasy. I half wondered if human-baguette marriage was legal in Catalunya.

A couple of steps further, and I landed in the seafood section. Squids with their spiral, ghostly forms lay next to orange-red prawns as large as my hand. Octopuses sprawled lazily on beds of crushed ice, their tentacles curled in a final, frozen dance. A fishmonger, animated and smiling, saw my awe and began gesticulating wildly and shooting off rapid-fire Spanish that I assumed was extolling the freshness of his fish. I couldn't quite understand him, but his enthusiasm needed no translation. I had no idea how to cook octopus myself, but I silently asked the universe to find me someone who could because I really needed more octopus in my life, like immediately.

I turned, distracted, and crashed into someone.

"*¡Ay, perdón!*" he exclaimed, his hands instinctively reaching to steady the basket of cherries that had nearly toppled from my grasp.

"No, *perdón yo,*" I replied, catching my breath. I steadied myself and looked forward—right into a chest. I then looked up—and up—as I noted how tall my accidental dance partner was. He was also absolutely gorgeous with a warm complexion with undertones of Mediterranean sun, a perfect canvas for the slight ruggedness that dusted his features. His hair was a dark tousled mess with just a hint of sunstreak. It suited him, framing his face with an air of casual nonchalance as if he'd just stepped off a beach. His eyes were a blend of sea-foam green and the soft gray of a stormy sky. *Annddd* I would be remiss if I didn't mention the way his forearms actually bulged. He wore a well-fitted shirt, sleeves rolled up to his elbows. He'd paired it with slightly distressed jeans, adding a raw edge to his overall look. The overall result told a story of a man who wasn't afraid to get his hands dirty. He smiled half-amusedly at my dumbstruck gawking, and I yanked my gaze away.

"Sorry, I was distracted," I said. "Um, *distraída,*" I tried. His smile grew wider.

"I speak English, it's ok," he said in perfect accented English.

"Oh. Wonderful. Well, um. I'm sorry. I was distracted."

"You keep saying that."

I laughed nervously and tucked hair behind my ears. Then I glanced down to his basket, eyeing the gelatinous octopus with bulging eyes. Well, hello, Universe. Look at the octopus. "That would make an excellent *pulpo a la gallega*," I said. The words were out of my mouth before I could even process them. He looked at me curious, then grinned.

"An expert opinion from a beautiful stranger, huh? Well, *pulpo a la gallega* sounds good, but have you ever tried octopus in a paella?" His accent was smooth and velvety with that slight lisp that Spaniards have.

I tilted my head. "Hmm. That's a bold move."

He tilted his head inquisitively as though mirroring me. "Are you a paella purist?"

"Undecided. I've only just arrived in Barcelona."

"Well, Señora, food, like life, is about mixing things up, isn't it? Why not an octopus paella?"

I folded my arms. "And here I was thinking paella was sacred in Spain."

He bobbed his head. "It's sacred in Valencia, si. But we don't like to follow the rules here in Barcelona. Rules get very dull."

I shrugged. "Well, who am I to argue with a daring... seafood connoisseur?"

He flashed me a look of feigned indifference. "I prefer the term 'seafood enthusiast'. 'Connoisseur' is just so... *stiff*."

The way he said the word made me blush. *Dios mio*, when did I become a teenager?

I chuckled. "Well, Senor Seafood Enthusiast, here's to mixing things up. Perhaps one day I'll taste this blasphemous octopus paella of yours."

"Please do." He reached into his pocket and produced a small business card. "I know just the place."

I took the card and sucked in a breath.

Rafa Santos, Chef and Owner
Santos California

I looked up. "This is your place?"

"Si. It's opening in two weeks. See you there, hopefully. If you are still in Barcelona. *Mucho gusto.*"

"Mucho gusto," I said in barely a whisper as he walked off, realizing I hadn't actually given him my name.

I swallowed a lump as he sauntered off with his haul. Well, that just got a whole lot more complicated.

Chapter Six

My head was in the puffy marshmallow clouds as I strolled down a winding alley of the historic Gothic quarter. Barcelona was a bustling, vibrant city full of life, full of sensory experiences. But this was my favorite neighborhood. It had been fifteen years ago, and it was keeping a strong hold on its position.

Rafa, the octopus chef, was occupying a little too much real estate in my mind, and not because of his delicious features. No, because his restaurant was the top reason I was in Barcelona. And the fact that the proprietor looked like he had just stepped off a sexy chef calendar was quite inconvenient.

As I turned a corner, a window display of incredibly artistic little tapas caught my attention. I stopped to admire the way they were artfully displayed, seemingly begging me to pluck one right through the glass. I glanced at the sign and saw that, while the place was empty, it was open. I noticed the name:

Pintxos Celia. I laughed. This was the other place the hotel concierge, Sandra, had recommended. Hopefully, it would be more hospitable than the last place.

I pushed open the aged, wooden door, a rich patina betraying its decades of service as the gatekeeper to this little hideaway. The warm glow of antique lanterns bathed the interior, casting playful shadows that danced along the walls. Faint rhythmic flamenco music resonated in the background. It was a compact space, but every nook and cranny of the establishment told a story—Gaudi-inspired mosaics adorned the floor, leading me through a labyrinth of family portraits gracing the earth-toned walls.

My senses perked up at the smell of sauteed garlic.

"Buenas tardes," a sweet, female voice said from the back.

"Buenas tardes," I replied.

A woman emerged from the back and took her position behind the small tapas bar. A mess of inky curls were piled into a messy bun, and she sported a flowing floral maxi dress with a nipped waist.

"*Bienvenida a Pintxos Celia*," she said.

"Gracias. Are you Celia?" I asked in English, then tried to phrase it in Spanish. "¿Tú eres Celia?"

She laughed. "Sí, I am. This is my little place. Por favor, have a seat or help yourself to the pintxos. Do you know how it works?"

I eyed the display of small skewered delicacies. I recalled my experience with them the last time I was in Spain. "I think so. You select the ones you want, and then you keep your toothpicks for the end?"

She nodded. "Sí. It's very simple."

"And very traditional," I added.

She tilted her head and studied me, then shrugged. "Si, it's how we've been doing things here for a long time. Why change?"

I laughed at the way she said it. There was no defensiveness —just a simple acknowledgment of her approach, like she couldn't care less one way or another which way the culinary tides were turning.

I selected a couple of delectable options, ranging from bite-sized salty fish on crostini to a golden, buttery potato morsel drizzled with something bright red. I settled into a small high-top table next to the window and gazed out at the bustling afternoon passing by. It was a quiet street off the main drag, but plenty of people were still strolling about.

"Would you like some wine to go with it?" Celia called over.

"I couldn't possibly refuse," I replied.

Without asking me what kind I wanted, she brought over a bottle of chilled white wine. She filled a small glass and set it in front of me.

"This is the best wine for the pintxos you've selected," she informed me, putting the cork back into the wine.

"Is that what these are? *Pintxos*?" I asked, saying the word awkwardly. "Not tapas?"

"They are not exactly tapas, no. Tapas are more like smaller versions of larger meals—tortillas, patatas bravas. Pintxos are small snacks like this. The word actually means 'spike,' hence the toothpick," she made gestures with her hand while she spoke.

"Well, they're incredible. Thank you."

"Are you American?"

I nodded hesitantly. "Is it that obvious?"

She laughed. "You say that like it's a bad thing. Nothing

wrong with being an American. Nothing wrong with people knowing you're American."

I laughed shyly. "Thank you. I suppose we all need a little validation from time to time. I'm Vera."

"Mucho gusto, Vera. I hope you enjoy. I'll be in the back if you need anything," she said as she started to leave, but then hesitated.

"Would you like to sit with me?" I offered. "There's nobody here, and I wouldn't mind hearing a bit more about the restaurant and the neighborhood."

She looked at me with a little surprise, her thick eyebrows raised over wide hazel eyes, but then smiled and nodded. She wiped her hands on the small black apron tied around her waist and slipped into the chair opposite me.

"Si. Why not? This is the dead hour, as you can see. How do you like them?"

"They are fabulous. I love the flavor combinations. Are these your own recipes?" I sipped my crisp white wine, noting how it brought out the richness of the little salty fish.

She shrugged. "More or less. But honestly, they are all favorites of our community. We've been making these kinds of things at family parties forever. Every bar in Barcelona carries something similar."

I studied her. She was young to own her own place, probably in her late 30s. She was quite pretty with long false lashes and thick, wing-tipped eyeliner in contrast to an otherwise fresh-face earthy look.

"You're very humble about your work," I observed.

"Is it humility to be just honest?"

"Yes, I think so. Most restaurateurs and chefs want to wax lyrical about how they are the best thing since sliced baguette."

She let out a genuine laugh. "That is apt. Do you work in the restaurant business, then?"

"Sort of. To be very honest, I'm a restaurant critic."

Her eyes went wide. "Oh," she said, surprised.

I shook my head. "Don't worry, I'm not here undercover or anything. I was honestly just walking by and was intrigued by your window display. I had to come in. And actually, my hotel's concierge recommended you, too."

"Si? Which hotel?"

"Casa Gòtic. Her name is Sandra."

Celia looked touched. "Ah. Sandra. Si. She's the best. And I'm honored. Are you here for work then?"

"Yes. I'm based out of New York, but I'm here on assignment. I'm writing a piece about the traditional food scene contrasted with the more modern, fusion-style restaurants that are popping up. Barcelona is becoming quite the foodie central. A real talk of the online town."

She pursed her lips. "*Si, yo se*. Seems like every day there's some new trendy spot popping up, even in the seedier neighborhoods. Visionaries are coming in and making trendy bars out of places angels fear to tread."

I laughed. "I like the way you phrased that. How do you feel about that?"

She looked at me slyly. "Off the record?"

"I'm not really that kind of journalist, but sure. Off the record. Just between you and a fellow food lover."

"This is not a popular opinion for us locals, but honestly, I think there's room for everyone. There are millions of people here, and even more come as tourists every day. Everybody has different preferences, so I say, why not let everyone just do their own thing? People get really worked up about it, like the integrity of our recipes is something to fall on the sword for. It always seems like a bit of wasted energy."

"I've noticed some rivalry. Maybe some of the old guard feels a little threatened?"

She drummed her fingers against the table, then nodded. "Si, I think so. But there's really no reason to be. If you're new to Barcelona and you're here on vacation, you're looking for something that's authentically Spanish, aren't you?"

"I would think so."

"Right, so that's where a place like mine comes in. Do you want an authentic pintxos experience? Then you come here. Or you want traditional Catalan dishes and tapas, you go to say *Cocina Vila*. The owner Martí has been doing the same thing for years, but he's famous for it. But if you're a local who's lived here your whole life, maybe you're sick of tapas, you know? It doesn't make you any less Spanish to not want to eat Patatas Bravas one day."

I laughed. "I don't know. I live in New York. You can literally get anything you ever crave at any hour. Honestly, it's a little overwhelming. Sometimes I wish my options were more limited."

Celia looked wistful. "New York. I have always wanted to go there."

I smiled. "I hope you get to."

She went on, clearly passionate about the subject. I could obviously relate. "There are some really great traditional restaurants here. And those people should be very proud. We have a long, beautiful culinary history. But that doesn't mean people can't experiment. I don't know." She shrugged.

"Have you heard of that new place, Santos California?" I asked, picturing the enigMartíc octopus chef and trying not to smile.

"Oh, sí. A lot of people are talking about it. It's supposed to be very innovative. The chef is young and very talented— Rafa Santos."

"Do you know him?"

"Un poco. We are acquainted through the industry. He's becoming something of a celebrity. You should have seen him at the farmer's market last week. Surrounded by people." She waved her hands wildly. She had a very animated demeanor that warmed me.

"Is that right?"

She grinned wickedly. "Have you seen him?"

I shook my head, then corrected myself. "Well, yes. I met him by chance this morning at the market. But we only talked for a minute."

"Do you have Instagram?"

I shot her an incredulous look. Did I ever. "I do. Why?"

She nodded at my phone sitting on the table. "Look him up."

I unlocked my phone and opened my Instagram app, which was, of course, the top app on my phone. I typed 'Rafa Santos' into the search bar, and sure enough, @ChefRafa popped right up. I clicked on his profile and sucked in a small breath. Given the chance to stare freely at his face without looking like a psychopath, I allowed myself to fully appreciate his glory.

Celia laughed. "I told you."

I glanced at her. "What exactly did you tell me?"

"OK, maybe I didn't tell you exactly, but can you see why he's so popular?"

I glanced down again at his profile. I most certainly could. He was, in a word, gorgeous, and his photos were... delicious. Vibrant shot after shot with perfect lighting of Rafa dicing, sprinkling, tasting. Oh, look, a video of him slicing tomatoes on his balcony. Shirtless. I'm pretty sure his chiseled, bronze muscles actually rippled in the sunlight. It was basically food porn.

"Well, he is nice to look at," I said almost under my breath.

Celia laughed. "That's an understatement, I think. But supposedly, his food rivals his good looks. If that's not a winning combination, I don't know what is." She kissed her fingers like a cartoon chef.

Indeed, I thought. I closed the app, making a note that I might do some Instagram stalking later tonight over a good glass of wine. I also revisited my initial reaction that this was going to be trouble. It was so much harder to be mean to sexy people, wasn't it?

"Is the five-star review already writing itself?" she teased.

I clicked off my phone and rolled my eyes playfully. "I'm not that easy." I popped my final pintxo into my mouth and savored it. "Mmm. Celia, these really are divine. Places like this aren't really on my radar for this piece, but—"

Celia shook her head. "That's OK. This isn't exactly an innovative place. Our people love us, and that's what matters."

"I'd like to give you a little shout-out on my Insta, if that's OK? I kind of do two things. One is I officially write for *Travel Luxe & Leisure* Magazine."

Her brow went up. "I love that website."

I smiled. "We do good work. But those are assignments that I can't really deviate from. But then, on my personal blog, I love to give small reviews to local places I find. Places I think deserve a little love. Street noodles, the best taco shops—or pintxo stands, in this case."

She looked genuinely grateful. She had such an earnest demeanor. "That would be wonderful. Muchas gracias."

"I wouldn't mind maybe doing a small interview if you're open to that?"

"What kind of interview?"

"Just a little history on the place. How you got started, where you're from—you know, standard fare."

"Sure, I have a little time right now if you do. I don't expect much of a crowd for a couple of hours now."

"That would be great." I pulled out my notebook.

She held up a finger. "Uno momento. I think I'm going to

need some wine of my own for this."

She hopped up and returned moments later with another glass. She topped off my glass and then filled one for herself.

"All right, then. Fire away," she said, taking a sip.

I turned on the recorder feature on my phone and leaned back. "Ok, obviously, this is a little impromptu, so bear with me. Are you from here?"

She nodded. "Born and raised. Proud Catalan."

"Do you speak the local language?"

"I do. We learned it in school. We take a lot of pride in it, especially since everything Catalan was banned during the Franco years. He tried to crush our culture and identity. I don't know if you knew that."

"I remember reading about it. I came here once when I was young as a backpacker. Toured the Catalan museum and learned so much. Such a wild history you have."

"It was before my time, of course, but it affected my parents deeply. And their parents even more. From the 30s until he died in 1975, he worked to crush our traditions, dances, language." She shook her head. "It was a very dark time for Spain. It took us a long time to recover, you know? As a country. And there are certain regions that still haven't really recovered—Catalonia, Valencia. They were hit very hard, and their individual cultures really suffered."

"That's very sad. We, of course, have some dark history in America, too. But I think people forget how recent some of these events were here in Europe."

"We're still feeling the effects of much of the 20th century. But anyway, you're not here for a history lesson. So yes, I am a proud Barcelona native, many generations deep."

I smiled. "And cooking? Was that always something you enjoyed?"

"It was. Mi mama loved to entertain, and she made me help in the kitchen for as long as I can remember. I probably learned how to put together tapas in nursery school. For our family—I think for most Spaniards—food is about more than sustenance. It's a way of life. The thing that binds us."

"And when did you start your own business?"

She glanced up to the ceiling as though thinking. "My brother, Pau, and I opened this place, actually. He's not one for hospitality or customer service or anything like that, but he's a good businessman. Loves Excel sheets, the weirdo. I always just wanted a little place of my own. We found this old building vacant, and this part of the neighborhood was just starting to become up-and-coming. It was perfect for what we wanted to do—low profile, traditional, and easy. The kind of place people come to after work for a glass of wine to socialize and snack. It's just a very Barcelona way to be."

I clicked off the recorder and took another sip of my wine, savoring the rich flavors as they blended with Celia's candor.

"Thank you for letting me into the world of your cozy little establishment. You're a testament to why Barcelona's food scene is so...well, magic." I laughed. "Sorry, that sounds cheesy. I blame the wine."

She grinned widely. "I think magic is a good word for it. Gracias for your kind words."

The door chimed, and a group stepped in. "Ah. Good timing. I better get back to work. Nice to meet you, Vera."

I finished up and paid, then stepped out into the bustling Barcelona street, my heart and notebook full, already anticipating how to weave these beautiful threads into the fabric of my upcoming piece.

Chapter Seven

If I had fallen in love with Barcelona as a teenager, I was now officially head over heels for the city. I was overflowing with energy. It was a global city, a melting pot of dynamic cultures from all over the world. And the food was, in fact, to die for. I once had an argument with one of my fellow writers back home about the lack of flair in Spanish food. They thought it was all fried potatoes and salty fish, but they were so wrong. I could already feel my waistline expanding, and I didn't care one bit.

Today, day three, I was going to do my first Instagram Live of my trip. I usually did about one per week from a newly discovered—or tried and true favorite—foodie spot. Today I'd chosen a lively corner with a vibrant modern mural behind me and the pulsing energy of the city in front of me.

Admittedly, I didn't love social media when I first started out. I found it cumbersome, exhausting, and completely artificial. And it was yet another thing I felt like I *had* to do every day. And while some days it still felt like all of those things, I'd found a hungry audience that actually cares about what I have to say. For them, it became about more than just the food—it became about the experience, the lifestyle. People like that I don't just talk about what I enjoy eating, but also about how it makes me feel. Everything from the texture of the napkins to the shape of the silverware factors into my holistic dining experience. And it isn't just about fine dining. I take into account the surroundings and the audience. I don't expect a local, family-run taqueria to offer the same experience as an upscale French bistro in the heart of Manhattan. But are they authentic to their audience? Do they put real thought and energy into their food? What's the vibe I get when I walk through the door, whether it's a place slinging pitchers of margaritas or fine Bordeaux?

I positioned my portable lighting and tripod and set the phone just right to catch my good angle. I reapplied my peach lip gloss and wiped away any rogue mascara. I took a breath and hit the button.

"Hola, everyone! I'm coming at you today from amazing Barcelona, Spain. If you've been following me, then you know I finally got my dream assignment with TLL, and I've come here to cover the vibrant food scene with an emphasis on a handful of new concepts in the Barri Gòtic. Today, I'm sitting outside the market where I've tried some fresh squid that I assume came right from the sea over there. You know, the Iberian Sea that's part of the *Mediterranean*? Right here, I have some amazing fresh mangoes and a glass of incredible Spanish wine. Which did you know is like three euros a bottle at the market?" I paused for dramatic effect and took a long sip. "What do you guys think of Barcelona? Have you been here? Let me know in the comments so I can answer back. And feel free to ask me anything as we go."

I scanned the screen as questions floated in.

@SunnyD: What's the best thing you've eaten in Barcelona so far?

I read the question out loud.

"Oh, that's a tough one. I've tried so many amazing dishes already. But if I had to pick, I'd say the *napolitana de chocolate* I had yesterday was out of this world. Whoever decided to put gooey dark chocolate into a buttery pastry deserves a medal."

@MrsKelley: It looks so vibrant there! How would you describe the food scene there?

"I love your questions, keep them coming. Ok, it's absolutely electric. No other way really to say it. From what I can tell so far, the food is a mix of traditional Catalan cuisine, modern fusion flavors, and a whole lot of passion. It's a true food lover's paradise."

@Books2readgirl: Any tips for finding the best local food spots?

"Always, always ask the locals. Look, guidebooks are great, but so much can happen between the time the guide visits, writes and publishes the book, you know? Places close. Management turns over. But locals will guide you to the best spots right now, often tucked away from the main tourist areas. Also, follow the crowd. If a place is packed with locals, it's usually a good sign."

@HollyBerry What are you looking forward to trying next?

A smile played at my lips as the first answer rose to my consciousness. "I've heard there's a local chef doing pulpo paella. Can't wait to see what that's like."

@EarthMamaJo: Any interesting foodie encounters so far?

I felt my cheeks warm as my thoughts drifted back to Rafa. Grr, ok he was already proving to be an inconvenience, and I didn't even know him.

"I've already met some really interesting people here. I had a fascinating conversation with a... let's say "seafood enthusiast" here in La Boqueria yesterday. We might not have agreed on everything, but it was a fun, lively debate. I can't wait to immerse myself more into the scene and hopefully have all kinds of stories to tell you."

As I glanced down to read the next question, I sensed a buzz of activity burgeoning around me. Before I knew it, a group of exuberant tourists on a walking tour enveloped my little setup.

I was so caught off guard that, for a moment, I was in a deadpanned stare into my phone camera. One woman in floral leggings and Birkenstocks pulled out her phone and snapped a photo of me. Um...did they think I was a street performer?

I tried to ignore them and read the next question.

@FabulousRickRick: What's the one dish you would recommend to someone visiting Barcelona for the first time?

"That's an easy one—pintxos! If you don't know about pintxos, they are sort of a tapa but more of bite-sized delicacies served on small slices of bread with a toothpick. It's the perfect way to sample a wide variety of flavors in one meal."

A man shouted from the walking tour crowd. "What's your favorite site here in the city?"

I blinked. Well, then, this was unexpected. "Um, well, I haven't explored much, but the Market has been the highlight for me. And—"

Floral Leggings snapped another picture, pulling me from my concentration.

"What do you think the city is going to do about all the pickpockets?" A woman with a heavy British accent said.

"Um, I—I don't know." My mind was a blur as I tried to salvage this situation. I breathed and flashed a smile to my followers. "It looks like I've been mistaken for a tour guide!" I said with a laugh. "For those of you just tuning in and for my new walking tour friends, I'm Vera Stone, food critic and blogger for *Travel Luxe & Leisure*. And I think that's all the time I have. Stay hungry and see you soon!"

Just as I thought I'd regained control of the wacko situation and was ending on a good note, a curious pigeon deemed it the opportune moment to poop on my shoulder. The pigeon took flight again, perhaps satisfied with its short-lived fame, leaving me to marvel at the beautiful chaos unraveling before my live audience.

I ended the livestream and exhaled my tension. I resisted the urge to glare at the walking tour, who were all still standing there, staring.

"Well, she's not very useful, is she?" The British woman said to her companion. I rolled my eyes and went about wiping the poop from my shoulder.

But as I checked my phone, a satisfying sense of accomplishment washed over me. Heart and laughing emojis and thumbs-up icons filled the screen, digital confirmation that my audience was engaged and eager for more. Apparently, people really loved the pigeon.

I couldn't help but marvel at how technology had bridged the gap, allowing me to share the culinary delights and cultural intricacies of Barcelona with people thousands of miles away. It was surreal, and yet it felt so right.

I put my phone down and took a moment to absorb my surroundings—the vibrant market colors, the enticing aroma of fresh produce and seafood, the low hum of vendors chatting with customers. I was at the crossroads of tradition and modernity, where age-old Spanish culinary arts met the digital age. The juxtaposition was beautiful, almost poetic. I sipped the last drops of my wine, feeling incredibly grateful. Even for the pigeon.

"Excuse me?" A high-pitched American voice grabbed my attention. I snapped around, ready to be annoyed. A woman was beside me, looking sheepish. Her earnest expression melted my frustration.

"Hi," I said.

"Um, sorry about the pigeon. That was—unfortunate."

I eyed the lingering remnants of the pigeon's very generous gift on my shoulder and tried to laugh. "Not the best timing."

"Um, I know this is weird. But I actually totally follow you. On Insta. Like before seeing you just now."

"Wow, you do? What a small world."

She blushed, looking down. "Would it be totally creepy if I asked for a selfie with you?"

I laughed. "Not at all."

She beamed and pulled out her phone.

I couldn't help but chuckle at the unexpected turn of events, my livestream transforming into a spontaneous meet-and-greet session.

Chapter Eight

Rafa watched her face come through the livestream. It was a lovely face, he had to admit. Big blue eyes and high cheeks. Nice full lips. And for being someone who ate for a living, she had a great figure—curves in all the right places.

But he couldn't quite get a read on her tone. She was definitely funny. He got why she had so many followers. She had a certain dry humor, reminding him of an American comic.

And the way she handled those weirdo tourists and the pigeon—he'd be laughing about that for years.

But he already knew she was tough. Watching her live feed, her footballing questions and answers, and then reading her past reviews on both her blog, and in *Travel Luxe & Leisure*, he was having a full-blown panic attack. It was going to take more than just one really good dinner to impress this woman.

"You are obsessing," Lorna said with an exaggerated sigh as she stepped into the back office where Rafa was staring at his phone.

He flashed her a look, then pushed the phone away. "This is my very livelihood, Lorna. Obsessing is part of the game. And have you even met me? I am an obsessor."

She flicked away his words. "What are you hoping to find by watching that over and over again?"

"A chink in her armor. The secret to her undoing," Rafa said with a smile.

"Yes, she's a hard person to impress. We know that. But all food critics are. Don't get so worked up. You can't please everyone."

Rafa sighed and ran his hand through his hair. "I know that. But I would very *very* much like to please this one. This is an opportunity we won't get again. It's the kind of thing that gets you enough notoriety to get a Michelin Star."

"Do you know they say that people who get Michelin Stars go into a deep depression because they can't live up to it?"

"They don't say that," Rafa said. Lorna grinned.

"It might be true. I think it sounds rather reasonable. Like lottery winners who can't handle the windfall."

"I'll take my chances."

Lorna sighed and hopped onto his desk, right on top of the inventory printouts. "Then we need a plan. You need to offer her more than just a nice dinner."

"Like a bribe? Seduce her?" Rafa said, joking but also maybe not really.

Lorna pulled the papers from under her butt and moved them aside. "Those shirtless tomato videos are enticing, but no, I don't think she can be seduced into a good review. She strikes me as rather professional."

"Bright ideas then?"

"You need to show her the true Satos California experience. Show her your passion for this project. Show her the *why*."

"The *why*?"

"Si. Explain to her why this means so much to you."

Rafa shook his head. "Have you seen this?" He gestured

toward the Instagram reel playing on repeat on his phone screen. "I don't think she's the kind of person to be swayed by sappy stories. This isn't some American cooking show where the contestants end in tears over living up to their sick *abuela's* expectations."

"I know. And everyone has a sob story. I'm not telling you to give her a sob story. I'm telling you to show her behind the curtain a little bit." She made an explanatory gesture of pulling back a curtain. "Explain why these ingredients matter to you. Tell her about your parents."

Rafa folded his arms. "That's personal."

Lorna rolled her eyes. "Get over it. Explain why you are the person to tell the story of this food."

Rafa raised an eyebrow. Lorna could be a little eccentric and esoteric, but she usually had a good instinct for these things. She was great at operations and had a creative flair that allowed her to see problems from different angles. Something he often struggled with, being far too close to the art himself.

"The story of the food?" He said it has more of a statement than a question. But he was curious as to what she meant.

Lorna hopped off the desk and paced the office for a moment, eyes darting about. "Yeah. You've said it yourself. You're not just creating food. You are creating an experience. Your food tells a story. So what is that? She's not a popular food blogger because people really care about what she thinks of crunchy asparagus. She tells a *story*. She offers a glimpse into a certain way of life. Her stories give you a holistic dining experience."

Rafa chewed on her words. She made a very good point. What was his story, and how did he tell it to her?

"Think about, Rafa. Ok, I must away. I have to get to the bank before end of day."

"Si, ok."

Lorna turned to go, then stopped. "Oh, and I spoke with Mari. She says you need to post on your Insta today. Preferably something to do with octopus and preferably shirtless." Lorna wiggled her eyebrows.

Rafa glowered. "I'm not a piece of meat, Lorna."

"Oh, but darling, you really are. The tenderest piece." She blew him a kiss and left.

Chapter Nine

The morning was crystal clear, with a perfect breeze coming in off the ocean. The crisp air was a nice reprieve from the sticky early fall days. I tightened my laces, strapped on my water bottle, popped in my earbuds, and stepped out onto the Barcelona streets. I mapped out how to get to a running trail that led to a path along the water. I geared myself up for it. I had a love-hate relationship with exercise. Maybe most people did. I hated gyms with their musty smells of body odor and sweat. I hated being too close to other people and dodging strange men who insisted on getting in your business and mansplaining the squat machines. But I did enjoy running outside. I enjoyed the fresh air, the cadence of my feet hitting the ground in a nice rhythm. The way I could let my mind wander and allow thoughts to blossom. I could get myself into a state of trance, allowing my creative muse to flourish. And it was a traveler's best friend. Anywhere you went in the world, you could find an open path to run.

As I jogged along the gravel paths, the sun just beginning to edge its way into the sky, I felt like I had the whole place to myself. I turned the bend, and then like a welcome mat, the Iberian Sea stretched out into the horizon. I stopped in my tracks and stared at the wonder of it. The tide ebbed and flowed in a gentle cadence, kissing the sandy shoreline and then retreating gracefully. I breathed in a shot of salty ocean air and picked up my feet again, turning down the boardwalk path.

Just when I was settling into a good pace, listening to a podcast about food trends, a familiar voice pierced through my thoughts.

"Vera?"

Was someone calling me?

I tapped my earbuds to stop the podcast.

"Vera!"

I glanced up and ran smack into Rafa. We stumbled, and he caught me, holding me steady. Wait, nope. Not steady. We both went tumbling to the ground. I yelped as he landed on top of me, his chest nearly crushing my nose. I took a moment to smell him.

"I'm not one for public displays of affection, but I suppose I can make an exception," Rafa said.

Dios mio.

I righted myself and then pushed myself to seated. Rafa stood and helped me to my feet. He was wearing running shorts and a casual sweatshirt and had a light gleam of sweat on his brow. And wow, his running shorts were, um, *short.* And, my, were those some sculpted thighs.

"Sorry!" I said, sweating and breathless. "I wasn't paying attention."

He smirked. "Obviously. Seems to be a habit of yours."

"Um, wait, how do you know my name?" My mind raced back to our one and only encounter. I hadn't even introduced myself.

He looked a little sheepish. "I might have figured out who you were." He rubbed the back of his neck. "My PR person, Mari, arranged for you to come review the restaurant. Naturally, I looked you up and realized you were the octopus girl from the market."

My brow went up. "Octopus girl?"

His lips twitched. "Sorry. My English is no good."

I shot him an incredulous look. "I think your English is perfect. What are you doing here? Were you looking for me?"

A smile tickled his lips. "I might have Googled you, but I hardly know your exercise habits. I was running. Same as you. I love this path. Maybe I'll live-stream it for my followers. Watch out for pigeons, though," he teased, grinning as if he'd just won a minor victory.

"Oh, you saw that, huh?" I felt my cheeks warm, and my eyes hit the ground. I studied my shoelaces.

"It was enlightening. Especially the part where you made friends with the local walking tour."

"I am quite charming and irresistible. What can I say?"

"I've noticed," he said, his iris flaring just slightly. I swallowed. His entire demeanor made me second-guess myself. Was he flirting? Or was this just Rafa being his usual charming self? Was Rafa charming? I had no idea who Rafa was other than a collection of very enticing Instagram shots.

"You might not livestream with pigeons, but you have a healthy following of your own," I said.

His expression lightened with amusement. "And I'm not the only stalker."

I shrugged nonchalantly. "I particularly like the shirtless tomato-slicing segments."

He chuckled. "You and Mari. She drives me crazy, but seems to have a knack for what sells."

"It works for you." My body flooded with heat as I said

the words. Ugh, why was I suddenly a big blob of stupid? "So, you usually run here?" I asked, steering the conversation back to safer ground.

"Sometimes," he replied, his eyes meeting mine. "Though mornings this beautiful are rare. Makes it worth waking up early. Especially if I run into an Instagram celebrity."

I offered him a clipped laugh. "My reviews can't be bought with flattery, just so you know."

He held up his hands. "I would never. I can sling insults if you prefer."

The air between us felt charged, and I found myself unexpectedly conscious of the slight sheen of sweat on my forehead and the less-than-glamorous ponytail I'd thrown my hair into. Ugh, when had I last washed my hair? I probably had days' worth of dry shampoo building up. I must look like I just rolled off an all-nighter in the red-light district.

"We should probably keep running," I said, suddenly aware that we were both just standing there, enveloped in a moment that felt both ordinary and laden with possibility.

"Absolutely," Rafa agreed, but not before his hand lightly brushed against mine as he moved to resume his run. "Race you to that fountain?"

I followed his gaze to a fountain at the end of the path that had some sort of sculpture that, from this distance, looked like a little boy urinating.

"Only if you're ok with losing," I quipped, feeling a rush of endorphins that had little to do with jogging.

"Tres, dos, uno, go!" Rafa said rapidly before I could compose myself.

"Hey, cheater!" I yelled as I took off after him.

As we took off down the path, my heart pounding in my chest, I couldn't help but steal glances at Rafa. His muscles rippled with every stride, and sweat glistened on his skin in the morning light. I shook my head, trying to clear my mind and focus on my feet. But it was no use. He took up all the space in the room. Or the beach in this instance.

I pushed myself harder as my competitive nature kicked in, determined not to let him win. But as we approached the fountain, he pulled ahead, his strides strong and steady.

He slowed down as we reached the fountain, laughing as I caught up to him, nearly knocking into him again.

"A valiant effort, but alas, defeat in the end," Rafa said.

I glared. "Not fair. You cheated."

"As it goes, in love and war."

"And he's a poet."

"You're too competitive," he said, his voice teasing.

"I can't help it," I replied, gasping for breath. "It's in my blood."

Rafa leaned in, his eyes meeting mine. "I like that quality in a woman."

Ah, hell. He was flirting. And it was doing its job. I felt the words right down to my pinky toes.

He smirked and sat on the edge of the fountain to catch his breath. I followed suit and stared up at the statue, which was, in fact, a cherub boy-type creature with wild Medusa hair and water coming out of his tender bits.

"What is it about boys peeing that inspires sculptors?" I asked, eyeing the statue.

"It's probably the first thing he saw on the street as he sat at his work desk."

The sun was fully up now, casting a warm glow over the beach. Birds were singing along with the crash of the waves. Beachgoers were starting to populate the scene.

"I made that pulpo paella," Rafa said.

"Really? I'll have to come try it. Although I have reasonable doubts," I teased.

He leaned closer. His words came out in a husky whisper. "I can be very convincing."

Nope. Too flirty. That was my cue. I hopped up. "I'm sure you can. But I better get going. Lots to do today."

I didn't wait for him to reply before jogging back toward my hotel.

Chapter Ten

My running app buzzed to indicate that I'd crossed another mile marker just as I turned the corner onto my hotel's street.

Phew, five miles in the bag. More than I thought I had in me today, I thought. It was much needed, though, as I envisioned another round of *pan con aceite* and a bottle of good wine. Or maybe a chocolate croissant or three. Fitness influencer and food critic were never going to be synonymous, I was afraid.

My phone buzzed again, and I glanced down. My eyebrows rose to see a FaceTime call coming in from my senior editor in New York, Joanne. She never FaceTimed me. In fact, I barely spoke to her other than some curt emails now and again. I swiped it open and flashed my best smile despite my exhaustion and sweat.

"Vera!" she said with noticeable surprise, as though she didn't expect it to actually be me on the other end of the line.

"Joanne, hi."

"Are you ok? You look out of breath."

"Oh, I was just running in the park."

Her face made an attempt at surprise, but the Botox held her features in place, resulting in a strange plastic contortion.

"On purpose, or were you being chased?"

Her expression was so deadpan I had no idea if she was joking. "On—purpose?"

"That sounds—terrible. But other than that, how are you? How are things going there?"

I wiped sweaty hair from my face. "Oh, great. Things are really great. Have I mentioned how much I love this city?"

Joanne laughed lightly. "You might've mentioned it a time or two."

"Right. Was there something wrong? Or something you needed?" I asked.

"Nothing is wrong, no. Actually, it's quite the opposite. I'm calling with some good news. Well, it should be good news, anyway."

Not knowing why, I suddenly felt uneasy. I waited, but Joanne seemed distracted by something on her computer. She clacked her keyboard a few times before clearing her throat and turning back to me.

"Sorry. Super busy morning here in New York." I checked the clock and did the math.

"Jo, it's like 4 a.m. there. Why are you even awake? And working?"

"Like I sleep. Not with reorganizations happening right and left. Anyway, what I was going to tell you is that your trip has been extended."

I waited a beat, an incredulous smile hanging at the corners of my lips. "What do you mean, 'extended'?"

"Well, the editorial board has been following your Insta, of course, and you're getting sooo much traction. And they love this modern fusion versus the traditional angle you're taking. It's great, especially for the time right now. So, they want the story to be part of the quarterly feature."

I blinked, certain I had misheard her.

"Vera? Are you there?"

I shook my head and sort of half laughed, half grunted. "Yeah, sorry. Did you say 'quarterly feature'?"

"Yes. How do you feel about that?" Her tone was all direct, with no fuss or emotion.

I couldn't believe the words coming out of her mouth. I dug a nail into my palm, making sure I was actually awake and talking on the phone to my editor.

"Of course, I'm ecstatic. The quarterly feature? That's huge." I pressed a hand over my mouth, afraid of revealing too much. Joanne never reacted well to too much emotion. I think it offended her facial muscles' inability to move.

"It is. The board did a deep dive into your work and determined they love your voice. I really think it was that post you did on the '*Many Faces of New York's Saurkraut*' that did it. I mean, if you can make pickled cabbage sexy, I really think you have something. So they're extending your trip by another two weeks so that you can do a more in-depth report."

In typical Joanne fashion, the words came out in a rapid cadence that took me a moment to process. I almost couldn't believe my fortune. Not only was I getting the quarterly feature, something I'd been dreaming about for the past five years working at *TLL*, but I was also going to spend another two freaking weeks in probably my favorite place on the planet. The stars were aligning, and I couldn't believe it. The quarterly feature was usually reserved for in-depth essays by world travelers, not food critics. I was well-known as far as food writers went, and I was proud of it, but this was a whole new level.

"Vera?"

I snapped back to attention and realized Joanne had said something. "I'm sorry, what was that?"

Her expression softened a little. "I'm glad you're excited, Vera. This is a fantastic opportunity, and you deserve it."

"I hope that I do. And I'm grateful for the opportunity. This is going to be a stellar piece, I absolutely promise." The excitement was mounting uncontrollably in my tone.

"I know that it will be. So, to get started, I'm going to need an outline from you on how to expand the piece further. I want you to interview some more chefs. I know you went with a top three to review, but I want to get a general feel for the whole scene. Are there even little tapas stands on the corner doing something innovative? Really dig deep and tell me anything you can find. Maybe by Friday, you'll have an outline for me?"

The more Joanne got excited about it, the more her up-speak continued. I nodded fervently.

"You've got it. I've already been eyeing places I've been dying to talk about. It's going to be fantastic." I could feel my whole body vibrating. My feet started to move back and forth.

"Right. Ok, then, I guess you're on it. I've got to get back to things here—we have this massive editorial redesign happening. You know how it goes in New York. Anyway, take care of yourself over there, and don't fall for any wooden Spaniards."

The last line was said with such speed that I almost barely caught the weak joke at the end.

"I will. Or won't, rather. Ok, bye!" I barely got my salutation out before the line clicked off.

I leaned back. My head was spinning with a mixture of fear, anxiety, elation, nerves, and excitement. But most of all, I was proud. I had worked so hard to build a name for myself. I was a stellar employee who took her job seriously. And I was proud of my writing and the work I'd done. Now I was finally getting the opportunity to do something bigger, something more. I slipped my phone into my shorts and ran up to my room to bask in a long, hot shower.

Vera, you have arrived!

I swallowed as the reality sunk in. Crap, now I had to live up to the hype. I was going to need more *napolitanas chocolate* stat,

Chapter Eleven

My love of food started early. As far back as I can remember, my mom cooked elaborate meals with painstaking care and love. Food was to celebrate, food was for comfort. Food was part of the fabric of our very lives.

Mom was always meticulous about fresh ingredients, too. She never skimped on buying the best produce, organically grown where she could. She always went for the highest quality meats and went out of her way to get farm-fresh eggs, which, luckily, weren't too hard to come by in Upstate New York. She believed that whatever we put in our body was represented in the rest of our lives.

Cooking was also something to be done as a family. And it rarely felt like a chore. It was meant to be pleasurable.

She also demanded, almost comically, precise feedback on every dish. Dinners became something of a game, eventually, and my brother and I created our own food critic organization —*Stone Cold Critics*. Vera and Liam Stone, get it? As we got older, mom would ask us about specific flavors and pairings. How did things go together? What would we do differently? I guess looking back through the lens of time, it's no shock I became a professional food critic. I'd been training my whole life for it.

My first official assignment was for my high school newspaper. I decided to review the new menu at our neighborhood breakfast café. When my harsh criticism of Jorge's steak omelet came out, it was met with uproar. I couldn't say such mean things about a local business! Why not? I wanted to know. Didn't everybody want honest feedback? How did a person get better if they didn't know what needed improvement? It made perfect sense to me, anyway.

The teacher overseeing the paper pulled the article. I secretly had it put back in by tipping our student editor $10. The result was us both being excused from the school paper.

The incident infuriated me but also lit a spark in me for idealistic truth in food journalism. I've been accused of being someone who doesn't actually *like* food. But that couldn't be further from the truth. I think most people just don't have any respect for food. Most people take perfectly good ingredients and butcher them with too much salt and poor-quality oil. Or they don't respect their customers and serve them low-quality food to begin with. If you don't take respect and pride in your own work, how can you expect me to? If you cut corners and load my meal with corn syrup and fake bacon, why should I reward you for that? No. This is a cutthroat business with competition up to your eyeballs. If you really want to stand out, if you want my seal of approval, then you have to bring something extra to the table. I don't call the X-Factor for nothing. And now, of course, I had a reputation to protect. As it turns out, the people who called me bitter now beg for a review from me. They were willing to risk my negative review for my stamp of approval. That's about as high as you can climb in my business.

But I don't take it lightly, either. This isn't a game to me. I'm not purposefully toying with people's futures. I fully understand the power that I wield with my pen. I take great pride in doing my job to the best of my ability. And that means not cutting corners, not playing favorites, or giving in to favors. I will, never, repeat *never*, take money for a review that doesn't come from a paycheck signed by *Travel Luxe & Leisure*. My integrity means too much to me in this business.

It's also why I make a point of never reviewing a restaurant if I have a personal relationship with a chef or the owner. I just can't risk an unbiased opinion. Oh, it's definitely caused some problems in my personal life. The thing is, I like the restaurant industry, and I do have friends within it. But I can't play favorites. My reputation is on the line.

My mind flashed instantly to Rafa. And that was why the Universe needed to stop with the random meet-cutes with seductive innuendos. Thanks, Universe!

The first restaurant on my list for an official review for my feature was *Las Brisas*—a newly opened place tucked away in a recently remodeled church, promising a true throwback to Catalan cuisine. They were pricy and took limited reservations each night, with the idea that each plate was a work of visual art prepared right at your table. Raving fans called it personal, critics called it pretentious.

As I pushed open the intricately carved wooden doors, a gust of air-conditioned comfort welcomed me into a sanctuary of elegance. The interior was a seamless blend of the old world of its church foundation but with updated contemporary flair. Dark wooden beams intersected the ceiling, paying homage to rustic Catalan architecture, while tasteful modern chandeliers dangled like droplets of liquid gold, illuminating the room in a soft, ethereal glow. Walls adorned with faded tapestries depicting historical scenes from Catalonia's storied past sat in captivating contrast to sleek, minimalistic table settings.

A subtle, complex aroma hung in the air. I detected wafts of roasting meats mingled with the sweet, smoky scent of piquillo peppers. A hint of garlic was omnipresent, like a refrain in a well-loved song. The perfume of fine wine—redolent of berries, oak, and an earthy robustness—added another layer to the olfactory tapestry.

So far, so good. Maybe I was just a little high on Barcelona, but my usual discerning eye wasn't finding much to complain about ambience-wise.

The clinking of fine china and crystal glasses orchestrated a melodic background, a gentle symphony that blended with soft conversations.

"*Bienvenida a Las Brisas*," a chipper hostess greeted me. She wore a black cocktail dress and a full face of heavy makeup. They were going for upscale, I guessed.

"Hola. Yo soy Vera Stone con *Travel Luxe & Leisure*."

The young woman's eyes went wide. "Ah, si! Bienvenida. Please, come. I have your table."

I smiled and followed as she led me to a small table in the back of the room draped in crisp white linen. A single red carnation in a slim vase served as a minimalist centerpiece, inviting without overwhelming. The menu was a leather-bound book, its pages thick and textured, each dish described in detailed Spanish that I would need the assistance of Google translate for once I was alone. I glanced around and wondered how the chef was going to cook right at the table.

"*Buenas Noches*. We are delighted to have you here." I

looked up to see the chef approaching my table, holding out a bottle of sweating white wine. "May I start you?"

"Just a small glass, por favor. Gracias."

He smiled and poured a couple of ounces into my glass.

"I am Julio, the chef and part owner. We are so honored to have you tonight."

"I'm excited to be here. And very curious."

He smiled thinly beneath a trim black mustache. He gestured toward the menu. "Now, you must please order whatever you wish. But I am happy to also bring you a curated tasting menu of what I think are our best dishes."

I closed the menu with a smile. "I always defer to the master. And you prepare it right here?"

He chuckled lightly. "Si. Don't worry, you will be impressed."

"I don't doubt it."

"Muy bien. I will get it started. Please, do not hesitate to let anyone know if there is anything you need."

I sipped my wine slowly as I patiently waited. It didn't take long for Julio to return with cart packed with everything one would need to prepare a meal. He went to work with shocking speed and efficiency and in no time, he was arranging colorful, succulent ingredients into tiny sculptures.

First, a Catalonian spin on carpaccio featured thinly sliced jamón ibérico that practically melted on my tongue, its rich, nutty flavor awakening my palate. For the main course, I was presented with a plate of '*Mar i Muntanya*,'—a marriage of mountain and sea—tender rabbit and succulent prawns stewed in a well-spiced sauce. While it was tasty, something about it felt safe. I couldn't pinpoint, but maybe the spices were just too familiar.

As I took the last bite and savored the lingering fusion of flavors, spontaneous applause erupted from a far corner of the restaurant. A couple had just gotten engaged, their joyous celebration another testament to the magic that seemed to imbue the very walls of this place. I couldn't help but smile.

"So much joy," Julio said, approaching my table. "We have already become a local favorite for engagements."

"I can see why. The atmosphere is very romantic. And it's an old church, so that seems appropriate."

"And the food? To your liking?" His dark eyes were wide in anticipation.

This was always the tricky part. I didn't want to give people false hope or lie. And I didn't like to give away my initial thoughts until I'd had a chance to ruminate.

I glanced down at my half-eaten crema Catalana—the pièce de résistance of my meal. The caramelized sugar crust had shattered at the tap of my spoon, revealing a creamy, citrus-infused custard beneath. This piece I could rave about. Each spoonful was a radiant blend of tart and sweet.

"This crema is divine. Truly," I said with a smile. Julio beamed.

"It is our most popular *dulce*, to be sure. Everything else?"

I smiled and pushed my plate away, quite full. "It was all really lovely. Thank you."

Julio didn't look too thrilled with my simple answer, but he smiled and bowed politely. He was clearly professional and wasn't going to give anything away.

Admittedly, the food was good. Very good. It was fresh and flavorful, beautifully designed. And the atmosphere was cozy and romantic. But there wasn't really anything that notable about it—at least if we were talking pure *innovation*. And that was my angle, supposedly. This is what I always found difficult with my job. There were plenty of places that were quite good. Places I couldn't necessarily say had any glaring character flaws. Places where I doubted any local or wandering tourist would be disappointed.

But did it deserve a write-up in one of our coveted features? This is why I started utilizing my own social media as well. It gave me bite-size opportunities to offer up my thoughts on restaurants that maybe didn't necessarily deserve a major write-up in *TLL*.

I jotted down some tasting notes in my little notebook, very aware that the management was watching me with an eagle eye. I wasn't exactly under the radar here, and I didn't aim to be. I wanted to give them an opportunity to impress me. To give me the best of what they had. I understood how easily things could go wrong in a restaurant at any given moment. Everyone was only just one accident away from a horrendous mystery shopper review. That wasn't how I operated. I wasn't trying to blindside anyone. Rather than a random observation, I consider it more of an audition. Give me the best you've got.

"Rabit was tender and well cooked. Could use more unique spices...Crema Catalana deserves most of the credit..."

I wrote out a few more thoughts and signaled for the bill and set down my company Amex.

My mind wandered to Rafa and Santos Calofirnia. Would it deliver on its promise of innovative fusion? I was set to go there last, but I found myself growing increasingly obsessed.

After running into him and doing some solid Instagram stalking, I, of course, did some more in-depth internet research. I'd come across an interview in one of those little magazines that do fluffy features on all things local.

Rafa Santos grew up in Barcelona but was also half-American, his mother being from Santa Barbara, California. She'd come to Spain during college and fell in love. And she never left. She passed her love of fresh California cuisine down to her son, Rafa. Hence the name of the restaurant, I supposed.

Rafa's dreamy eyes flashed in my mind—like a forest in twilight mist. I shook the thoughts away. I couldn't let a little budding chemistry with the chef cloud my judgment on his food and restaurant. While I did take personality into account when writing my reviews, it was more about how the chef and management interacted with the guests and the atmosphere it created. I wanted them to show their personal style, it was true. But, my desire to see if his abs were as hard in real life as they looked on Instagram—that should have no bearing.

The thought brought a small smile to my lips, regardless. It has been a while since I had a flirty interaction with a stranger. I'd been so busy with work lately I hadn't been dating much. Or at all. Sometimes, it felt futile anyway. Dating had become so mechanical back home. A series of casual coffee meetings squeezed in between other business meetings. Just a string of people looking for hookups. It didn't seem like anyone wanted anything serious or meaningful anymore. I wasn't even sure I wanted anything serious or meaningful. All in all, I loved my life. I had a career I loved, one that allowed me to travel across the country, even internationally. I had a healthy network of friends and work colleagues. I had extended family I saw on occasion. I drove up to see my parents at least once a month. I had my health. In general, life was good. I suppose I had always thought that I would settle down one of these days, maybe start a family. But I certainly wasn't in a rush. I had a lot of life left to live.

The host brought my check, and I handed him my company credit card. I signed, tipped, and headed out. At least I could say I was very full.

Chapter Twelve

"Buenos días, Señora," Sandra greeted me as I stepped off the lift and into the lobby the next morning, desperately searching for more coffee.

"Buenos días, Sandra. How are you this morning?"

"Very busy, in fact. But that's always a good thing. The festival has brought in a lot of overnight guests. Please, we have coffee and pastries in the lounge." She gestured toward the little cozy room with the fireplace just off the main lobby.

I eyed the breakfast display in anticipation. I turned back to her.

"Festival?"

"Ah, si. *Festival de Otoño. The Autumn festival.* It's in El Poble Sec neighborhood. One of many throughout the year, of course. But it's very popular with growers all around northern Spain. It's a great place for new restaurants to show what they've got. There's usually even a little competition at the end. It's all quite fun. We're here in Barcelona love nothing more than good food."

My excitement perked up.

"Precisely why I'm here. What time does it begin?"

Sandra glanced at the clock on the wall. "I think in another hour. But it will go all night. You can get there on the metro. There is a stop just at the end of the block."

I wandered into the lounge to get some coffee and plucked up some bread with tomato for breakfast. I didn't know how I didn't know about the food festival, but I was pleasantly surprised.

I typed out a text to Celia. "Are you by chance going to *Festival de Otoño?*"

She wrote back immediately. "Already getting ready. My brother is managing my booth today so I can mingle. Meet you there?"

* * *

As I stepped off the metro and climbed the stairs, I found myself plunged into the pulsating heart of *Festival de Otoño*. A wave of exhilaration washed over me. For a food blogger, this was paradise regained, a canvas of culinary artistry sprawled across the historic Poble Sec streets. The neighborhood was a vibrant and diverse section of the city located in the Sants-Montjuïc district. Nestled between Montjuïc Mountain and the bustling avenue of Avinguda del Paral·lel, it carried a rich history and a bustling modern life that married the old and the new in a delightful embrace. I was surrounded by a patchwork of architectural styles ranging from traditional Catalan to modernist and contemporary buildings.

The streets were dotted with a wide array of tapas bars, eateries, and restaurants that looked like they offered a delightful blend of local and international cuisines, but no one was inside today. The festival was already in full swing, filling the winding streets with activity.

Colorful banners fluttered overhead. Local chefs manned sizzling grills, their faces flushed from the heat, while others showcased a mosaic of colorful, traditional tapas.

In one corner, a stall was heaped high with ripe tomatoes and olives in a mosaic of colors. Another stall displayed a mound of cheeses, and next to that, an artistic display of various breads.

Wine vendors swirled and poured local Spanish wines, and a hip young couple was pouring fresh Sangria packed with colorful fruit.

The sounds of sizzling pans, the clink of wine glasses, and the murmur of excited chatter filled the air, underscored by the rhythmic strumming of a nearby flamenco guitarist. Every so often, the crowd would break into applause as the chef completed a flamboyant demonstration.

In one corner, a small stage was set up and a group of young men and women in full costume was performing Sardana dancing.

I wandered, taking in every sound, every smell. It was all so overwhelming, it was hard to know where to even begin.

A particularly succulent-looking display caught my attention, and I ambled over. A handsome but very sweaty and disheveled chef was stirring a giant pot of what looked like a form of paella but was inky black. That looked like a good starting point.

"Would you like a sample?" A young woman behind the giant vat said. She slid me a small sample dish with a little fork.

"Gracias," I said, I glanced down at the little cup of black rice. I took a bite of the aromatic, slightly salty concoction.

"That's incredible. And unique."

The woman spared a glance back at the chef. "Martí is magic," she said.

At the sound of his name, Martí glanced up, and I felt a

little tingle in my belly. Well, hello, blue eyes, I thought to myself. What was it with Spanish chefs?

"*Buenos días*," he said with a subtle smile.

"*Buenos días*. This is incredible." I held up my sample cup.

He pressed a hand to his heart. "Gracias. Squid ink arroz. There is much more where it came from."

The words were innocent enough, but I detected a slight innuendo.

"I bet," I said, throwing the flirtation back his way. I could play, too.

"How is it that every solo woman in Spain finds their way to Martí?"

I turned at the female voice and smiled to see Celia ambling over. She had a cheeky grin across her face. She wore a maxi boho skirt and cropped white top, and her dark hair was in a messy but chic top knot.

"Because I am a comfort to their wandering souls," Martí said, winking at me. He turned to Celia. "Come to check out the competition, Celia?"

Celia smirked. "Oh, Martí, we all know we can't hold a candle to you." She rolled her eyes at me.

Their competitive banter seemed friendly enough, but I had to wonder if there was something more there. She had mentioned a chef named Martí, hadn't she?

"Nice to see you, CeCe," Martí said. There was the ghost of a smirk playing at his lips and a hint of annoyance dancing on hers. The tension thickened around us.

"Come back this afternoon. There is a little competition going on, and I think you might be pleased with the winner," Martí said back to me.

"Is that so?" I said.

"Maybe I'll even take you to dinner to celebrate my victory."

I half-laughed but admittedly blushed a little. This guy

was really trying to embody the Latin lover, I guess.

"Oh, please. Can you tone it down?" Celia said with an eye roll. "Come on, Vera. Let me save you from this viper."

I flashed Martí a look, and he winked.

"Nice to meet you. Enjoy the festival, *Vera.*"

"Stay away from Martí," Celia said as we sipped Sangria. I thought I liked Sangria until now, but now I know that I *love* true sangria from a market stall in Barcelona.

"What's the story there?" I asked.

"Hmm?"

"There is obviously some history with Martí."

Celia shook her head and laughed half-heartedly. "Everyone has a story with Martí, I'm afraid." She paused and sipped. "It's a small world, the culinary scene here. We dated for a very short time. A *very* short time." She pinched her thumb and forefinger to demonstrate. "Trust me, he's not boyfriend material. But he smells fresh female blood like a shark in the Med."

* * *

As the day progressed, the air buzzed with anticipation of the aforementioned cooking competition. A small, open-air stage had been set up, draped with the vibrant red and yellow of the Spanish flag. A hearty crowd was already packing around the stage.

The stage was a spectacle in itself. It was set up like a culinary coliseum, complete with fully equipped cooking stations. Each station had a large, polished countertop that gleamed under the warm afternoon sun, a professional-grade gas range that looked like it could handle anything from sautéing to flambeing, and an assortment of gleaming knives and specialized kitchen tools arranged neatly on a magnetic strip. Each station also featured a large wicker basket filled to the brim with fresh local ingredients—artichokes, asparagus, fresh fish on ice, and a variety of colorful peppers, from what I could see. It was like a still-life painting you could eat right off the canvas.

Above the stage, a giant LED screen was mounted, ready to give the audience a bird's-eye view of each chef's workspace. Close-up camera angles would allow us to see the chefs' precise knife work, the sizzle of ingredients hitting hot oil, and the transformation of raw elements into culinary art.

"Wow, this is no pop-up event. This is a big deal," I said.

"It always is. Locals love it. Martí never misses a chance to show off."

"They let him participate every year?"

She shrugged. "Honestly, I'm not sure it would be the same without his smug face." She hid a smile in her second sangria.

A rustic bell clanged loudly, cutting through the chatter and laughter that filled the air. The competition was about to begin.

Five local chefs walked onto the stage, their white aprons starched and their faces set with a mixture of determination and excitement. Martí stood front and center, his charisma lighting up the whole stage. His eyes swept over the crowd before landing briefly on mine, and he winked. In that split second, I felt a shiver of intrigue. I shook it off. *That* was the last thing I needed.

The rules were announced in Spanish, then repeated in English, through a booming microphone: *"Damas y caballeros,* each chef has been provided with a basket of fresh, local ingredients. The objective? To create a dish that not only tastes extraordinary but also embodies the spirit of Catalonia. And they must do it within one hour!"

With that, a large digital clock projected on the screen began its countdown. The chefs opened their baskets, their faces lit by the golden glow of the spotlight, each unveiling the array of local produce and proteins they'd been provided.

Martí, his sleeves rolled up, wasted no time. He grabbed a bunch of fresh herbs and began to chop them finely, his knife moving in a rapid blur. The camera zoomed in to capture his technique—each slice was clean and exact. He had skills.

The audience watched in rapt attention as the chefs worked their magic, their expert hands moving in a choreographed dance of chopping, stirring, and seasoning. The sizzling sounds of cooking food and the mouthwatering aromas wafting from the stage added to the festival's lively atmosphere.

As the clock ticked down, it became clear that each chef was bringing their unique flair to the competition, an individual thumbprint of style. The announcer gave little bios of each chef as they went along. Sofia, a seasoned chef who specialized in Catalan classics, was working on a modern interpretation of *escalivada*, a dish traditionally made of grilled vegetables. Sofia's version included smoke-infused eggplants and bell peppers, plated in a way that "resembled a vibrant Catalan landscape." But what caught everyone's attention was when she took a small bottle of truffle oil and began to delicately apply droplets to her creation. The pungent aroma wafted through the air, causing murmurs of excitement in the crowd.

Across from her was Javier, a "young and ambitious chef who decided to forego tradition entirely." He was making a deconstructed Spanish *tortilla*, turning what is typically a humble dish into an Avant-Garde culinary statement. With a focused expression, he layered thinly sliced potatoes on a spherification spoon, placing them gently into a liquid bath.

And then there was Lucia, whose approach was a celebration of the sea. She was grilling local fish and drizzling it with an emulsion made of olive oil and seaweed, "capturing the spirit of Catalonia's coastline in her dish."

Then there was Martí. With a calm but intense focus, he was skillfully crafting a traditional paella. But his twist? The previously tasted base of black squid ink rice that oozed "sophistication and mystery," as he said. His hands gracefully moved as he adjusted the heat, his eyes scrutinizing each grain of rice as it absorbed the saffron-infused broth.

"That's about as innovative as he gets," Celia quipped, glaring at Martí at work. I flashed her a look. She definitely had some lingering resentment there. I could probably take a wild guess at who ended things.

Feeling the buzz in the air, an idea popped into my head. "My followers have got to see this," I thought out loud. I whipped out my phone, tapped a few buttons, and before I knew it, I was live on Instagram.

"Hey everyone, it's Vera!" I said, making sure to capture the hustle and bustle behind me. "I'm at this insane food competition in Barcelona at *Festival de Otoño.* The atmosphere is like...it's electric."

I spun the camera around to showcase the chefs, who were engrossed in their culinary creations. "If you could smell what I'm smelling, you'd forget all about grandma's cooking—no offense, grandma!"

I swept the camera back and forth, highlighting each competitor, giving a small description of what each chef was up to, doing my best Caesar Flickerman from *The Hunger Games.*

The real announcer went on in the background. "Each chef here, in their own way, is keeping the spirit of Catalan cuisine alive in their creations. Whether through reinvention, elevation, or faithful adherence to tradition, they all pay homage to the culinary heritage of the region."

The crowd clapped and roared.

The electric energy on stage was palpable. It was a culinary orchestra and each chef was a virtuoso in their own right. The clang of pans and the rhythmic chop of knives against cutting boards were like percussion instruments, underscoring the melody of hisses and sizzles from the stovetops. The crowd was entranced, living and breathing each moment of culinary craftsmanship as if it were a high-stakes sporting event.

I did my best to narrate the events as I panned my phone camera.

As the competition began to wind down, I wound down by stream. "Alright, my lovelies, gotta dash. These dishes won't critique themselves. Besos from Barcelona!"

As the last few seconds on the clock counted down, each chef took a step back to admire their work—dishes that were as much works of art as they were food. Even I was impressed. The bell rang out once more, echoing the finality of the moment. It was done.

As the applause settled and the audience began to disperse, Martí, the freshly-crowned champion of the festival—shocking—hopped off the stage and started mingling with the crowd. His eyes darted around, absorbing the congratulations and praise with a self-assured smile that straddled the line between confidence and arrogance. When his eyes met mine, they lingered a moment too long. Then, he began making his way through the crowd toward me.

"Vera, isn't it?" he said, his Spanish accent smoothing over the syllables of my name. "The visiting food critic from New York?"

"Guilty as charged," I replied, holding up my hands play-fully. I wasn't sure if I was flattered or alarmed that he knew who I was, but I guessed it was a small circle. If word got out, he would have looked me up.

His lips curled into a smile that I couldn't quite read. "I

enjoyed your last piece on molecular gastronomy. Brilliantly written, though a bit... safe?"

"You read *Travel Luxe & Leisure*?"

"Who doesn't?" There was an unsettling glint in his eye.

I guffawed.

"What did you think of the show?" he asked.

"Talk about safe," Celia reappeared with two cups of wine. She handed me one.

Martí snorted. "I think I just defied culinary tradition in front of a live audience." His voice carried a teasing tone, but there was also an undercurrent of challenge.

"Even my daughter can make squid-ink paella," Celia said.

Martí pursed his lips and pulled a teasing *just ate a lemon* kind of face.

"I appreciate creativity," I countered, "as long as it serves the dish and not just the chef's ego."

His laugh was hearty, and his eyes seemed to sparkle a bit. "Touche! You do have a point, Senorita Vera."

"Martí, you hate trendy food and anything innovative. Stop pretending," Celia said.

He looked dramatically affronted. "You wound me, CeCe."

Just then, someone from the crowd called out his name, and he turned his head, breaking our eye contact. "Duty calls," he said, giving me a wink as he took a step back.

As he rejoined his admirers, I stood there, a little dazed. He was undeniably charismatic, but that final wink? It felt more rehearsed than genuine, like a well-timed garnish on an already complex dish.

"He's a talented chef, but his ego is going to be his end one of these days. Mark me," Celia said. "Come on. There is an entire tent dedicated to *dulce.*"

Chapter Thirteen

The cacophony of *Festival de Otoño* danced all around, but Rafa heard or felt none of it. He was laser-focused on one thing—Vera talking to Martí beneath the competition stage. He almost didn't watch the competition. Like he needed to see Martí peacocking yet again. But it was always good to check out the other chefs participating.

A surge of anger bubbled within him at the sight of them together, talking and clearly flirting. There was also something like fear wedged in there. He really needed to stop being so anxious about this thing, he just had so much riding on it. He had poured everything he had into this endeavor, both financially and mentally. And selfishly, stupidly, he wanted all of Vera's attention on him and *his* restaurant, on *his* food. Martí had a way of needlessly getting in the way of what Rafa wanted. He didn't want Vera distracted or muddled talking to Martí or getting sucked in by his silly, run-of-the-mill tourist trap of a restaurant. Just because Martí had gotten himself into a famous guidebook, he thought he was really hot stuff.

And he had been riding that fame for years now. But honestly, his food was so commonplace. It belonged in a guidebook because it was stuff for the masses. And look, there was nothing wrong with that. Everyone should just do what they did best, and he didn't begrudge Martí from making a living. Or did he? Sometimes he wondered if it was more that he begrudged Martí for his arrogance than his talent. He was talented, sure, but he wasn't creative. But he acted like he was a king of the culinary scene in Barcelona.

"If looks could kill," Lorna said, coming up beside him.

He spared her a glance. "And what is that supposed to mean?"

"Well, you're shooting daggers out of your eyes right now. And it looks like it's trailed on Martí. What he do this time?"

"Do you see that woman there?"

"The pretty tourist?" Lorna said, tilting her head and studying Vera.

"Yeah, her. She's the blogger."

"That's Vera Stone?" Lorna said, her voice ticking up.

"Yep. The one and only. We've run into each other a couple of times. While we were at the market. Then running on the beach."

Her brow went up. "You run on the beach? Are you trying to be some kind of sex-symbol cliché?"

"Focus, Lorna. She lives up to her reputation, it's true. But what is she doing talking to Martí?"

Lorna chuckled. "You are too much sometimes, Rafa. She's a food blogger. Of course, she's going to talk to any chef she can. She can't fly halfway around the world just to see you, no offense."

"I know," Rafa snapped too harshly. Phew! He was wound up. Obviously, she didn't, he thought. But would it be nice if she had? A part of him — a foolish, hopeful part — wished she had flown halfway around the world just for him.

"Is this because she's talking to *any* other chef or because it's Martí specifically?" Lorna asked.

Rafa said nothing.

"Are you two ever going to move past your little boyhood rivalry?"

He glared at her. "It's not my fault. He's the one who's holding the grudge."

"Mature, the both of you. C'mon, will you relax already? It's not good for the food for you to be all negative."

"And here I thought it was my broody mood that gave it its edge," Rafa said. He half smiled, trying to find lightness in the situation.

"Come on," Lorna said, patting his back. "Let's get things wrapped up. We have prep work to do tonight. The opening is like days away. You're not the only one who is a ball of nerves right now. Ok? Stop being so selfish." Lorna winked.

Rafa smiled and nodded. "*Si, claro.* Let's get going." Rafa started to walk, then paused. "I heard a rumor about something."

"You shouldn't believe rumors, Rafa. You should know better."

"Sometimes they are true. And sometimes they're useful."

"So what's the rumor?" Lorna asked as they walked back to his booth.

"I heard there's a developer looking at the district two streets over. Thinking about revitalizing it, turning it into some sort of hip culinary strip." He started to pack things back into boxes.

Lorna's face looked like she was contemplating the idea. "How do we feel about that?"

Rafa scratched at a few days of stubble on his chin. "Yet to be determined. Revitalizing old streets is always a good thing, I guess, in theory. Just in practice it doesn't always go the way you think it's going to. The next thing you know, it's just a whole bunch more tourist traps, taking the soul of the city away. Sometimes I feel like ours is the last authentic Street in Barcelona."

"And here I thought you were the innovative one."

Rafa flubbed his lips. "I know. I'm contradicting myself. But I'm part of Barcelona. I'm local. Born and raised here. I hate the idea of investors who don't understand the pulse and the soul of the city coming in and tearing everything up."

"We have foreign investors, remember?"

"It's not the same as some developer coming in and slapping neon signs on old buildings advertising oversized, overpriced, tourist food. Just to make money."

Lorna sighed. "I know. It's tragic to think about. But there's not really anything you can do in situations like this. You kind of just have to embrace the change." She shrugged.

Rafa considered it. "Do you think it threatens the business?"

Lorna furrowed her eyebrows. "What? If a bunch of hot trendy restaurants go in one street over?" She smirked incredulously.

Rafa rolled his eyes. "I know there'll always be competition. I think we have enough hungry bellies for everyone. I just mean...if the neighborhood changes. Really changes—"

Lorna put her hands on his shoulder. "Rafa. Stop. You hear me? Stop. Worrying. Stop worrying about things outside of your control. Focus on what you do best. Making god damn delicious food and that will impress the designer pants off that food critic."

Chapter Fourteen

I was scrolling through my morning updates, checking my comments, direct messages, and email. An Instagram comment I was tagged in caught my attention. I got tagged in a lot of things, and sometimes it was hard to keep track. A lot of times it was just spammy promotions trying to get me to collab on chintzy jewelry or buy followers, so I had to be discerning about what I pay attention to. But this one had weight. It was a comment responding to another account, which I thought I recognized as another food blogger.

@Tastyjoy "@VeraStoneEats taste is so low-brow. She doesn't know innovation when she sees it. Not sure why she has any authority to review Barcelona hot spots."

I blinked and reread the words. Ouch. I was used to vitriol on the internet. Anyone with even a modicum of an online social presence had to accept it as part of life. The trolls were real, and they were out there. And they would come for you. But what caught my attention about this was that it wasn't from a troll or even just a random follower. This comment was made by a fellow—or maybe I should rival considering the comment—blogger. Granted, she didn't comment on my profile, but I had been tagged in her conversation. That was either a total oversight or this person wanted me to see it.

I continued to read. The original post went on to reference how my particular style of critiquing was outdated, a relic of old journalism practices, and how, at the end of the day, I didn't even have very good taste in food.

I closed the screen. I knew I should just ignore it. That I shouldn't let it hurt me, but it did. The words *low brow* echoed in my mind. Sophistication wasn't something I came by naturally. It's not like I was from a total backwater, but I was from a rural part of New York where we didn't exactly use the right fork at every course. I'd had to teach myself everything I knew about fine dining in Manhattan and my expertise was hard won. The Manhattan restaurant scene was not a place for the faint of heart or the easily deterred. It was the kind of place that would eat you alive and laugh as it digested you whole.

So seeing those words had all my insecurities flaring to life at that one little post. And besides, we were supposed to be in this world together. What was even worse was that it was a fellow woman. Being a writer, especially in journalism, was already a tough road for women. We were constantly overlooked, overworked, and underpaid. Our work wasn't taken seriously. And even in the blog space, something like food was still considered a man's domain. What bothered me was that she had decided to take a jab at someone who was on her side. Why couldn't there be room for more than one food critic? It seemed absurd. Weren't we all allowed to have opinions, to share our thoughts?

I shook my head. I wasn't going to let it get to me. I had faced tougher critics than some up-and-coming influencer. This is the nature of our business. Friends are fickle, and enemies are plentiful. The internet gave people a sense of anonymity. People felt like they could say whatever they wanted about you as long as it was in the form of a tweet or a post. They didn't have to actually say it to your face and face the consequence of your real-life pain. They were thousands of miles away, with no chance of ever encountering you in real life. It gave people a sense of entitlement. I had mixed feelings about how public things could be and how much we put out there online. But what choice did I have? It was the way I made my living these days. The magazine paid well enough for a journalism gig. But at least half of my income came from sponsorships and such. And I hadn't paid for a meal or travel in the last few years, so that was a plus.

I shook it off and poured myself another cup of coffee. I had a long day of sightseeing ahead, and I wasn't going to let this derail my plans for a fun day. With my working holiday extended, I felt like I could afford a bit of downtime to stir the creative juices and get inspired. Barcelona wasn't just about the food, of course. And to me, food wasn't just about how it tasted. It was about the experience, the culture. What made food the way it was. How did generations create these individual dishes? How did new generations turn everything upside down?

So, like a true tourist and inspired by my walking tour friends, I signed myself up for a walking tour of my own. What better way to see the city than from an eager local who wanted to tell you stories? Call me nerdy, but I loved walking tours and went on them every chance I could get. I was often alone in my enthusiasm for such things. I recalled my 30th birthday when I wanted to do a haunted ghost walking tour of New Orleans, and my group of friends, basically falling asleep, left me halfway through to hit up a Bourbon Street bar offering five-for-one shots. In a test tube. I stayed the course, absorbing every morbid tale my enthusiastic guide could muster. I learned to accept and embrace my nerdy interests a long time ago.

Lately, I operated in a silo, anyway. I had a group of friends in New York, sure. But I was a little bit of a lone wolf. And frankly, I was OK with that. Solidarity tended to fit me just fine. I liked being social when I needed to be and then going home without commitments. That's why the writer's life worked. In my younger years, when I first landed in NYC for college, I'd forced myself into every social situation I could think of, thinking it gave me a sense of purpose or belonging. When I finally allowed myself to embrace my extroverted-introvert nature, I finally found a true sense of peace.

I slipped on my trusty walking sneakers and a comfy black cotton dress, then slipped on my day backpack and headed out. I wandered the narrow, winding streets of the Barri Gòtic, making my way to my tour meeting spot. The streets buzzed with afternoon energy. Tourists mix with locals, each going about their day amidst a backdrop of Gothic architecture and history.

I arrived at the corner of Las Ramblas, where an eager group of about six awaited with sunhats and guidebooks. It was a collection of couples and one family with a teenage daughter who looked like she'd rather be walking on flaming hot coals than be there with her parents. The tour was being conducted in English, so I made a safe bet that they were all Americans, Brits, Aussies or Canadians.

"*Buenos Dias!*" the young woman leading the tour said with fervor as I approached. She flashed me a wide smile.

"Buenos Dias," I said, weaving myself into the group.

"Welcome to our famous walking tour of Barcelona," she said with enthusiastic hands. She was young and thin, with a glowing, fresh complexion. I'd say she was probably a university student, or at least of that age.

. . .

"My name is Cristina and I'll be your guide through the enchanting streets of the Barri Gòtic. A place where every stone tells a story."

I already knew this was going to be good. I pulled out my phone to take notes.

The guide began her introduction with the enthusiasm of a professor.

"Barcelona is a magical city full of history and legends and rich culture. And the Gothic Quarter is the pulsing heart of Barcelona. As you might guess from the name, is famed for its stunning medieval architecture. But the roots of this place stretch back even further." She waved a hand at the ground. "Underneath your feet are remnants of a world from over two millennia ago, to the time of the Romans who set up a colony called *Barcino* at the end of the 1st century BC. The colony had some thousand inhabitants and was bounded by a defensive wall, the remains of which can still be seen in the old town."

A couple of tourists gasped dramatically as they glanced down at their feet, looking down as if they might catch a glimpse of ancient Rome through the cobblestones. I tried to hide a smile at their earnest enthusiasm. Cristina's words did bring it all to life.

Cristina went on. "And right here, this maze-like area was once the center of Roman life."

I zoomed my camera app in to catch the intricate details.

"For over 200 years, Barcelona was under Muslim rule, and, following the Christian reconquest, it became a county of the Carolingian Empire and one of the main residences of the court of the Crown of Aragon. The fruitful medieval period established Barcelona's position as the economic and political center of the Western Mediterranean. During this time, this quarter was the heart of the city. Imagine merchants selling their exotic wares, poets reciting their newest verses, and children playing in the courtyards."

A chill ran down my spine as I heard the echoes of the past laughing off the ancient walls. A little girl ran past at that moment, laughing with gusto as she waved a streamer through the air. We all jumped as though she'd walked right through time.

Cristina chuckled. "Some things never change. Now, for a fun fact: is anyone here a fan of mysteries or legends?"

All hands shot up, including mine. Why not?

"Bueno! You see that narrow alleyway?" Cristina pointed to a shadowy path between two tall buildings. "Legend says that during full moons, a ghostly knight emerges, seeking his lost love. Locals call him '*El Caballero de la Luna*' - The Knight of the Moon."

I made a mental note to Google that later. It would add some delightful color to my article. I really wished I could livestream this whole performance right then. I loved the way Cristina spoke in a lyrical, poetic way—every word a song lulling us right back to the past.

"Now, whether you believe in such tales or not, there's no denying the palpable sense of history here," Cristina said, her hands waving about theatrically. "From the majestic Barcelona Cathedral, with its breathtaking Gothic spires, to the intimate plazas where locals gather for a café or a chat, Barri Gòtic is a testament to time, culture, and the resilient spirit of its inhabitants."

"Are you American?" A middle-aged woman in a loose floral dress and sandals leaned in to ask me, snapping me from my moment of reverie.

"Hmm? Oh, yes. I'm from New York. You?"

"New York! How wonderful. We've always wanted to go there. We're from Toronto." She gestured toward a red-cheeked man beside her. He sported a short-sleeved button-down shirt over cargo pants and the type of sneakers you see on woodsy running trails.

"Oh? Well, you're only over the water, really," I said.

"Yes, I know. We're here on our honeymoon, if you can believe it. I'm Katie. This is Jack."

The woman beamed at her partner. They weren't exactly young lovers, but you could still see the youthful adoration in their eyes.

"How wonderful. I'm Vera. You picked an amazing city for a honeymoon," I said.

"You might wanna tell her that," a British woman said. She nodded playfully toward her teenage daughter, who was staring down at her phone, thumbs whirling way over the keypad with a constipated look etched on her pale features, completely oblivious to the world-class environment in which she stood.

"I might have been the same at that age," I said. Although, that was probably a bit of a white lie. I think I would've given anything to be here as a teenager. I hopped on a plane with a backpack as soon as I turned eighteen and flew across the ocean. But, some kids will never understand how lucky they are. "Someday, she'll look back and think of this fondly," I said.

"One can only hope. Hopefully, she at least appreciates the price tag," the dad said dryly. The mom rolled her eyes at her husband as though this were a familiar dance.

"*Vale*, then, let's proceed with the tour," Cristina said. She splayed out her hands and led the way down the next winding alleyway.

She went on about the history of the city as a whole, about the region of Catalonia, and about each individual neighborhood. She talked about the famous artists who strolled the streets and crowded into cafés, huddling over cigarettes and politics. She talked about the dark years of Franco's oppression.

"They try to crush our soul, but we would not let them," she said, echoing what Celia had said. If was learned anything about the people of Barcelona was that they were a proud and determined bunch.

We continued our tour, hitting the highlights, and Cristina touched on many of the other things we might want to see and experience while in Barcelona.

"It is a big city, and you could spend a long time here and never see all it has to offer. I highly recommend a bus tour if you're so inclined. It might sound silly or touristy, but it is a wonderful way to see all the sides of the city, new and old."

We concluded the tour by stopping for some light tapas and wine at *Café Jamon*— a traditional tapas bar, complete with hanging ham hocks and Picasso prints. We gathered around a tall pub table, chatting away, getting a feel for what brought us all to Barcelona. I knew my own draw of the siren's call, but I was always fascinated by other people's motivations. It helped me understand my work better.

"Well, I saw an Anthony Bourdain Special years ago on Barcelona, and I always knew that I just had to go here," the Canadian woman—Katie—said with a sigh. "Rest his soul."

I nodded. Anthony Bourdain had been one of my heroes. His tragic, untimely death had cut me deeply.

"I remember watching his shows when I was young, and dreaming of all the exotic places he went. His love of food and culture was one thing that really hit home with me," I said.

"We're trying to get this one a little culture," the British dad, who I learned was named Lyle, said, elbowing his daughter in the side. "Spends all day on her bloody Tock-Tock."

"Dad, stop it," she whined. Her posh British accent did little to hide the fact that she was still a petulant teenager. "And you're such a *dork*." She shook her head as if to say, *I can't even.*

I tried not to laugh. Not being a parent myself, I could find a comedy in it. I'm sure living the experience of teenager-hood was far less funny.

"And we brought you here, dear?" the British mother, Rose, asked.

"Oh, I'm actually here for work. I'm covering the food scene for a magazine I work for."

"Oh, how glamorous!" Katie said. "Isn't that a glamorous job, Jack?" Katie turned to her husband, who looked more enthralled with the FC Barcelona football match on TV.

"Mmm, yes, of course," he said, not looking our way. I hid a smile.

"It's a fun job, I admit. I'm lucky to have it. Although sometimes it's hard on my waistline," I said with a laugh.

"That sure beats my job in human resources," Katie said. "Also hard on my waistline, but that's mostly from the terrible donuts every morning that I can't seem to resist, even though they taste like powdered sugar parchment. Not like the pastries here. Have you *had* the pastries here?"

I pictured the chocolate croissants and had a Pavlovian drooling reaction.

As we made small talk, another loud laughter rose above the din of the restaurant. Something familiar pricked my attention, and I followed the noise with my eyes. There, standing at the tapas bar, clutching a small glass of wine and laughing with another man, stood Rafa. I stared for a moment, his chiseled jaw and haunting looks catching me off guard as they always seemed to do. He just stood out in a room like a storm cloud at a garden party.

Then, as if sensing my eyes on him, his head slowly turned toward me. When he spotted and recognized me, his mouth turned up in a subtle smile. He waved gently. I waved back. For a moment, we were caught in a silent stare-down. Then he gestured for me to come over. My stomach flopped. I don't know why it made me nervous. I was being ridiculous. Just go over there, Vera!

I inhaled and stood. "Um, if you'll excuse me for just a moment. I see someone I need to chat with. About work," I added nervously.

"You really do have a fun job," Katie said as she spotted Rafa, a knowing little smirk spreading across her face.

I resisted the urge to roll my eyes, but just politely excused myself and strolled over to where Rafa stood.

"*Buenos tardes,*" Rafa said, the smooth cadence of his Spanish sending a little chill down my spine.

"*Buenos tardes.*" I turned toward his friend. "I'm Vera. *Mucho gusto.*"

"*Mucho gusto*, Vera," the man said. He was a little older than Rafa, with a tall, lean frame and a slight salt to the pepper. He had a tanned face that had obviously seen a lot of beach days, but a nice sharp jawline.

"This is my uncle, Tio Rafael," Rafa said.

"Tio and namesake," Tio Rafael said, winking. He leaned in to kiss my cheeks. "He gets his good looks from me."

"Vera here is—well, she's a restaurant critic," Rafa said. The words came out with a touch of uncertainty.

Raphael's eyebrows went up like two fuzzy caterpillars. "I see. Is she friend or foe?" He had a lovely cartoonish Spanish accent when he spoke English.

"I like to think a friend," I said. "But I suppose that's yet to be determined." I flashed Rafa a cheeky look.

"Yet to be determined indeed. We are still getting to know one another, are we not?"

"Indeed," I said.

Tio Rafael tapped the bartop. "Well, I find the best way to get to know each other is with wine. *Señora! Una botella de mi rioja favorita, gracias.*"

A moment later, the woman behind the counter had set down a bottle of red wine with a beautiful gold label and three fresh glasses.

Rafael filled each.

"Oh, I probably shouldn't," I said as he slid one to me. I spared a glance back to my group. Rafael's eyes followed mine.

"You would refuse a dying man his last wish?" Rafael said.

I smirked. "And what wish is that?"

"I've always wanted to share my favorite Rioja with a pretty American." He nudged the glass toward me.

"And are you dying?" I asked.

"Of course. I have been dying since the day I was born."

Rafa rolled his eyes at his uncle, but I laughed.

"How could I possibly refuse?" I picked up the glass, and we clinked. I took a long, luxurious sip.

The wine was like silk on my tongue. The atmosphere euphoric. Who cared about a jealous blogger when I was here, living my life in real-time, in color?

"When should I expect you at my restaurant then?" Rafa said oh-so-casually.

I smirked. "Didn't your manager put it in your planner?"

"Probably. I'm not very good at paying attention to details."

"I'll be there tomorrow. Are you ready?"

His eyes narrowed with playful competition. "I think, *guapa*, the question is, are *you*?"

Chapter Fifteen

As a general rule, when I'm working on a long piece rather than just a blog post or Instagram update, I give the restaurant in question three chances. This approach serves several purposes. First, I have a voracious appetite and aim to sample as much of the menu as possible, pairing dishes thoughtfully. I am literally always hungry. Second, I want to offer the staff and chef multiple opportunities to impress me. I strive to be fair in my evaluations, and everyone has off days. Third, the magazine's reputation is important both to me and the publication itself. We aim to be at the forefront of dining and travel journalism. If a restaurant receives a feature on my website, the public knows that it has been thoroughly vetted. I make a clear distinction between what I post on Instagram and what I write for the magazine. In a casual post, I might say that I had a great experience and hope it will be the same the next time I visit. But if I feature you on the website, people know you've undergone serious scrutiny.

I kept this in mind as I strolled in for my first experience at *Santos California*.

I was instantly struck by how much it felt like an actual

coastal California restaurant. It was difficult to articulate precisely why—it wasn't kitschy decor or anything blatantly obvious. Rather, it was a subtle vibe—someone had paid meticulous attention to the small details—the large windows, the airy decor and twinkling porch lights dangling from the ceilings. The second thing that captivated me was the aroma— a perfect dance and blend of spices, garlic, and fresh bread that all combined in a harmonious medley. My stomach grumbled in anticipation.

There was a balance to strike when I attended one of these tastings. I wanted to arrive hungry, of course, but not so famished that I gobbled down the food without really tasting it. Also, if you're too hungry, everything tastes amazing, which can skew your judgment. You have to be just the right amount of hungry.

I know, my job really is glamorous.

"Buenos dias," a female voice said with a British accent. I turned to see a young woman in a black pantsuit coming toward me. "Welcome to Santos California," she said in a chipper British accent.

"Hello. I'm Vera," I said.

"Yes, of course. We've been expecting you. I'm Lorna, the general manager. Please, come in. We have your table ready."

I glanced around and noticed I was the only person there.

"We aren't open for another week. At least not officially," Lorna said as though reading my thoughts. "We do have some special events and a soft opening coming up, however."

"Well, I'm very honored to be one of your first guests then," I said.

"We are just so grateful that you have taken the time to come all the way here to try out our little passion project."

I smiled thinly. If only she knew how excited I was to be here. And as I took in every meticulous detail, I thought *passion project* wasn't giving it its due.

"I've heard great things about your concept. I'm very excited to try it." I tried to keep my tone neutral.

"How did you hear about us?" Lorna asked, almost timidly, though she must know.

"Our magazine has scouts all around the world in the global cuisine scene. I think your PR team must have gotten the ear of the right person. And I was very intrigued when I read about what Rafa was doing."

Lorna nodded, whether satisfied with my answer or not, she didn't lead on.

"Wonderful. May I bring you out a glass of wine?"

I nodded. "Please." The second trickiest part about this job was not to get too drunk on the job. The restauranteurs and chefs were always eager to supply you with wine—too much wine. Most people enjoyed their meal a lot more when they were a little tipsy. But I'd made that mistake one too many times in my early days. Now, I really tried to pace myself. Loosen up with one glass and only small tastes that pair with the food thereafter.

But at that moment, as I pressed the crisp Garnacha Blanca to my lips, I nearly abandoned my entire philosophy on drinking. I could just guzzle this all day long.

"This is wonderful," I said.

Lorna smiled. "Thank you. It's one of our favorite local wineries. They do marvelous work. It's the perfect opener to your meal, I promise."

I smiled briefly and took small sips. Lorna hesitated by my table for a moment, a nervous energy dancing around her. Finally, she nodded curtly.

"Right. Well, the first course will be out in a moment."

As promised, a few minutes later, I was staring down at a Catalan caprese salad bursting with colorful Heirloom tomatoes, a salty local Catalan cheese, and fresh basil. There was something else I couldn't identify—a spicy, citrusy infusion that took me out of any notion of Caprese being solely for Italy.

Next was an Avocado Gazpacho—a cold soup hinting at a traditional Spanish gazpacho but with a creamy ripe avocado texture—a beautiful nod to California's favorite fruit obsession, I gathered.

"And what do we think so far?" Lorna asked as the server cleared away the first course and another set down the next round.

"The flavors are remarkable. What was the infusion on that caprese?"

Lorna smiled a little wickedly. "You'll have to talk to Rafa about that later on. Ah, here we have one of my favorites. The Tuna Tartare Tacos. Sashimi-grade tuna caught right here in Barcelona daily, California avocado, of course, and a drizzle of traditional romesco sauce in a mini corn tortilla made right here in-house. And the salads, you will have kale & escalivada salad, which consists of Tuscan kale, roasted vegetables, marcona almonds, and a sherry vinaigrette topped with *Bauma Carrat cheese*. It is a local favorite and definitely one of Rafa's favorites." The server returned with a tasting-size glass of wine. "Oh, and I recommend pairing this course with an Alella. The fruity notes really complement the cheese."

Even though I was already getting full, my stomach rumbled in appreciation.

"Gracias. This looks wonderful," I said.

Lorna smiled professionally and left me to my gluttony. I subtly pulled out my notebook and started jotting down my initial reactions. I was really starting to understand why Spanish food was served in small portions. How else could you taste everything?

"The main course," the server returned with tapas-sized portions of the next items.

"First is *Paella de la Baja*—a fusion of Baja California flavors and traditional paella, featuring *pulpo* and spicy Mexican chorizo."

"Chorizo?" I asked.

The server blushed, then said conspiratorially. "He'll probably be flayed alive by the traditionalists for that one, but it works. *Really* works."

I eyed the sizzling dish with ferocity.

"Next, we have grilled steak filet medallion and jumbo prawn served with a side of patatas bravas and aioli de casa, and *Brussels Sprouts al Ajillo*— Brussels sprouts fried in olive oil with garlic and chili flakes."

"I'm not sure I can get all this down. Hope you do take away bags."

She smiled thinly, probably unsure if I was joking or not. "And of course, no Spanish meal is complete without some *pa amb tomàquet*, which in this case is an individual loaf of San Francisco sourdough bread served with traditional Catalan tomato bread toppings. And a dry crianza will pair with this perfectly, I think."

"And what's your favorite?" I asked.

"Hmm?" she seemed taken aback.

"Of all the things Chef Rafa makes, what's your favorite?"

She looked uncertain, then grinned and leaned in almost insidious. "The paella. But don't tell my mama. She would never forgive me for eating octopus chorizo paella. It's a sin." She crossed her heart and winked.

I closed my eyes and melted into the ecstasy of it before diving in. *Dios mio*, she was right. The flavors on the paella were a constellation of devilish flavors. The filet was buttery soft, the prawn tasted like lobster. I chewed every bit with painstaking slowness, milking every ounce of flavor.

"How are you finding the food?"

I snapped from my food climax and looked up to see Rafa standing beside my table in his crisp, white chef's uniform, looking as though it had just come fresh from the laundry. Curiously, not a speck of food was on him. Should I be wondering if it was all a facade? Perhaps he wasn't the man behind the curtain? I thought wryly.

"It's very good," I said, keeping my expression purposefully neutral. I dabbed my white linen napkin to my lips and set it down. I wasn't trying to mean, just coy. The mean thing would be to let them think they were going to get a glowing review if I decided otherwise. But, as I chewed and severed, I knew it would be difficult to even consider giving this place a negative review.

"*Very good.* That's not very descriptive for a writer," Rafa said with a smirk. "And it did look like you and that *pulpo* were having an intimate moment."

I smiled, fighting my creeping blush, and set down my fork. "It's exceptional. Really, it is."

"Exceptional. I'll take that praise. Especially coming from you."

I tilted my head and flashed him a look. "What does that mean?"

He grinned. "Your reputation precedes you, Miss Stone. I know you're a difficult woman to please."

"In more ways than one," I said. I knew I was teetering on flirtation, but he made it too easy. He had the kind of face that was made for banter.

"We'll see if I can't be the exception, then."

"We'll see," I said.

"You still have the *dulce* course. We can talk after that. If you aren't in a coma by then."

"I nearly forgot about dessert."

He *tsk tsked* me. "I will pretend I didn't hear that."

On cue, the server returned with three bite-sized portions of deserts. She set them down in front of me.

"I'll do the honors, Sylvie," Rafa said. Sylvie nodded and made herself scarce. "*Vale*, here we have a Churro Sundae, which is Fresh churros, *helado de vainilla*, and a drizzle of crema Catalana."

"Decadent," I said, eyeing the crunchy churro with a rising fever.

"Si. And here is avocado and lime cheesecake. It's a dairy-free cheesecake featuring California avocados and a hint of Catalan lime. And finally, almond and naranja flan. A traditional flan infused with Californian almonds and Valencia orange zest."

"Where do I start?" I asked as saliva pooled in my mouth and my dress expanded.

He chewed his lip thoughtfully, and I noticed how full and lush they were. My eyes locked on the tiny motion of his teeth biting into the tender skin.

With a curt hand motion, he pointed at each. "Cheesecake, Flan, Churro. In that order."

I nodded, all business-like, and dug in.

"Uno momento," Rafa said and slipped into the back. He returned a moment later with a small bottle.

"A sweet wine to accompany. Don't worry, it's not that sweet. More raw cocoa than sugar."

He splashed a little into two glasses.

I eyed the ruby liquid in my glass, and an assertive *no thank you* was on the tip of my tongue—I'd probably had enough wine. But instead, I found the words coming out of my mouth quite contrary to my thoughts.

"Gracias. The wines tonight were also exceptional. But I'm guessing you can't take any credit for that."

"Only the selection process. It takes a keen palate to know what's going to pair well with food."

"A keen palate. I suppose I can quote you on that?"

"Quote away."

His confidence—or was it arrogance—was unusual. Chefs could be arrogant, but usually, when they knew I was in their midst, they turned into mushy balls of nerves. But not this guy. He was all swagger and confidence. It was like he didn't care at all what my review had to say. I couldn't decide if I liked it or not.

I slipped the first bite into my mouth and tried not to groan with pleasure.

For a moment, he just sat there, staring at me, hands folded across the table. Then he picked up his glass and raised it. "Salud."

I wrapped my fingers around the new glass and raised it as well. "Salud."

"So, Vera. Tell me about yourself."

I stopped chewing the flan, and half laughed. "Excuse me?"

He shrugged. "I thought we could get to know each other."

I leaned back in my chair and stared at him. "And why would we do that?"

"Because you are sitting in my restaurant. Because you're eating my food, my creation. Enjoying the wine, hand-selected by me. You are my guest. When people are my guests, I want to know them."

I swallowed my final bite and set down my spoon. "Is that so? And do you get to know every guest that comes through your door?"

He looked thoughtful for a moment, sparing a glance around his restaurant. Then he looked back at me and nodded assertively.

"Si, of course. At least I will once we open. I think it is a chef's duty to know what and who he is entertaining. Don't you want to know who is eating your food?" I chewed on his words for a moment, not quite sure what to say.

"Well, I don't really cook much."

His thick black eyebrows went up. "You don't cook? A food critic who doesn't cook?"

"It's probably more common than you think. I love food. Truly. But other people can just do it better than I can. So why muddy the waters?"

"Does that mean you don't *like* to cook?"

I sipped my wine. He was right. It was like drinking smooth dark chocolate in a glass. "I wouldn't say that. I actually do enjoy it. I just don't think I'm anything special. If I'm trying to impress somebody, I'm not going to serve them my pasta. It's going to be take-out from Trattoria Ramone down the block."

He snickered softly. "That's a shame. The best food is made by those who put love into it."

"That's a little cheesy."

He shrugged. "Is it? So it goes. Sometimes things are *cheesy* when they are heartfelt. Doesn't make it less authentic."

"I suppose that's true. So you love what you do?"

He smirked. "Do you know anything about the restaurant business?"

"A fair bit, I suppose. I spend a lot of time in them."

"Then you would know how difficult a business it is. Most of them fail. And even those that do succeed take many years to turn a profit. They are hell on relationships. On your health. On your savings."

"It is a brutal business indeed."

"So, *guapa*, you would know that anyone who is crazy enough to go into this business must love it."

I laughed. "You make a very good point, Rafa. The only people I know who run restaurants are investors and crazy people."

He raised a finger and pointed at me. "Exactly."

"Which one are you?" I said, teasing.

"You'll just have to find out, won't you?"

"Well, then. Since we're getting to know each other, tell me about this restaurant. I read that your inspiration was your mother?"

He nodded. "Si. My mother was from California. From Santa Barbara. You know it?"

"I do. It's a paradise."

"She came out to Barcelona when she was young and fell in love with my father. Never went back. But we went there often when I was growing up. I loved it there. Eventually, I went to culinary school in San Diego."

"No wonder your English is so perfect. When you want to, you hardly have an accent."

He smiled thinly. "That is very kind of you to say. Yes, I learned English from day one. I was raised bilingual, of course. But my mother, while she loved Barcelona and I don't think ever really thought of going back home, left her heart in California. And she would talk about how the food is very specific there. How you have a very fresh seafood and fresh produce. A focus on healthy and organic. Good appreciation for good soil and sustainable farming. Quality, conscious. It's very European, you know?"

I smiled. "Yes, I wish more of the country was like that."

"My father was a well-known chef here in Barcelona. But my mama loved to cook, too. I think it's her passion that truly inspired me. I knew someday I would have to infuse both my cultures into my cooking."

"Well, I think you've done a marvelous job in bringing that vision to life," I said. Perhaps the wine was loosening my tongue a little bit, but I felt like he deserved to know the truth.

He leaned in conspiratorially. "Does that mean we get a good review?"

I laughed. "Now I see why you opened the second bottle of wine."

"But of course. I needed you drunk and a little bit sloppy."

I raised my glass and drank. "It's going to take a lot more wine."

Chapter Sixteen

The sound of a glass shattering in the kitchen nearly pushed Rafa over the edge. He snapped up from his inventory list, and some choice words were on the tip of his lips when Lorna came into eyesight and shot him a look. Her cropped hair was pinned back, and she wore a casual tracksuit and bright pink trainers.

"Maybe it's time you lighten up a little, boss," Lorna said, her voice reverberating warmly in the half-lit restaurant, the scent of fresh herbs permeating the air. The mid-morning sun pierced through the wide bay-style windows.

Rafa flashed Lorna an annoyed look. His entire body was showing signs of stress from endless hours of preparation.

"When your dreams and livelihood are on the line, you can lighten up all you want. But until then, I will be as stressed out as I need to be. I would just like one day to go by without someone breaking something. It's not like the plates are free!"

He reined in his anger and breathed.

"Rafa. RE. LAX. Here, let me turn on the music." She switched on the surround sound and hit the button. A smooth, jazzy medley pierced the tension.

They both knew last night had been special, a ray of hope in the chaos of the pre-opening mayhem. Vera, the critic who held his future in her hands, had not just been pleasant, she'd been genuine, drawing out a lighter side of him that even he had forgotten existed.

Lorna leaned against the counter, staring at him thoughtfully.

"Why are you looking at me like that?" Rafa said with annoyance.

"She's getting to you."

His heart betrayed him with a skipped beat. "What do you mean?"

Lorna made a show of polishing a wine glass. She bobbed her head and started to hum.

"Lorna, what are you implying?" Rafa pushed, growing increasingly irritated.

Lorna gently set down the glass and flashed him a look. "I said, I think that food critic is getting to you."

He sighed dramatically. "Yes, do you think a food critic who could destroy the reputation of my yet-to-even-open restaurant would be getting to me?"

She shook her head. "Oh no. Don't play it like that. She's getting to you more than just professionally."

Rafa resisted the urge to growl. "I don't know what you mean."

"Yes, you do. You're a terrible liar, and you're terrible at being coy. You fancy her, and that's getting under your skin."

"*Fancy her*? C'mon, I don't even know her. I've met her twice. Ok, three times."

"That's all it takes sometimes. I saw the empty wine bottles this morning."

He shook his head. "She did a full menu tasting. It required wine."

"Mmm, hmm." Lorna said incredulously. "I'm sure it was *strictly* professional."

A flicker of images from the evening passed — Vera's laughter ringing in his ears, her inquisitive eyes locked onto his, the natural flow of their conversation that danced between playful banter and deep reflections.

"It was! Yes, she's cute. I'll give her that. But so what? Lots of people are cute. Her appearance doesn't render me unable to do my job professionally."

"Cute? Right. I'm sure that's exactly what you think when she comes in here batting those big, long lashes. And since when are chefs professional? You're no exception."

"I think maybe *you* have a crush on her," Rafa snapped petulantly.

Lorna smirked.

Rafa threw down his pen and crossed his arms. "Do you have a point to any of this, Lorna? Or are you just trying to annoy me?"

Lorna nudged him, a knowing smile spreading across her face. "I've known you for years, Rafa. I know when someone has gotten under your skin, stirred something in you."

"You read too many romance books," Rafa said gruffly.

Lorna grinned. "Like I said, maybe it's time you just loosen up a little. I don't mean professionally, but when was the last time you even went out on a date?"

He rolled his eyes. "I don't *date*. You know this. It's not like I don't have options."

She rolled her eyes. "I know. You're basically a celebrity around here. I'm pretty sure every girl in Barcelona wants to jump into bed with you. But yet you say no all the time. Women throw themselves at you, and all you do is bury your head in your work."

He sighed, the weight of her words settling on his shoulders as he looked around the restaurant, his dream inching closer to reality with each passing day. It was true—he had submerged himself in work, shunning the world, the joys and pleasures of life. But he had no choice.

"Because I have an awful lot of work to do. Maybe something you should take into consideration." He threw a bar rag at her. She ducked out of the way with a giggle.

"All right. It's none of my business. But look, Rafa. You're my friend. I want you to be happy. And frankly, as an employee, I also want you to be happy. When it's been too long for people since the last time they got busy, they get a little cranky, and that makes them bad bosses. You are cranky enough in your general state of being without adding a nonexistent love life into the mix."

"And when did you become a matchmaker? Just go back to organizing the menus, or whatever it is I pay you to do."

She shot him a cheeky grin and turned on her heel. "Just think about it!" She said over her shoulder as she walked back into the kitchen.

Rapha grumbled to himself as he turned back to his work. He had too much to do to think about Vera—professionally or personally.

He scanned through the inventory, going through anywhere they might cut costs going forward. He hated the very idea of cutting costs, but his accountant was on him. Quality ingredients cost money, Rafa insisted. But, he had to concede that it also cost money to keep a restaurant open. And his initial investment was dwindling. He had faith and confidence in himself that when the restaurant did finally open, it would be a smash hit. He truly believed it deep in his soul that he had something here. Something special, with a little bit of spark, that the neighborhood needed.

But he was also a realist, and he knew that most restaurants failed. Most businesses failed. The odds were not exactly in his favor. So maybe he should heed his accountant's advice and tighten the purse strings a little. The trick was, how did he do that without sacrificing the quality that he knew was going to make this place great? He was already running a pretty lean staff. And he got discounts wherever he could on ingredients. He contracted with a few local wine sellers to get good deals in exchange for featuring some local growers. But there was only so much they could do until the profit started rolling in. He sent up a little prayer that he wasn't insane.

Chapter Seventeen

As I was heading into my second week in Barcelona, I was really starting to get a feel for the city's rhythm. My body clock had adjusted, and I was creating my own morning rituals. Thoughts of Rafa kept popping into my head annoyingly, and I was doing my best to kick them right out. Didn't my subconscious know I had to focus? I couldn't get distracted by the first seductive local I came across.

Over morning coffee and *pa amb tomàquet,* I worked on my article for a couple of hours, then found myself back on Las Ramblas, soaking in the hustle and charm.

I took gentle steps down the vibrant pathway resonating with an energy so robust, so alive. The midday sun cast long, dancing shadows as people from all walks of life promenaded alongside me, indulging in the spectrum of sensory delights offered on this animated street.

Life on the boulevard was something straight out of a postcard—a vibrant mosaic of pulsing life.

With every step, I encountered a new scene unfolding — artists ardently sketching portraits with swift, precise strokes, their hands dancing gracefully across the canvas, as curious passersby leaned in to admire their craft. The stalls along the pathway were a cornucopia of textures and hues. Vendors showcased a colorful array of goods, from intricate lace mantillas to handmade ceramics. The flower vendors were a particular draw, a burst of vibrant purples, deep reds, and sunshine yellows and fragrances that greeted me with open arms. I paused at a stall laden with glassy amber jewels and delicate trinkets and bought myself a slim amber bracelet.

As I meandered further, street buskers offered a sound-track to my stroll—from the passionate strums of a Spanish guitar to the joyous rattles of maracas. I couldn't help but stop for a moment, allowing the rhythm to seep into my bones, igniting a warmth, a kind of happiness that buzzed silently in my veins.

A few entertainers got a little too close for comfort as I passed, and I pulled my cross-body bag tighter to me. I had been warned about pickpockets and street scams, especially in the super touristy areas, but felt pretty secure in my ability to spot trouble. I was aware of most of the hustles—the acci-dental "bumps," the distraction signs, the woman whose bags have been stolen. So I was on high alert.

As I strolled, I passed a mime dressed in classic black and white stripes, with stark white makeup and exaggerated facial expressions. He entertained passing pedestrians, making them laugh by mimicking their movements and pulling exaggerated faces.

I spared him a laugh as I passed by and then felt a presence behind me. I glanced back to see him two steps behind me. He mimicked my motions by also glancing back. I laughed again, as did he.

I took a few experimental paces, veering left and right, and true to his craft, he followed. Our little dance garnered a few chuckles from those around. Playing along, I gave a twirl, and he responded with his own flamboyant spin. But after a minute, the game wore thin, and it started to feel creepy. I waved goodbye and sped up my pace, thinking he surely didn't want to wander too far from his post. But, no, my little shadow kept on. Finally, I stopped and spun around.

"Ok. That's been fun, but let's stop now, shall we?"

The mime simply blinked at me, unmoving. I sighed and reached into my pocket for a euro. I handed it to him, and he accepted with an exaggerated bow and a little twirl.

Phew, ok. That was over with. I turned to go, but apparently, the laugh was on me. I felt a gentle tug on my bag, and my amusement faded in an instant. The sneaky clown was trying to unzip my purse! I slapped his hand away, but he was fast. He'd plucked something from my bag in a flurry of exaggerated surprise, he attempted to vanish into the crowd.

I wasn't having it. "Oh, no, you don't!"

Channeling my best vigilante impersonation, I pursued him, weaving through the crowd. Our chase was a ridiculous spectacle. I'd run after him, and he, in full mime character, would pretend to be trapped inside an invisible box or pull on an imaginary rope, trying to hinder me, all while keeping that comically shocked expression on his face.

I almost caught up to him at a fountain, where he mimed slipping on a banana peel. The surrounding crowds laughed and applauded. His comedic antics weren't enough to shake me off his trail, though.

"Stop him!" I yelled out to no avail. People probably thought this was all part of the act. Well played, little mime.

I continued my pursuit and finally spotted a group of musicians up ahead standing in the mime's direct line.

"Hey! Stop him! He stole from me."

The musicians took a minute to compute, then formed a wall against the rogue entertainer.

But just as I thought our chase had reached a crescendo, the mime spun around and came toward me, pushing me backward. I stumbled and fell right into a trinket stand. A small ceramic pot fell from the rack and smacked me right in the forehead, then shattered at my side. All around me, I heard the cacophony of laughter, applause, and angry Spanish.

I watched as black and white stripes faded into the crowd. I sighed and looked up to see a very angry tinker towering above me.

"How much for this pot?" I asked, defeated.

"Vera?"

Groggily, and with much embarrassment, I glanced up from my place of humility and squinted into the sun to see a tall figure looming over me. He crouched down, and I found myself face-to-face with Rafa.

"Um. Hi," I said.

He started to laugh. "What the hell happened to you?"

"Would you believe me that I battled a mime?"

Chapter Eighteen

"A mime, really?" Rafa asked incredulously as he pressed an ice pack to my head. I winced.

"Yup. Weird as it sounds." I held the ice to my head and tried not to die of embarrassment.

"*Un Cafe?*"

"Si. Please."

Rafa stood and stepped into his small adjoining kitchen to pop some espresso pods into his sleek, compact silver machine.

His apartment, conveniently just off Las Ramblas, was somehow exactly what I thought it would be. It was small and efficient, like most Spanish apartments, but it was more modern. The building was ancient, at least by American standards, but he'd clearly updated appliances and fixtures so that everything was a sleek, stainless steel. The furniture was Scandinavian in design, with muted colors and simple lines, and there was no clutter anywhere. The only real personalization was a few framed photos of what I assumed were him and his mom. It suited him, I thought.

He returned a moment later with two espresso cups and

handed one to me. It was so strong it sent a much-needed jolt right through me.

"So, tell me more about this mime," Rafa said with an amused smirk.

I laughed and sipped my espresso. "Well, I was minding my own business," I told him of my brief harrowing adventures to both our amusement.

"You're getting good material for your blog. What did he take?"

"You know, I don't even know. Can you hand me my bag?" I nodded toward my day bag by the door.

Rafa passed it to me, and I rummaged through it. With much relief, I found my small wallet, phone, and notebook were still there. Ah.

"Well, he is now the proud owner of an emergency kit. If he has a stomach bug, headache, or spider bite anytime soon, he should be all set."

Rafa chuckled. "Do you have lunch plans?"

I hesitated at the swift change in topic. "Um. No, I guess I don't."

He patted his leg. "Good. Then I will cook."

"On your day off?"

He waved my words away. "A chef never has a day off. Not in our nature. Come, sit at the counter while I work. Need more ice?"

I delayed standing. A personal lunch by the most up-and-coming chef in Barcelona? Any food blogger would give their career for this. So why was I hesitating? My eyes wandered down to those lips again. Yeah, that's why. He was dangerous. This whole situation was precariously dangerous.

But did I follow him to his kitchen? Yes, yes, I did.

Like a well-oiled machine, Rafa went to work pulling out ingredients. He worked like it was all choreographed, not pausing for a moment as he pulled garlic, paprika and veggies from various nooks and crannies throughout the small kitchen. The more I studied it, the more I saw how wildly modern and efficient the tiny space was. It was like a brilliant but upscale Ikea design.

He pulled out his chopping board and began working on the garlic. Instantly, the small space was a waft in the spicy aroma. He heated some oil in a large wok-style pan and tossed the finely chopped garlic in. It hissed and sputtered, then settled into a smooth oil bath, sending a signal right to my brain to begin drooling.

"Wine?" Rafa asked. "Or is it too early?"

"Never. And yes. I think my mime battles entitle me to a lunchtime glass."

"It's not *la comida* without wine. We usually have a small glass with *almuerzo* too."

"What's almuerzo?"

He plucked a bottle of white wine from his sleek fridge and poured two glasses. He slid one across the counter to me.

"Ah, si. Almuerzo—it is like a mid-morning snack, or early lunch. Something light to take a little work break. Maybe some *pa amb tomàquet* and a small beer or wine."

"Not a bad work break. Who needs Starbucks?"

He smiled. "Si. Starbucks is garbage. No offense. Then *La Comida* is the real lunch. It's our biggest meal usually and can take hours, especially on the weekend. If you're ever invited to *La Comida* on a Sunday, plan for the whole day."

I smiled. "That sounds like a nice way to live."

He tossed some shallots into the pan, filling the room with a sharp tang.

"It is. We are a lot more relaxed about life here than in the States. I loved living in California, don't get me wrong, but even so, everyone was so fast. Everything was fast and rushed and stressed."

"It's true that a five-hour lunch is probably not on most

people's agenda. Even on a Sunday. Most days, I eat lunch at my desk, and I actually appreciate food culture."

I thought of my one New York coworker and friend who considered a bowl of cereal in front of Netflix dinner.

Rafa tsked. "It's a shame. You miss out on so much living like that. And I think it makes people unhealthy."

"Oh yeah?"

He stirred the pan, the movements smooth and sensual. "If you don't appreciate your food, appreciate that it's more than just fuel but an experience, you shove it down too fast. You eat too much garbage, too many processed things from a bag or box. You rush through and eat too much without even thinking. But when the food is real, and you linger with good wine and good friends? You eat slowly, you digest. You show your body love by giving it the things it craves."

As he spoke, his hands never stopped working. The cadence of his chopping, the movement of his mouth as he spoke, and the smell of the sizzling herbs and vegetables had me in a trance.

"Is that your mom? In the picture on the wall?" I said, needing to take my eyes off the way his hands moved.

"Hmm? Oh, si. She's the best."

"So what's your story, anyway?"

Rafa said nothing for a moment. He continued on with his chopping and stirring. After a moment, he looked up at me. "My story?"

"Yes. Your story. Everybody has one."

"You already know my story. You can Google it."

"No. I mean the real story. What makes you tick, Rafa Santos? It's not just your mother's love for avocados."

He flashed me a small smirk. "Yes, I have a story. It's not that interesting."

"I'll be the judge of that," I said, taking a sip of my wine. Have I mentioned that Spanish wine is utterly delicious?

He covered the sizzling skillet and turned toward me. He picked up his wine and sipped. "Well, you know the highlights. I come from a long line of food."

I laughed. "That sounds like a good opening line."

"I told you my father was also a chef. He had quite a name for himself. And his restaurant was very successful."

"Is it no longer around?"

Rafa paused for a moment, then shook his head. "Sadly, he closed it down shortly after my parents got divorced. It was kind of a messy situation. Very expensive. And things at the restaurant got complicated because of the divorce, you know?"

I tilted my head, now intrigued by the family saga. "How so?"

Rafa started chopping a zucchini and looked contemplative. Finally, he sighed. "My father, he was a good man. And he was a good father, really. He was incredibly talented in the kitchen and a good businessman. But—he had a—wandering eye, you might say."

"Oh, I see," I said, suddenly feeling embarrassed for him.

Rafa half-laughed. "I don't know why I told you that. That's pretty personal."

I smiled comfortingly. "I'm sorry for prying. But it's OK. You can tell me whatever you want."

"Says the journalist." He smirked.

I laughed. "Fair. But we're off the record, I swear."

He nodded and added the vegetables to the pan.

He went on, unprompted. "Restaurants are not exactly great for that kind of thing to begin with, you know? A lot of late nights, people get very close. Lots of after-hours drinks. Anyway, it was always pretty harmless, you know, for years and years. My mama just didn't let it bother her. But then he got a little too close to one of his sous chefs. And it all kind of blew up. Mama found out they'd been sleeping together for months, and it was the last straw. Their marriage was already a little bit on the rocks. Running a restaurant is not exactly easy on a marriage. It's stressful, and the hours are terrible. You're kind of married to the job, *claro*?"

I nodded. "I've never run a restaurant myself, but I've certainly known enough chefs and owners to know the stress. Most of them fail, like you said." I saw the look flash in Rafa's eyes, and I corrected. "Most, but not all. There are obviously those that rise above. Like yours surely will."

He smiled thinly. "I appreciate the vote of confidence, but I don't need your platitudes. I know the risks. And I know what it takes."

"Is that why you are yet to be attached to the fairer sex?" I said playfully. He flashed me another one of those tiny smiles.

"Something like that."

He didn't say much more, and then I realized perhaps he wasn't into the fairer sex. Perhaps he liked to fish in his own pond.

"Most women like the idea of dating a chef, but when it actually comes to it, they don't want to be a part of the mess," he said by way of clarification.

Well, that answers that question.

"I imagine it's hard to be with anyone starting a small business of any kind. Start-ups are hard." I threw back the rest of my wine and pondered how I could ask for more without seeming like a complete lush.

"Si, they are. On everyone involved. So after that, things got kind of stressful. And he decided to sell the restaurant. He thought maybe he'd start over, but then, unfortunately, he got sick. And that was the end of that. He passed away about five years ago."

"I'm so sorry, Rafa."

He smiled thinly. "Gracias. But growing up, despite the toll it took on my family, I wanted to follow his path. Professionally speaking, anyway." He grinned. "I do hope my personal life goes a little better, eventually." He plucked the cork from the bottle and refilled my glass without asking. Yes, please.

"Is your mom still here in Barcelona?"

"Si. When my father was in a sour mood, she used to tease him that she grew up in paradise and would go back if he didn't change his attitude. But when it came to it, she didn't want to leave me or my sisters. And even though things didn't work out with my father, she was here for twenty years by that time. Barcelona is home to her. She loves it."

"I don't blame her. I'm not sure I want to go back either."

"She was also an exceptional cook, like I told you. In a different way, of course. Even though my father was a professional, it was really my mother who taught me to cook. Papa was always too busy. She was the one who spent time with us. She showed us the basics. She told us to love and appreciate food. How a good dinner made a home complete."

I smiled. I thought back on my own experiences with my mother, How cooking together, food, became this magical binding force.

"That's really wonderful. I'm sure she's really proud."

He smirked. "When I told her I was going to become a chef, she just about lost her mind. Lectured me on the toll it had taken on our family and did I really want that kind of life for myself. But I think, despite all her bravado, she knew there was only one path for me. Cooking is a lot like art. Some people are just drawn to it. You have no choice but to just create. That doesn't make sense to everyone, I know."

"I understand. I'm not exactly an artist myself, but I get the pull. I certainly share a passion for eating good food, even if I can't cook it." I smiled.

Rafa looked up at me with a wicked grin. "Who says you can't cook?"

"Me says."

"Nonsense. Come here." He waved me over.

I raised my eyebrows. "Huh?"

"Come into the kitchen. I will show you."

All my warning bells told me to grab my bag and run, but the pull to Rafa was stronger.

Harnessing my racing nerves, I slowly stood from my stool, sipped my wine for good measure, and came around the counter into the small space. It felt intimate and personal, the small room a canvas of many meals and memories. My heart was beating in tandem with the rhythmic sizzles that punctuated the room.

"Here, take this knife." Rafa extended a long, glinting chef's knife.

My hand was trembling as I wrapped my fingers around the sturdy handle.

He leaned in and said in a whisper. "Let's chop something."

Rafa's large hands guided mine with a gentle yet firm grasp, a reassuring presence as he guided my hand toward a pile of fresh green herbs.

"Not like this, *querida*," he murmured close to my ear. His breath was warm, his Spanish accent turning the word into a tender caress that seemed to linger in the air between us. "You must become one with the knife, feel its weight, its movement as an extension of your own self."

A shiver danced down my spine as I let myself sync with the rhythm he was setting, my grip on the knife becoming more confident under his guidance.

"That's very poetic," I said, trying not to sweat.

My skin was buzzing.

I pressed the knife down, slicing through each green spring and sending a burst of aroma into the air.

"Bueno," he said in a rich, deep murmur. A ringing started in my ears. "Now faster. Like a dance."

I swallowed hard and obeyed. My hands moved quickly as I finely chopped ingredients and tossed them into the skillet.

"Stir that for a moment," he directed. I did, hyper-aware of the heat from the stove, the heat from his body behind me, a tangible, electrifying field that seemed to pull us closer with every passing second.

I leaned down and inhaled the tantalizing scents. I turned back around, and my breath hitched as I found Rafa just inches away, his presence enveloping, yet not imposing, a firm warmth radiating from him. He stared down at me, and I was suddenly all too aware of how tall he was. How much space he occupied in a room.

"El arroz," he said, holding up a bowl of pre-cooked rice. He settled a hand on my waist and gently urged me out of the way. He tossed the rice into our mixture and stirred.

Then he turned back around.

His eyes were dark pools of warmth as he regarded me. His finger traced a slow, burning path from my hand up to my elbow as he took the spoon from me. "The moment of truth, bonita," he teased. He scooped up a tiny bite and brought the spoon to my lips.

The flavors exploded in my mouth, a riot of warmth, sweetness, and spice that danced across my taste buds in a heady rush of perfection.

"I think it's done," I said, voice barely audible above the pounding in my head.

He tasted it as well, those full lips pulling over the spoon in a way that just wasn't fair to everyone else in the room. Namely me.

"Sí. It's done. Shall we have more wine?"

Chapter Nineteen

"Should we have more wine?"

I had so desperately wanted to say yes. I had wanted nothing more than to lose my senses for a night, to give in to this thrumming at my core. But I didn't. I thought of my job. I showed restraint.

"I really shouldn't. I have a lot of work to get done," I'd said.

Rafa had smiled thinly and served up our *Arroz Espanol*.

I left his apartment full and confused.

I was now sprawled out on the plush couch of my hotel room as the sun set over my balcony, my laptop balanced on my knees. A cup of café con leche sat within arm's reach on the coffee table. I needed to focus on my work and not on sexy Spaniards. I was sorting through the photos I'd taken the previous day, ready to upload a couple of choice shots to my Instagram, when my phone buzzed.

I glanced down at my screen to see a text from my friend Willow, a podcaster in Los Angeles.

Hey, is this some sort of joke? Smiley emoji.

I tapped on the link she'd sent me. It opened an Instagram

profile eerily similar to mine—wait, no, not eerily similar. The exact same. The same profile photo, same bio, even the same damn font. I scrolled through the photos. Some were copied from my real account, and some looked like stock images. But the captions were different than my style. Low brow and snarky. Too much swearing. What the hell was this?

My heart thudded in my chest. I examined every aspect of the profile. It was an exact replica of my Instagram account. It even had 100k followers, although those were likely just bots. It was easy to craft a completely fake but seemingly legitimate online persona these days. There was no shortage of companies selling fake followers and likes. The username had a subtle tweak, just a single underscore added. And while I prided myself on crafting thoughtful, insightful captions, these were designed to provoke. The imposter was vocal about highly controversial opinions on food ethics and even politics—topics I never broached—all purportedly coming from me.

I'd been hacked. Or hijacked, rather. Was someone trying to capitalize on my following or just ruin my reputation? What could someone hope to gain from this?

My fingers flew across the phone screen as I captured screenshots of the profile and the posts. Part of me was in disbelief. Who would do this? Another part of me felt violated, as if someone had invaded my personal space, stealing my identity and replacing it with a distorted version.

I opened my laptop and sent an email to Instagram's customer service team with a detailed description and screenshots. I fired it off, then fixed myself another coffee while I waited.

My nerves were on fire as I pulled out my notebook and reviewed my thoughts. I tried to focus on Santos California—while trying *not* to focus on Rafa. I didn't want to think about the way he moved in the kitchen, the soft cadence of his accent. It was proving to be a futile task.

My phone buzzed again, and I saw it was an email notification from Instagram—my account was temporarily suspended pending review for 'harmful and abusive behavior.' You've got to be kidding me! An imposter was hacking my identity, my *work*, and I was the one being punished?

"No!" I yelled into my laptop screen. I massaged my temple. Which was starting to thrum. This could not be happening right now.

There was a line at the end of the email. "If you think this was in error, please contact customer service with your case."

I sighed and clicked the button with fervor. "*This is in error.*"

I leaned back. What the hell was I going to do? First, I needed to alert Joanne. I had an ethics clause at the magazine, and I needed to make sure they knew anything this imposter was posting was not me, just in case. I fired off a detailed email to her. I tossed back my coffee and sighed. Now what?

Then, a thought popped into my head. I pulled up my phone's contact list. I found the number and dialed.

"Karlo here," the groggy voice of my go-to IT director at *TLL* picked up.

"Karlo! Hi, it's Vera Stone."

"Hey, V. Um, what's up?"

"Sorry if I'm interrupting. I know you hate the phone."

He chuckled lightly. "All good. Just a long day implementing this stupid new firewall. Boring. Anyway. What's going on? VPN issue? We've been having some issues with the remote log-ins. I have a workaround if you need it."

I scratched at the wood on the coffee table. "Uh. No, that's all working fine. Um, hey, it's more of a personal issue. Do you have a minute?"

"How much coffee will I need?" He asked. I laughed lightly.

"Hopefully, not as much as I do. But you're the best IT nerd I know."

"Can always count on you for a compliment. Ok, what's up?"

I ran him through my Instagram predicament.

"And now they've closed my real account," I said, exasperated and panicked all at once. "And I know that seems like a minor issue—*oh, no, I lost my social media*—but it's my job, you know?"

"I get it. No need to defend it. Is the dummy account still up?" he asked. I heard the clack of the keyboard.

"Yes. Unfortunately. They're operating like they're me! How can they do this?"

"Happens way more than you'd think. And Instagram isn't responding?" He asked. More typing.

"I countered their violation of terms thing, but I haven't heard back."

"Okay, okay. Send me all the screenshots, and I'll see what I can do. Unfortunately, this crap is common. But fortunately, being common means there's precedent for solutions. Sit tight and don't stress. You probably got flagged by a bot and once a real human actually looks at the appeal, they'll reinstate you. If there are any real humans working there anymore."

I smiled weakly through the phone. "Ok, thank you."

I hung up and emailed him everything I could. I waited, nervously sipping my now lukewarm coffee that I definitely didn't need this late in the day.

Too much nervous energy to sit around and wait, but too agitated to work, I laced up and went for a run. Wine, coffee, and rice sloshed around in my stomach, but the distraction helped.

After managing to lose myself in a sloppy and ill-coordinated three-mile loop, Karlo rang me back.

"Tell me you have good news," I said, catching my breath.

"I've traced the IP. But it's cloaked."

"Cloaked? What does that mean? Sounds so ominous."

He cleared his throat. "It's how you hide your location. Without getting too technical, you basically access the internet through a second computer called a proxy server. The proxy server acts as an internet gateway while their IP address remains hidden. It's not that different from the VPN you use for your work computer. It can be a security thing for companies, or it can be to hide more nefarious activity."

"So you can't tell me anything?"

"Well, I can at least tell you that the proxy is local to Barcelona. Not too far from you."

"Barcelona?" I said with surprise. "Who would want to steal my identity here?"

I the clack of computer keys through the line. "Honestly, V, this move is so public and obvious, that I'd think less in the identity theft realm and more in the sabotage or just plain old messing with you. Jealous local? Someone who doesn't care for your controversial stance on tinned fish?"

I sighed. "I have no idea. Is there anything else you can do?"

"I'll keep digging. Maybe they left some breadcrumbs. But really, I think your best bet is to keep on Instagram customer service. Escalate the complaint. It's not hard to prove this. I'll email you over what found."

"Thanks, Karlo. I owe you a giant beer when I get back."

"Yeah, you do. Ok, stay safe, Vera. And change all your passwords on everything."

I hung up and followed directions and went about updating all my passwords. As I updated my last, I paused. Whoever was behind this was here, in Barcelona, maybe even closer than I realized. The thought sent a chill down my spine.

When Karlo's findings came through, I spent the next hour writing an email to Instagram's support team, attaching evidence, and pushing for the reinstatement of my account. As I hit "send," I couldn't help but feel a mix of vulnerability and anger. My one authentic platform to the world had been hijacked, and there was nothing I could do but wait and hope it would be sorted out. I was completely in the dark, trying to fend off an enemy I couldn't see.

After sending the email, I felt like I had hit a wall. I wanted to keep working, to keep fighting back, but with my account suspended, there was only so much I could do. I slumped into the plush hotel bed and stared at the ceiling, feeling the exhaustion of the day finally catching up with me.

That's when my phone vibrated. I lunged for it, hoping for a message from Instagram Support. Instead, it was from my editor, Joanne.

"Got your message. That sucks, darling. But hang in there. I've alerted the editorial board so they know whatever garbage this imposter is slinging isn't coming from you."

While it didn't change anything, the message lifted my spirits just a little. At least I knew that part of my career was safe. And it reminded me that I had a team of people on my side.

I finally caved into the fatigue and dozed off, my phone still clutched in my hand. I woke up a couple of hours later to a notification sound. I snapped up and opened my Gmail app. It was Instagram Support! "Thank you for contacting Instagram Support. We have successfully verified your identity and restored your account. The reported account has been removed for violation of terms. We apologize for any inconvenience this has caused."

I sighed in relief. One battle won, but the war was far from over. My eyes narrowed as I thought about the imposter. Whoever you are, I thought, you picked the wrong food critic to mess with.

Chapter Twenty

As I approached Vila Cocina, Martí's restaurant, I wasn't a hundred percent sure what I was doing. Once my Instagram had been restored, I found a direct message from him inviting me to dinner at his restaurant. His motive was unclear, however. I mean, I didn't live under a rock. I knew Martí was flirting with me at the festival. But how much of it was genuine and how much of it was to pull me into reviewing his restaurant, I couldn't be sure. I was always suspicious of these kinds of things. I couldn't help it. It was in my nature. I always assumed someone was out for a hustle.

Or was this supposed to be a date? That was also unclear.

I stepped into the restaurant, and it smelled delightful if not a little overpowering. It was hard to pinpoint the exact scent. I looked around, and the decor was decidedly Spanish. Legs of ham hung from the ceiling, and displays of gorgeous tapas were in glass cases. An entire wall of wine greeted me. It was the kind of place you'd expect to find in Spain. And there was nothing wrong with that, to be sure. You had to give people what they were looking for. An authentic Spanish experience? Check.

I'd looked up Vila Cocina, of course, and read that it had been featured in the 2019 Savvy Traveler guidebook as a top Barcelona eatery. The mention had naturally skyrocketed business, garnering Chef Martí tons of local media attention. He was still riding high as a top destination, although a more recent review in a local rag had described his restaurant as a "tired touristy concept that refuses to evolve." Ouch.

But I wasn't there to review or judge. I was there for—I wasn't really sure. Curiosity more than anything. Well, and food. I never really could say no to a free dinner.

"*Buenas noches*!" Martí emerged from the back. He was wearing a black button-down shirt with black slacks, what I assumed was his uniform when not actually cooking. The ensemble was quite form-fitting, showcasing a lean figure.

"*Buenas noches*," I said. "This is a lovely place you have."

He nodded and looked around with proud satisfaction. "Gracias. She is my pride and joy. And we have done very well. I'm grateful."

He gestured toward a table in the back, already lined with a place setting and a bottle of wine. "Please, will you join me for a drink?"

"Do you have work to do? Are you closed?" I asked.

"This is the day we are closed, si. But, I like to come here when it's empty. Is that terrible? That I eat at my own restaurant even on my day off?"

"Not at all. I think it shows your passion for what you do. And maybe it's your comfort zone."

"Comfort zone." He chewed on the words for a minute. And I realized maybe it was more of an American phrase. "Ah, si. Yes, my comfort zone. It's where I feel the most at home."

I took my seat, and Martí filled up two glasses of wine and slipped into the seat opposite me. "Salud." He raised his glass.

"Salud," I said, sipping. I could really get used to drinking Spanish wine all the time. Yes, you could find Spanish wine back home. Lots of specialty wine shops carried decent bottles. But I knew there were things you could only get here at the source. There were a lot of small winemakers that just didn't distribute outside of their local regions. And the glory of it all? It was always so inexpensive. Back home, we treated wine like a luxury. And if you weren't willing to shell out $20 a bottle, you were likely drinking swill made in inhospitable inland areas. But here, wine was just part of everyday life. They took pride in even a simple table wine.

"I hope you don't mind, but when you said you enjoy eating just about everything, I took the liberty of preparing a menu for you. I know, on a proper dinner date, you would be choosing your own menu, but I didn't really think this was a dinner date," Martí said.

"Oh? Then what is it if not a dinner date?" I asked, swirling my wine. I sipped, waiting for his answer.

"I don't know," he bobbed his head. "I think I just want to show off my pride and joy to a beautiful woman."

I half chuckled. "I think that sounds like a dinner date."

"OK then, you said it. It is a date."

I smirked, not entirely convinced either of us really thought that.

"Honestly, it's perfectly fine that you selected the menu. I love a chef that takes pride in his work. And I trust your judgment is the best," I said.

"What kind of chef would not take pride in his work?" Martí said, echoing Rafa's sentiments. They both had a point. This was a brutal, unforgiving business. Even those with absolute passion and pride in every speck of basil often failed.

"Always do everything with your full ass, I say," I said.

His expression contorted, utterly confused. I laughed.

"It's just a thing my boss used to say. Don't half-ass things, Vera. Do everything with your full ass."

Martí chuckled as he registered the joke. "I like that. And it makes a lot of sense. If you're going to do something, just do it right?"

"Most definitely."

"OK, are you hungry then? Can I bring out the first course?"

"I think you better before I have too much of this wine." He shot me a flirtatious smile and shot out of the room into the back. A moment later, he emerged from the kitchen carrying a tray of starters.

"Some of my favorites." He set down the tray of small, sliced bread topped with a variety of delicacies. My eyes went wide. Much like the decor, they were all things you'd expect to find in a Spanish restaurant. Tiny smoked fish, cheeses, various tomato purées. But they were definitely elevated. I could tell just by the presentation and the aromas, this wasn't prepackaged, fast food Catalan. It might be traditional, but it looked decidedly authentic. That was his whole thing, wasn't it?

"Please forgive me, as I absolutely stuff my face," I said.

"I appreciate if you don't stand on pretense," he said with a laugh.

"No, I've never been accused of that. I'm afraid I tend to say far too much." It was true. I had a habit of putting my tiny foot in my big mouth. But honestly, I'd stop caring a long time ago what people thought about what I said. When I chose to be a somewhat public figure, in the sense that I was putting my work out for the public to read and critique, I had to give up having sensitive skin. People were going to say all kinds of horrible things to me online and in the comment section. I got nasty emails from people who did not appreciate my thoughts. Apparently, even other bloggers wanted to take me down. At first, it got to me. At first, it made me want to reign in the personality I was cultivating online. It made me not want to not be myself, to walk a more delicate line. But then I thought, screw it. I've got one life to live and one job to do, and I'm going to do it the way I want to do it. If people don't like my personality, the way I write, or my opinions? There is a beautiful Unfollow button.

"You're known for your very traditional approach, aren't you?" I ventured as I savored a particularly zesty bite of fish.

Martí snickered, leaning back with a confident air. "Traditional. People make it sound like it's a bad thing."

I shrugged, swirling the wine in my glass thoughtfully. "I think some people equate traditional with a lack of innovation."

Martí's face grew serious, and he leaned forward, resting his forearms on the table. "Innovative? Interesting choice of word. Tell me, why should we be innovative? Why change something that has been perfected over thousands of years? Why innovate recipes we fought so hard to protect during the 20th century?"

His passion on the subject was palpable. I considered his point, feeling the weight of culinary history in his words. "One could argue that innovation drives progress. But I do see your point. Not everything requires an update."

He waved dismissively, though his eyes twinkled with amusement. "I am not discussing societal growth or politics here. I mean, why do we need to 'innovate' food? Traditional flavors, pairings — they satisfy the soul, fulfill what the body craves."

The man clearly had a fierce dedication to his culinary heritage. I could admire that. "Being different isn't inherently bad, though, is it?" I argued, unable to resist playing a bit of a devil's advocate.

Martí sighed dramatically, throwing his hands in the air for emphasis. "Not bad, per se. But it alters the perception of what Catalan food represents. Fusion cuisine, while interesting, can overshadow traditional dishes, eroding the essence of our culture over time. People already don't know the differences between what makes the food here different from the rest of Spain."

"Why don't you tell me?"

He flashed me an impish smile. "Is this a test?"

I laughed. "No! I'm sitting here thinking, maybe I don't even really know."

"Our food is deeply related to other regions of Spain, especially Valencia and the Balearic Islands, but also to the south. A lot of people from Andalusia and Extremadura came to work here in the 20th century. So we here love gazpacho, *tortilla de patatas*, and paella as much as in the rest of Spain, obviously. But we have some differences that the rest of Spain doesn't do. We mix meat and seafood in the same recipe—gasp!" He put his hand over his mouth dramatically.

"What do you think of Rafa Santos' new concept?"

At the mention of Rafa's name, Martí's eyes went a shade darker. "What about him?"

"Do you know him?"

Martí took a long drink of wine. "Si. We've known each other our whole lives."

Curious.

"Is that right?"

Martí shrugged. "It's a small community, really. And I think...I think I wish him the best of luck."

There was more here. "I'm featuring his restaurant in our magazine as an innovative new Barcelona concept."

"Really? I may need to rethink my perception of you as a critic," he teased, raising a playful eyebrow.

"Tread carefully, Chef."

"I am teasing of course. It's just, you have to be careful about these chefs," Martí said.

I flashed him an incredulous look. "These chefs?"

"The newcomers. They're so desperate to make their ventures work they'll say anything. Especially to those who wield the sword of culinary destiny."

Laughter burst from me. "Is that what you think of me?"

He shrugged. "You do carry some weight. Just be careful about getting too close. You know us Spaniards. We have a reputation." He winked.

"And are you any different?"

Martí grinned. "Once upon a time, maybe not. But now, I think my reputation is pretty well secured. My restaurant is, how do I say it without sounding too arrogant? A hit."

"Oh, so you don't need any publicity?"

"Not the same way."

I popped some cheese in my mouth. "You make it sound like you don't trust Rafa."

He worked his jaw. "Maybe I don't."

"That's interesting. Those are some pretty strong words."

Martí shrugged. "I just say how I see."

"Would you care to elaborate?" I sipped the last of my wine and chewed a tomato.

Martí sighed and looked pensive.

"I don't like to gossip. And if you can't say nice things about people, you probably shouldn't talk at all, right?"

"So the adage goes."

"But, let's just say, he says he will do one thing, and then he will do something entirely different. He uses people to get what he wants. And with something like you, he wants very much for your stamp of approval. He wants—no, he *needs*—that feature article you're writing to go well. And I think he'll use all kinds of tactics to get to you."

I considered Martí's words. I wasn't sure what tactics Martí thought Rafa could use to get to me, but I suppose I wasn't a complete stranger to the idea. I wasn't naïve. I'd been offered all kinds of things in exchange for my stamp of approval, as Martí put it.

"I appreciate what you're saying, Martí. But I assure you I can take care of myself. I've had plenty of chefs and owners try to bribe me and otherwise earn my favor. I'm not so easily manipulated."

Martí shrugged and offered me a thin smile. "I'm sure you're not. I just would never want you to be taken advantage of."

I tried not to take offense to the idea that he thought I was the kind of person who could be taken advantage of. I suppose anyone was susceptible, but I was one of the last people who was going to fall prey to some bush league tactics.

"Well, enough about that. Why don't you bring the next course? I'm suddenly starving."

Martí leaned back, his face wearing a slightly worried but hopeful expression. "Then I must impress you. It seems I have a significant task ahead of me."

"I am ready to be impressed whenever you are, Chef Martí."

Chapter Twenty-One

"The cooking here is more than just a pastime or an occupation. It's a part of people's souls. It is woven into the fiber of their beings, their life tapestry..."

#Foodscene   #barcelona   #barcelonacooking   #foodwriter #foodcritic

I typed out the Instagram post with a vibrant photo of last night's traditional fare—*Escalivada* with aromatic roasted red peppers and eggplant. *Esqueixada de bacallà*—salt cod and tomato salad. And the famous *Arròs negre amb allioli*—squid ink rice—a bizarre but shockingly satisfying concoction. I was still tasting the garlic.

I clicked "post" and sent my words into the ether. So far, my culinary adventure was everything I'd hoped it would be, but I was struggling to find that real spark—the heart of the article. If this was more than just a feature on which restaurants to try for a top-ten list, then what was the true beating heart of the thing?

I glanced at the clock and noted it was time for my interview with Rafa.

Martí's words echoed in the recesses of my mind—he couldn't be trusted. Rafa wasn't like that, surely. I thought back to our moment chopping and swaying in his tiny kitchen. The heat of his body, and the tantalizing scent of garlic enveloping us, trapping us in a moment. I shook my head. I was letting the romance of Barcelona cloud my judgment. This was all professional. "And here were two chefs, clearly with some sort of historical rivalry, possibly using me. I could see that, and I wasn't going to be tossed about like a mouse between two cats.

* * *

"There are a lot of people who think what you're doing is not really Catalan cooking," I said as I sat across the table with my trusted notebook.

Rafa stopped arranging the pintxos for a moment but said nothing. Finally, he turned around and faced me with such sincerity it melted my icy heart just a little.

"People always say that when you're a threat to the status quo. When you try new things. People have said that about art from the beginning. Do you know how many artists were cast out and burned at the stake here because they dared to try something different?"

I tilted my head. "Is that really true?"

He shrugged and chuckled. "Ok, maybe not the burning at the stake part, but cast out of polite society, definitely. People do not like change. I'm not just talking about the ancient Catholics. I'm talking about even now. How many times have you seen a piece of modern art for the first time and thought, what the hell is that supposed to be? Show me the Monet."

I laughed. He had a point. The very first time I visited the New York MoMA, I scratched my head as I stared at a single brick painted black.

"You've called cooking art before. Is that what you feel you're doing?" I said.

His lips turned up into a subtle smile. "Of course. Cooking is art. And like any art, there's a recipe, a formula. And you learn that, but then you put your soul into it, and you find a new path, a new way. You are creating something from nothing. From raw ingredients. And through that thing, you create an experience for your audience. The right food can move you to tears."

"Or indigestion."

He snickered. "You like to use humor as a defense mechanism."

I turned my eyes down and pretended to jot down notes. "And how would you know that?"

"I've known you long enough to sense that about you. This whole snarky façade is just that, I think. A façade."

"My dry humor is just part of the job. It's what people like about me."

He smirked. "I see."

"Well, I admire it. Cooking."

"Do you?"

"Of course," I said, laughing. "I wouldn't be in this job if I didn't respect cooking. People have accused me of hating food. I'm just very discerning. The truth is, I love food. I love everything from taco trucks to five-star Italian bistros. It all has a place in the world."

"You made a wonderful arroz espanol," he said in a low husky tone that tickled my spine. I cleared my throat. Rafa grinned and went on. "And so, what do you think of innovation then?"

I drummed my fingers and thought. "I think—I think we

are comforted by the traditional. I think, as you said, the newness sets people on edge a little bit. But we need innovation. We need to test our limits, whether it's through art or through food. I think sometimes it gives us a greater appreciation for the traditional. But other times, it opens our eyes to brand new things. Experiences we never could've imagined."

He nodded. "Can I expose you to something you never would've imagined, then?" He said, with a slightly more serious tone. There was something about his voice that was indicative of sultry Barcelona nights.

"I was hoping you'd say that."

Rafa turned back to his work and then set the platter down in front of me.

"*Pintxos ala Rafa Santos.*"

I eyed the masterpiece in front of me piled onto small slices of baguette and skewered with toothpicks. My stomach grumbled. "What are we looking at?"

He lovingly pointed to each creation. "*Cochinillo*—suckling pig. *Angulas*—which are eel fried in olive oil, pepper and garlic. A personal *favorito* of mine."

I eyed the worm-like sea creatures with skepticism, but I was rolling with it.

"This one is simple. Bacon-wrapped dates. But I have the dates flown in from California, and the drizzle is a balsamic reduction."

Saliva filled my mouth, and my body went numb. This was all a giant tease.

"And *finale, morcilla cocida pinchos* topped with fried quail egg."

"And what is *morcilla cocida*?"

He grinned like a naughty child. "Blood pudding."

The way he looked at me over his creations sent a chill down my spine. I had to be honest that from the very first time I saw him, I felt a little jolt of lightning. But that's how I knew he was all wrong. Nothing about the situation was a good thing. Professional implications aside, men like Rafa only came with trouble. The sexy brooding Byronic hero—no, I'd had plenty of those in my life. The kind of men with whom you have that raw chemistry—it never goes anywhere. It's explosive. You can't trust that kind of chemistry. It clouds the brain, the senses, and you end up in a melted puddle of wax on the floor like a candle left to burn out. You can't have a functional relationship with that kind of chemistry. Not that I knew a whole lot about functional relationships, having never really had one chemistry or not.

Thoughts of Alex suddenly permeated my mind. Oh, Alex, my college boyfriend and perpetual nice guy. He was smart, kind, from a good family. And he wanted to settle down. Settle down with me, no less! I wasn't the kind of girl you settled down with. Not then, not now. No, I was too driven, too focused on making a career. I was selfish, but rightfully so. I had been burned before by men swearing their allegiance and then stabbing me in the back. A nice guy like Alex couldn't withstand my thunderstorm of determination.

It was like I needed that kind of raw chemistry to be satisfied, but it always got me in trouble. What was wrong with me? Why couldn't I like a nice and normal guy like Alex? Why did I always have to fall to my knees over broody jerks? Why were women such idiots sometimes?

I read an article once in *Psychology Today* that men were attracted to unhinged women and women were attracted to jerks. There was no real logic to our species, I guess. How had we survived?

"You seem 1,000,000 miles away?" Rafa said.

"What's that?" his words snapped me from my reverie.

He flashed me a flirty grin. "I just said you seem distracted. You didn't respond to the last thing I said."

I shook my head, dismissing my meandering psychological

pondering. "Oh, sorry. I'm just thinking about work. I suddenly had an idea for how to phrase something, and I was sort of mentally writing it down."

"I do that too."

"What's that?"

"When I get ideas for something. It can stop me in my tracks. I could be in the middle of running a marathon, and I will just stop and mentally take a note. Hopefully, write it down if I can."

"And what kind of ideas would those be? Like recipes?"

He nodded. "Si. Like recipes. How to modify something. A menu. Maybe something seasonal, an ingredient to try. Just like art, you get ideas, you get inspired. And it can take over your whole life until you get that idea out there."

"Totally. Even though what I do isn't exactly creative writing, there is some art to it. At least, I like to think so."

"Who says it's not creative writing? Just because it's nonfiction doesn't make it any less creative. Lots of things are creative that aren't made up. I read your articles. You have a wonderful way with words. You have a way of bringing the reader right into the kitchen."

I blushed. "That's one of the nicest things anyone's ever said to me," I said. I buried my embarrassment in a glass of wine.

Rafa stared at me a little too intensely. His eyes bore into me like hooks right into my soul. I wanted him to look away, but then again, I never wanted his eyes to leave me. As if sensing my discomfort, the corners of his lips turned up. It was subtle, but I caught it.

"You look uncomfortable," Rafa said, his voice dropping just a little. It had a deep, throaty sound that sent vibrations down my spine. I swallowed.

"I'm not uncomfortable. I'm just tired. It's been a long week."

He nodded, doing a poor job of containing a smirk. He reached for the wine bottle and tilted it over my glass. I quickly shook my head.

"No, I shouldn't," I said.

I heard the words, but my tone was weak. Because who didn't want another glass of delicious Spanish wine in an incredible restaurant in my favorite city with a sexy Spaniard staring me down? Yeah, the whole situation sounded *terrible.*

"But you say one thing, and your eyes tell me something very different. You do that a lot, you know."

"What's that?"

"Pretend you don't want what you actually want."

I swallowed again. We were dancing a dangerous line. A little too close to the edge.

I said up straighter. "Fine, I will have another glass of wine. Fill it up."

He grinned, wiggling his brow, and topped off my glass. He filled his as well and placed the empty bottle back on the table.

"What else do you plan to do while you're here in Barcelona, Vera Stone?"

I popped another bite into my mouth and took a long time chewing, biding my time as blood pudding filled my mouth. "I don't know. I don't have a lot of plans. Probably just eat a lot of food and try not to get too fat."

He laughed. "Didn't you know the calories in our food don't count?"

I raised an eyebrow. "Oh, is that so? Fascinating science you have."

"It's true. I think it's the saffron. It creates a negative calorie balance. You can look it up. Cutting edge science."

"Since I would desperately like that to be true, I'm going to believe you."

"You should really get out and see more things, though. Barcelona is the best city in the world."

"I don't disagree. I'll probably hit the top tourist sites when I can."

Rafa shook his head. "You need to do more than just see *La Sagrada Familia*, as wonderful as it is. There's a whole vibe to Barcelona that you're not going to find in a tour book."

"I'm sure there is. Every city has one. I just don't necessarily know what to look for. And I'm not sure I have that kind of time. I have a lot of work to do." I said, lowering my eyes.

"Stop that," Rafa said.

"Stop what?"

"Stop pretending you don't want to do what you want to do. Do you want to see the underground? I'll take you. Do you want to go to the hottest flamenco club? You got it. Do you want to eat the best gyro in the world that will probably give you a horrible stomachache? You got it."

I sighed longingly. "There is nothing better than a dirty gyro, is there?"

"Nothing in this world. The sicker you are the next day, the better it was."

I hesitated and played with the pages of my notebook. My mind was screaming at me to finish up, go home, and work on my article. But my heart...my heart was much louder and far more convincing.

"All right then. I can make myself free for a little underground exploration." I closed my notebook with assertion.

Rafa tapped the top of the table with gusto. "Excellent. Finish your wine and will go."

"What, right now?" I said with surprise.

He shrugged. "Why not? You're done working for the day, aren't you? Besides, these kinds of places, they don't heat up till late. Now is the right time to go. And you're already out. And you're already dressed for the occasion."

I glanced down at my flowy red dress, which I had seen as tourist chic, not Flamenco club. "Am I?"

Rafa leaned in. "Yes. You look incredible. Maybe even a little too incredible. Spanish women can be very jealous, so watch out." He said with a wink.

I pretended the comment didn't faze me, but secretly, my entire insides were exploding. He needed to stop whispering things in my ear. It was going to get us all in big trouble.

Chapter Twenty-Two

As Rafa led a very nervous but elated me through the narrow, labyrinthine streets, I couldn't help but feel the transformation of Barcelona around me. We were venturing into El Raval, a district that hummed with a life force all its own, a neighborhood that had shed its former skins many times over to reveal the dynamic hotspot it was today.

Rafa seemed to sense my curiosity. "Have you ever been down here?"

"I think when I was here in Barcelona before, but that was fifteen years ago."

"El Raval has a complex history. It was once the *Barri Xinès*—a term that didn't really have anything to do with China but rather indicated its seedy reputation. Over the centuries, it's been many things—a refuge for minorities and outcasts. A hotbed of revolutionary activity. Even an enclave of artistic brilliance. Dalí, Picasso, them and their kind all spent time here."

My imagination flared to life as I pictured the artists and outcasts huddled over cigarettes and sketchpads, dreaming of a more enlightened Spain.

As we walked, the district seemed to embody this eclectic past. On one corner, an elegantly restored Art Nouveau building stood like a grand dame, commanding respect. Just across from it, colorful street art adorned the walls, defiant and irreverent, like a rebellious teenager declaring autonomy. Squat, centuries-old taverns coexisted with avant-garde galleries—a halal butcher shop was neighbors with a vintage boutique.

The air was thick with scents that defied easy categorization. The smoky aroma of grilled lamb skewers floated from a tiny kebab shop, mingling with the floral notes of incense wafting from a New Age bookstore. Over it all, the earthy smell of worn cobblestones carried the whispers of countless souls who had trodden them before. The result was a sort of delirium.

Finally, Rafa stopped in front of a nondescript door that I would have easily missed. "And arrived," he announced, pushing it open. As we stepped inside, I felt as though I'd been transported to another world—a world where the rhythms of Flamenco guitar reverberated through the very air, compelling even the most reluctant feet to move.

The door closed behind us with a soft thud, muting the cacophony of El Raval and enveloping us in a dimly lit cocoon of raw emotion and intense focus. The club was an intimate space—its walls swathed in plush, dark red velvet that seemed to absorb both sound and light. The room felt like the inner chamber of a heart, pulsating to the rhythm of its own lifeblood—Flamenco.

"Have you ever been to a Flamenco club?"

I shook my head. "I've seen live performances. But I didn't realize there were clubs for it. That normal people just go dance flamenco."

His brow furrowed. "Then you are in for something very special. Come on, let's get *una cerveza*."

I couldn't help but notice the stage, no bigger than a small bedroom, but it commanded attention as if it were a grand arena. The wooden floor looked worn, likely a testament to the countless footfalls and heel-clicks that had been imprinted on its surface.

The air in the club was rich with the mingling aromas of human intensity—sweat, a trace of cologne, the faint bitterness of spilled beer, and the sharp tang of anticipation. Smoky incense curled in the air, lending a mystical vibe to the place. Scattered around were tables covered in deep red tablecloths, each adorned with flickering candles casting dancing shadows. I almost expected vampires to emerge from the shade.

Lively music bounced off the walls and dancers of all kinds were clicking and clacking across the floor with flamenco moves. Some even had the castanets, clapping them over their heads as they moved.

"Can you dance like that?" I asked.

Rafa shot me a half smile. "Maybe. We shall see."

We made our way to the bar where Rafa shouted over the noise to grab us two cold Estrella beer bottles.

"Salud, Vera," he clinked his beer against mine. I didn't drink beer often, but the cold liquid was the perfect pairing with the sweaty room.

Before I could take it all in, the strumming of a guitar filled the room. The room hushed. It started soft, almost like a whisper, but grew into an attention-grabbing roar. Then came the clapping, the rhythmic handclaps as integral to Flamenco as the guitar itself. They punctuated the melody like heartbeats, giving it life and vigor.

The room collectively held its breath as a dancer—her back ramrod straight, her face an unreadable mask—stepped onto the stage. As she moved, her ruffled, blood-red dress seemed to become an extension of her, mimicking her fervor and passion. When she stomped her heels, it was like an act of defiance, an assertion of her existence and a demand to be seen. My eyes were riveted to her every movement, her swirling red dress becoming a blur, as if she were a painter's brush bringing a vivid portrait to life on an invisible canvas.

She finished up her first set and the room erupted in applause. She smiled with a tight satisfied smile. Her piercing eyes scanned the audience, and for one unnerving moment, they locked onto mine. Dumbly, I waved. With a playful smirk, she beckoned me to join her on stage. My stomach did a somersault.

I shook my head and stepped back. She opened her arms to me like a welcome.

"Senorita!" she shouted. "*ven aquí.*"

Everyone around us cheered me on.

I turned to Rafa in mild panic, but he just chuckled. "Go on. That's Blanca. She's very nice. Doesn't bite too hard."

I wondered if he was speaking from personal experience.

"You're used to a live audience, Vera."

I glared. "Online! Not like this." I shook my head wildly. "I don't know how to Flamenco."

"Just follow her lead and feel the music," he said, that familiar grin stretching across his face as if he were privy to a private joke.

I felt every pair of eyes on me. Blanca began a rhythmic clap from the stage, and the room followed. Oh God. I was backed into a corner. I mustered my courage and smiled as brightly as I could, feeling like a lamb being led to a rather rhythmic slaughter. I rose and climbed onto the stage. Everyone applauded. Blanca greeted me with a smile that said, "Welcome to my world." The crowd was a blur. My ears buzzed with the thrumming guitar and handclaps that filled the space like a palpable energy. It was terrifying but also thrilling.

"*Vale*!" the guitarist shouted before he strummed the first chord.

Awkward and uncertain, I took my first tentative step. Blanca, reading my hesitancy, started to guide me. Her hand on my shoulder felt like a grounding force, and I started to forget where I was—or who I was supposed to be at that moment.

My movements were far from graceful, a clumsy imitation of the spectacle I'd been watching. But something began to shift. As the room clapped along, their rhythmic encouragement seeped into me, dissolving the stiffness in my bones. When I glanced at Rafa, his eyes met mine, and what I saw there—unfiltered joy and affection—gave me the impetus to lose myself in the music fully.

Emboldened, I attempted a spin, my arms reaching for the nonexistent stars in the dim room. But my bravado exceeded my balance. I stumbled, my world tilting sideways, and just when I thought I was about to hit the ground—Rafa was there. He'd leaped onto the stage and caught me, steadying my world both literally and metaphorically.

Laughter and applause erupted around us. Even the stoniest of faces were transformed by smiles, and Blanca, the stern Flamenco dancer, who had been all fiery intensity a moment before, chuckled and gave us a warm nod of approval.

"*Vale. Muy bien. Dos cervezas aqui*!" She shouted to the bartender, pointing to us.

As Rafa and I made our way off the stage, our hands unintentionally entangled, I felt a rush of exhilaration and vulnerability, but I also couldn't stop laughing.

"You were great," Rafa said, clinking his beer against mine.

"That was a first. I almost wish I got in on video to post."

"I can almost guarantee someone here did."

"That was a lot of fun. This place is great."

"Si. Nothing like Flamenco. My mother loves it. My sisters followed suit. Nuria, the youngest, she's an accomplished dancer. Performs here sometimes."

"That's so cool. I'd love to meet her sometime," I blurted out, then halted, realizing the implication of my words What was I saying? I wasn't going to meet his family any time soon. Or ever.

"I'd like that," Rafa said.

"What a surprise."

We both turned to see Martí standing in front of us. I swallowed a lump. Whoops. This didn't look good.

"Martí," Rafa said curtly.

"*Hermano, que paso?*"

Rafa pursed his lips, clearly not sharing in the casual camaraderie.

"This is Vera—"

"Vera Stone, I know," Martí said, leaning in for a cheek kiss. "We've met."

"Oh?" Rafa said, surprised.

"Si. Did you enjoy dinner the other night?" Martí said.

Hells, bells. Was this really happening? I forced a smile. "I did, thank you. Um, Martí was kind enough to treat me to a private tasting. At his restaurant." The words came out in a wobble. I don't think anyone in Barcelona missed the vitriol that populated Rafa's expression.

"How nice," he said dryly.

"Glad to see you're getting around town, Vera," Martí said, his tone laced with innuendo. "So much to see here. I'll catch you both later. Meeting some friends. Adios."

Rafa said nothing as Martí turned from us. He flashed me a look. I had the urge to cower, but I kept my spine straight. That was awkward, but I didn't owe either of them anything, including explanations. I lifted my beer and conveyed as much in my expression. To Rafa's credit, he seemed to get the hint.

* * *

As we wandered back through the intricate streets of El Raval, the city took on a softer hue, the moon draping ethereal shades across the historic stone pathways, morphing stark realities into gentle dreams.

We paused at the beginning of the narrow alley leading to my hotel, the ambient noises hushing as if to grant us a pocket of privacy. I turned to face him, and as our eyes locked, I glimpsed a reflection of the raw and rich experiences that the night had gifted us—a kaleidoscope of feelings and discoveries mirrored in his eyes. My heart rate crept up.

"That was fun," he said. "Even with Martí's obvious attempts at sabotage."

I laughed. I was glad he could find humor in it. "It was. What is his deal anyway?"

Rafa rolled his shoulders slightly. "It's nothing. Just a long history."

I let it go. It was none of my business. "Well, thank you for getting me out of my shell. Showing me something new."

I looked up at him. In my flat sandals, he must have been a full foot taller than me. The world around us seemed to condense to this single point of magnetic pull, a silent agreement forged through lingering eye contact. His hand found its way to my face, fingers gently cupping my cheek, thumb drawing tender paths across my skin.

"I know—I know this is probably a terrible idea, but—"

"I like terrible ideas," I whispered the words I shouldn't have.

He stepped into me, and I was pulled irresistibly toward him. He leaned down—he was so much taller than me—and skimmed my lips with his. A bolt of lightning went right through me, and I leaned into him harder, parting my lips to him. He tasted of cinnamon and sea salt and faint traces of hops.

He pulled away a moment later, leaving a pulsing vacancy where his lips had occupied space.

The reality of the situation crashed into me, and I stepped back. "I should probably call it a night."

He smiled understandingly. "Will I see you tomorrow?" he grazed my lip with his fingertip.

"We'll see, won't we?" I grinned and turned to walk back to my hotel.

Chapter Twenty-Three

I was getting too close. Nope. Not getting, had already gotten. I traced my lips, feeling phantom lips on mine.

No, no. I could not let this happen.

I stared at myself in the mirror, noting the sun-kissed glow of my skin—a testimony to the time spent under the baking Barcelona sun. Or maybe it was the new zest for life I was finding.

As I readied myself for the day, applying sunscreen and makeup and pulling my hair back, I chided myself for all my idiocy. I risked damaging my hard-earned reputation if any of this got out. The thought looped through my mind—how could I possibly give an unbiased review now? Rafa's restaurant was everything I hoped for—innovative, bold, and centered around fresh ingredients. But had I jeopardized everything with a moment of weakness? A stupid kiss— or was it more than just a kiss? Was it his strategy for a better review? Martí's words echoed. The trust in Rafa's awareness of my stringent professionalism wavered.

No, I shouldn't have allowed this complexity to evolve. I grabbed my coffee, sipping it with determination. I needed to redefine boundaries, to communicate that despite the magnetic setting, the enchanting dances, and the wine that flowed like water, I was here to do a job, not to star in my own personal rom-com. I resolved to cease the flirtations, the personal tastings, and the after-hour drinks, to retain the focus on the culinary art that brought me here.

And not just with Rafa but Martí as well. The realization dawned that the allure in me may not be personal at all but rooted in the influence of my professional standing. Yes, there was a certain thrill, a heady rush of power acknowledged in Martí's teasing nickname for me—the Sword of Culinary Destiny. But this dynamic, this flirtation with the sway of power, could easily spiral into the manipulative tendencies I despised in some critics. No, I championed the art, the dedication, and the pure joy of culinary mastery.

With a deep breath, I mapped out the conversation in my mind, affirming the need for clear boundaries to protect both my integrity and Rafa's hard work. I hoped for mutual understanding, a shared desire for authenticity. I would have that conversation...sigh, maybe tomorrow. I couldn't face him just yet.

.   .   .

And first, Celia awaited. With a sense of purpose—and a slight hangover—I grabbed my handbag and slipped on my leather sandals, ready to face the world yet again.

As I stepped out, another sunny Barcelona day greeted me with open arms. I navigated the ancient streets down to Celia's bar. I walked through the front doors into the empty restaurant. I stopped short when I heard the soft humming of a high-pitched voice. I glanced around and then I spotted something very curious behind the counter—a little girl. I wasn't a great judge of children, but she had to be only been six or so. Her tiny hands were assembling a beautiful pintxos display. Her fingers worked dexterously while she hummed a little tune. Her hair, black as night, was pulled up to a high ponytail with curls at the end. She wore a floral sundress with a small apron over it. Her face was set with concentrated determination.

"Buenos días," I said as I stepped closer.

She stopped what she was doing and glanced up at me with wide brown eyes.

"Buenos días," she said in a high-pitched voice. "*¿Quieres probar mi creación?*"

I resisted the urge to laugh but smiled nonetheless. "I would love to. Um, Sí, por favor. Gracias."

She blinked at me as though trying to sort me out, then casually slid her most recent creation toward me.

"I make it up myself," she said in accented English.

"Do you speak English?"

She shrugged in that nonchalant way little kids do. "Some time."

I picked up the little slice of bread piled high with cheese and peppers and popped it into my mouth. The flavor combination was incredible—a smooth mix of salt and cream. I chewed slowly, savoring it, and swallowed.

"That was delicious. You didn't make that up, did you?" I teased.

She nodded eagerly. "*¡Sí, lo hice!* I took one of Mama's, and I made it better. Don't you think it's better?"

"Well, having not had the original recipe, I couldn't quite say. But that one was delicious."

"She thinks very little of my recipes," Celia said, coming around the back.

I looked up with surprise. "She's yours?"

Celia sighed as if she was exacerbated by the little girl, but then grinned. "Sí, I'm afraid she doesn't fall far from the tree. Vera, this is Aitana. Aitana, this is Mama's friend, Vera. She loves to eat food. So much so that she eats food for a living."

Aitana looked up at me and blinked a few times as though trying to process her mother's words. Finally, she said skeptically, "How do you eat food for a living? That's not a real job."

I tried not to laugh. "I know, it's not much of a real job, it's true. But I like to try delicious food that people have made, and then I write stories about it. And I put the stories on our website."

"Like a blog? I love blogs," Aitana said.

I flashed Celia an amused look. "Exactly. A blog about travel and food."

Aitana tilted her head and studied me. "Well, that sounds like the best job in the world. Mama, can I do that job?"

I laughed out loud this time. Her earnest innocence filled me. "You know, Aitana, I think it is. And I bet you could."

"Did you come hungry?" Celia asked.

"If you've asked a food critic whether she's hungry, then clearly, you've never met a food critic. I would love something to eat, something cold to drink, and some good conversation."

"Well, you've come to the right place for all of those

things. Please, sit over there, and I'll join you." She gestured toward a booth in the back of the café. She turned toward her daughter. "Will you finish assembling those and then move on to the ceviche?"

"*Si, mama. Si, puedo,*" she said with a slight petulance that comes from a child learning independence.

Celia mocked glared, then turned toward me with a headshake.

"Dios mio, she takes years off my life every day."

I laughed but saw the love in her eyes.

"She's adorable," I said.

"Gracias. She is the heart of my life."

I took my seat, and Celia returned a moment later with a plate of snacks and a cold bottle of white wine.

"How are you finding our magical city today?" Celia asked as she filled up two wine glasses.

"It's definitely magical. Even more than I remember. I might never leave this time."

She smiled. "It has that effect on people. And how is our favorite celebrity chef?"

I hesitated, then sipped my wine to bide time. "Fine, I guess. I wouldn't know."

Her expression held back thinly veiled amusement.

"What's that look for?" I asked.

She shrugged. "It's a big city and a small town all in one. *Mi hermano* and his girlfriend Violeta were at Rival last night and said Rafa was all over some pretty tourist. Was that tourist you?"

I felt my cheeks ripen like a tomato. "Small town indeed," I muttered.

Celia spared a glance back at her daughter, then back to me. "You don't have to be embarrassed. Dancing with a sexy man is not a crime. Neither is impromptu Flamenco performances."

I snapped up, and Celia grinned. "Si, there is a video on the club's Insta," she said.

I dropped my head and rubbed my forehead. "Dios mio."

She laughed from her belly. "Don't worry about it! You and Rafa are having a good time."

I sighed. I sipped my wine, savoring the crisp fruit, and contemplated.

"I know. It's just—how do I explain? I have a professional duty to be unbiased. And getting close to Rafa on a personal level—well, you could see how that definitely muddies the waters, as we say. And the thing is, Martí was there too, and he saw us and—" I shook my head. "I don't know. It all suddenly feels very messy."

"*Ah, claro*. I guess you better stay away from those *machismos* and spend more time with me." She winked.

"Actually, now that you mention it. I have a favor to ask you."

"Un favor?" She said with a raised eyebrow. "I am intrigued."

"I'm going to be doing an Instagram live tomorrow from Barri Gòtic. And I'd love to have you on to talk about your restaurant."

Celia looked taken aback for a moment. She started to say something, then closed her mouth again. Then opened it again.

"My restaurant? You want me to talk about my restaurant on your Instagram? I've seen your Instagram, Vera. You have like one million followers."

I laughed. "Not quite that many, but yes, I have a lot of followers. And I want to tell all those people about this place. I was going to just do a blog post about my experience so far, and I thought you're exactly the kind of small place I want to support. And now that I know you're a mom, even more so."

"A single mom," she winked. "Even more of a tragic sob story."

"See? You're the perfect fit. A single mother running her own business, sticking to her roots in one of the hottest food scenes in the world. The story basically sells itself."

Celia chuckled. She took a long sip of wine, then popped one of her creations in her mouth and chewed.

"Can't see why I would say no to that, would I? But me? Are you sure? I'm not very interesting."

"Don't insult my creative insights."

She smirked. "Ok, *La Americana* knows best. What time?"

"Say noon?"

Celia considered it, twirling her wine glass by the stem. "Let's do it during siesta. Two o'clock, OK? The business will have died down during that time, and people are more likely to be sitting around scrolling on their phones."

"And she's a marketing genius to boot," I said.

"I don't know about that. I just know Spaniards."

I chuckled. "Your humility is admirable. Maybe I need to have you along on my journey here, put me in the right direction."

She shrugged apathetically. "It couldn't possibly hurt you. You can easily be led astray in the city. One wrong turn down the wrong corridor, and you're paying six euros for a cup of cigarette coffee water."

I nodded earnestly. "I have discovered that."

"The best places, the places the locals go, are sometimes very hard to find. They are tucked away in little alleys, with nondescript storefronts. You walk by the wrong time of day, and it looks like a boarded-up wall. You come by during happy hour? And all of a sudden, that little corner is transformed into the hottest bistro in the city. Bursting with people. There are two Barcelonas. Sometimes it's impossible to know where to look. Even your Rick Steves can't always tell you."

"Do you know Rick Steves?"

She laughed. "Every American wanders in with that blue book."

"He is our guide," I said dramatically, folding my hands into a prayer move. "OK, I'll come by here after lunch and will get set up."

"Mama!" Aitana was rushing over, carrying a plate. "See what I did here?"

Celia's eyes went wide. "I—see."

I glanced down to see a bowl of colorful, fresh ceviche peppered with something black. Was that—

"*Chocolate*!" Aitana said with glee. "It makes everything better."

Celia hung her head and crossed her heart. "Dios mio."

Chapter Twenty-Four

It had been ages since Rafa ventured into the world of dating, a realm he had willingly forsaken, consumed by the relentless demands of his culinary career. Time, that ever-elusive entity, scarcely allowed for casual encounters, let alone anything serious. His work was all-consuming. Both in terms of time and mental energy. He didn't have anything left to give at the end of the day.

With Vera, though—she stirred something long-dormant in him. It was the first time in a long time he had even *entertained* the idea of bringing anyone into his life. And, of course, it had to be the one person he was most likely not to spend his life with. Not only did she live thousands of miles away, their jobs were literally in conflict of interest. The rub lay in the very thing that brought them together—food. It seemed a stupid thing, and it wasn't exactly like either of them were doing life-or-death things, but could he really date a food critic and vice versa? Wouldn't that call into question all of her professional integrity? And if he got a glowing feature piece in *Travel Luxe & Leisure* and then it came out that they were romantically involved, it would discredit both of them. As silly as it all seemed, considering their entire livelihood depended on food, it did put them both at risk. Besides, she was annoying. She was an enigma that mirrored his own guarded disposition. Despite the undeniable attraction, he could tell she was the kind of woman who never let anyone get close. And if he was honest, he was the exact same. Not exactly the best foundation for a relationship.

He shook his head. Maybe he was making excuses. Or maybe he was just overanalyzing things like he always did. That was definitely a character flaw about him. Lorna would attest to that. It made him an excellent artist, but a terrible boss. He knew he drove most people in his life crazy. Even his wonderful mother often told him to get his thoughts out of his head. He overanalyzed things to death. It could be a professional detriment too. His drive toward perfectionism in his work could often lead to analysis paralysis. It took him a long time to finally have the courage to want to do his own thing because he felt like he could never get it right. It was something that he couldn't admit to people that while he absolutely loved cooking, it was also the source of anxiety. Nothing ever seemed perfect. Nothing ever seemed done. It turned out that when you're cooking for somebody, you do eventually have to feed them. You can't toil over the recipe in the kitchen in perpetuity.

His pot started to boil, and he quickly turned it down, giving it a stir. Tonight's choice of dish, a humble yet soul-satisfying fish stew, paid homage to his Basque heritage — a recipe passed down from his father's mother. It was a dish undemanding of perfection, offering comfort in its rustic simplicity.

. . .

It wasn't exactly innovative, so it wasn't going to make the cut onto the new menu, but it was his soul food. Fresh clams, mussels, and octopus. Spicy tomato broth. His papa's mother, from the Basque region, had brought with her a little spice not commonly found in the rest of Spain. They didn't get in a lot of the rest of Spain. When he was going to culinary school in California and tried traditional Mexican cooking, he had nearly passed out from the heat. And then he developed a terrible addiction to habanero. How did they not have this glorious thing in Spain?

He tasted the stew and determined that it was as done as it was going to be, considering his stomach was grumbling. He ladled some in a bowl and tore off a crust of day-old bread. He brought it out to the dining room and plucked a bottle of hearty table red wine from the cabinet. He popped it and settled in.

"Please tell me you made more of that?" Lorna strolled into the dining room in tight black pants and a lacy top. Rafa wasn't a top judge of female fashion, but Lorna's svelte figure allowed her to pull off slinky looks while maintaining an air of class.

"You look nice. Hot date?"

"Mmm. With my girls. We checked out the happy hour at Sol Cocina in L'Eixample."

He raised his brow. "You're *cheating* on me?"

She laughed and set down her black handbag. "I have to scout out the competition."

"What are you doing here?" Rafa asked.

"I left some inventory paperwork here this afternoon. I was going to get a jumpstart on it, so I came back. And here I find you having a date with yourself."

"A man needs alone time."

"I won't read into that. I knew you made fish stew when no one was looking," she said accusatorily but with a wry smile.

"I am supposed to be innovative and hip, did you not know? I can't be seen eating peasant food."

"But we are all peasants at heart," Lorna said. "Is there more?"

"Si. There's a whole pot. Help yourself. Bread is on the counter. Grab a wine glass and join me."

Lorna looked like she was already salivating as she ran back into the kitchen. She came back a moment later with a heaping bowl and plopped down across from him. She said nothing as she dug in.

"Rafa, if this new concept doesn't work out, promise me you will open up a shop dedicated entirely to fish stew."

Rafa chuckled. "I'll consider it. But I doubt I can sell enough to keep you on the payroll."

"Pay me in fish stew." She smiled and slurped down some wine greedily. "So, what's going on with you?" She said after a few bites.

Rafa took a long sip of his wine. There was something about a hearty table wine that just paired perfectly with peasant stew. You couldn't have something too pretentious to upset the balance.

"I don't know what you mean."

"Don't avoid me. You seem broodier than normal."

"Hey, I was just here minding my own stew when you had to disrupt everything with your interrogations."

She raised her brow expectantly.

Rafa sighed. "Are you dating anyone?"

Lorna looked taken aback. "Interesting diversion. Are you asking me out?" She said incredulously.

Rafa laughed. "No. I learned my lesson from my dad. Don't get involved with your employees. No, I'm just curious. Do you find time to date given the demands of this job?"

Lorna leaned back and considered the question. "I get out from time to time, I guess. But I don't really have anyone exclusive right now. To your endless point, we've been working pretty hard. It doesn't exactly bode well for making new connections. Maybe once the restaurant opens and things calm down, which I know is never, maybe I'll get out there again. Why? Are you dating anyone?"

Rafa didn't answer. He wasn't quite sure how to explain it. No, he wasn't dating anyone, and he wasn't really sure if he wanted to.

"Not exactly. I was just thinking about logistics. If—never mind." He stuck his spoon back into his stew and moved it around, prodding the bits of seafood.

Lorna tilted her head and studied him. "This is about Vera, isn't it?"

Rafa shook his head vigorously. "Of course not. That's ridiculous."

Lorna smirked. "You're a terrible liar, Señor Santos. If you like her, just ask her out."

"You know it's not that easy. There are...complications."

"Only if you make it complicated. Sure, this isn't the most straightforward situation you've ever encountered, but the complications are mostly in your head."

"Yeah, well, what do you know about any of it?" Rafa said with a smirk. "Just eat your food and be quiet."

Lorna rolled her eyes. "You're the one who brought it up, Romeo. I think sometimes you forget to let yourself be happy, Rafa."

"Happiness is overrated. Don't you know?"

"Says the miserable. I happen to quite like being happy." She slurped down a huge bite.

Rafa considered her words. "Are you? Happy?"

Lorna tilted her head. "Yes. I think so. As happy as one can be, I think. The world is a complicated place. I think happiness is fleeting. But I think we can all find moments of peace, moments of contentment, to hold onto. Those are the things that fill our lives."

Rafa felt a stirring within him at her words. Moments of joy. Of peace. That's the way he felt in the kitchen. With open flames and sizzling garlic and the melodic rhythm of clanging pots and clinking dishes. Of the chatter and the shouts and the banter. The music in his head—the soundtrack that was all his own. Those were moments of utter peace despite the chaos. Was he happy? He hadn't slowed down enough in the past few years to even consider the question.

He pictured Vera and her snarky smile and quick wit. Those lovely lips and the way they folded over his creations. The way they had felt pressed against his so briefly beneath a street lantern. Those moments definitely brought him joy. And maybe that's what life was all about. Maybe that was all it had to be about.

The front door buzzer sounded, jolting them both from the conversation.

Lorna looked up. "Well, well. Speak of the Devil."

Chapter Twenty-Five

I approached Rafa's restaurant with trepidation. My nerves were rattling around inside me like bones. But, this had to be addressed. The other night, well, the other night was magical. There was no other way to describe it. But it was also the exact opposite of how all of this needed to go. I blamed myself, really. I should have never put myself in that situation. I'd let myself be seduced by the sultry Barcelona night and all that entailed.

The door opened and Rafa stood there with a shocked expression. His sleeves were rolled up, revealing strong forearms punctuated by muscle and veins, which I imagine he sculpted over hot flames in the kitchen day after day. Even from my limited encounter with slicing and dicing in his kitchen, I knew it was hard work.

"Vera."

"Hi. Um, sorry to just come by unannounced."

His shocked expression melted into something welcoming.

"You never need to apologize. Or announce yourself. You are always welcome."

It might have been in my head, but he sounded a bit like a hotel concierge. There was a strange formality to his tone. I got it. We'd gone and made things awkward. Super awkward. I glanced behind him and spotted Lorna sitting at a table with a bottle of wine and soup bowls.

"Am I interrupting?"

Rafa spared a glance back at Lorna and shook his head. "Not at all. We were just talking about work. Come in, por favor."

I stepped into the inviting restaurant, so peaceful in the late hours.

"Vera, nice to see you," Lorna said.

"You too. Sorry to interrupt."

She stood then, setting her napkin in her chair. "Not at all. I was just finishing up. I'm going to be in the back getting that inventory paperwork sorted, Rafa."

I nervously tucked a lock of hair behind my ears as I stood there, not quite knowing how to broach the subject. Rafa cleared his throat loudly.

"Would you like to sit down? Are you hungry, or thirsty?"

I bit my lip. Then I shook my head. "No, thank you. I actually just needed to talk to you about something."

"Ok."

We stood awkwardly. I opened my mouth, but the words were lodged in my throat. God, why was I so nervous? How was one supposed to act after everything that had transpired?

The smile on his face wavered. "Is everything all right?"

"Um, yes. Fine." I folded my hands together. "I just think we need to talk about what happened the other night. After the flamenco club." I heard my voice go up in a squeak.

Rafa's expression tightened, and I could tell he knew exactly what I was about to say. He nodded in an understanding way.

"I think we both got a little carried away."

I exhaled a small breath I hadn't realized I was holding. I needed so much for him to be in alignment with me on this.

"It's not that it wasn't wonderful. And I had so much fun, really, I did. And it's not that you're not wonderful, and—"

"Vera, stop. It's ok. You don't have to clarify. We both have a professional obligation, and we might have, in a moment of lowered defenses, blurred the lines. And we need to take a step back from that. Realize that we can't be reckless with this. This opportunity means too much to both of us. To both of our careers."

I didn't know what to say at first. I wasn't sure what I had expected him to say, but I was prepared for pushback or even resentment. Agreement and total understanding weren't what I was expecting.

After a moment, I nodded fervently. "Thank you. I really appreciate the way you're handling this."

He offered me a thin smile that didn't quite touch those dreamy eyes. His expression gave away nothing.

Finally, he said, "But of course. I'm sorry if I pushed you into something that made you uncomfortable."

I shook my head. "No! No, really, it was both of us. We just got—carried away. If the situation was different—" I stopped myself. What was I even saying? I was successfully making this situation way more awkward than it needed to be.

"Si. In another life, this could be much different. But, here we are."

"Here we are," I echoed in a whisper.

Tension swirled around us as we stood in silence. The tick tick of a clock punctuated the stuffy air. Rafa's breath came in slow, collected cadence. I swallowed, hearing the echo of it like a drum beat.

"Well, I suppose I should go—" I started, but my feet stayed glued to the floor. I felt something like grief wiggling through me. Grief for what? Perhaps the loss of potential. Of what might have been. But I didn't have time for might-have-beens. I had to live in the real world.

"How about something to eat before you go? Are you hungry? Wait, I know the answer to that." He grinned, and I laughed, the stiff tension seeming to melt away.

"You know me well. And why not? I can't get enough of your spice."

He flashed me a look, and I wanted to take back to innuendo-laden words.

"Is that a stew you're eating?" I said, eyeing the depleted meal.

"Si, but I have something else I'd like to share with you. Something new I am debating putting on the menu, but I'd love to get your opinion. If it can be off the record, that is. It's not perfected, so your discretion is appreciated."

I felt a little wobble in my stomach, but I forced myself to smile. "I'll be as honest as I can be. Off the record."

He turned and went back into the kitchen.

I plopped into a seat and waited nervously. He returned shortly with a steaming terracotta dish radiating spices.

"Did you seriously just make that in the thirty seconds you were gone?" I asked, already drooling.

"Didn't I tell you I was a magician?" Rafa said, wiggling his eyebrows. "She's been simmering on the stove just waiting for a sharp food critic to come test her out."

I eyed the stew-like concoction filled with vegetables, thick tomato sauce and fried eggs.

"And what is it I'm testing here?"

"*Huevos a la Flamenca*, with a twist."

"Flamenca," I murmured.

"Si, I was inspired the other night by—well, anyway. It's a dish that is popular in Southern Spain, but I have made it my own, of course." He set down the skillet and placed a plate in front of me. "You have a smoky tomato sauce with onions, plenty of garlic, smoked paprika, and roasted peppers. Fresh vegetables and patatas, topped with crispy jamon serrano and spicy chorizo y *los huevos*."

"Is this the traditional recipe, or is it a fusion twist like everything else you touch?"

He wiggled his brow. "But of course, it would not be a Rafa Santos creation if I let the recipe live in peace, would it?"

I chuckled. "I would be so terribly disappointed."

"And that would break my heart. No. I have made some alterations. I can't give you all of my secrets, but you will notice it is spicier than is traditional. I have included a more robust variety of vegetables, and I have added serrano peppers to the sauce. My fellow Spaniards won't know what hit them, but my global warriors, I think, will appreciate it. Por favor, try it." He handed me a large serving spoon.

I ladled some onto my plate and, with much-delighted anticipation, tipped a small bit into my mouth. I closed my eyes as my mouth welcomed the onslaught of flavor. Smokey, garlicky, savory, and—wow. He was right about the spice. The serranos sliced right through my tastebuds, but it wasn't overwhelming. He'd struck the balance perfectly to where the heat raced through your body like small flames that only toyed with the idea of pain. The result was a sort of euphoria that begged for more. I opened my eyes, feeling the heat in my cheeks.

He was staring at me expectantly. I swallowed and felt my lips turn into an uncontrollable smile.

"Perfecto."

Chapter Twenty-Six

I was a bundle of nerves as I approached *Casa Batlló*, one of the most iconic and admired works of the renowned Catalan architect Antoni Gaudí. Located at Passeig de Gràcia in the heart of Barcelona, the building was a testament to Gaudí's unparalleled genius and his ability to push the boundaries of architecture and design.

And tonight, the building stood as the backdrop to Sabor del Mundo, a private cocktail party for the travel and food media world. My stomach was in twisty knots. Some of the absolute *who's who* were going to be there, and I had no idea how my editor had managed to get me an invitation.

"You can't pass up this opportunity, Vera!" Joanne said last night on a hurried FaceTime.

"I don't have a cocktail dress with me," I said in a panic.

She rolled her eyes. "Then go buy one. They have dress stores in Barcelona, yes?"

"Yes, I guess, but—"

"And skip the H & M, will you? Get an actual dress and put it on the company card. Keep it under $500, and I'll approve the expense."

I nearly spit out my Perrier. $500? For a single *dress?* Phew! I really had made it up the ladder a notch.

So now I stood in a sleek black V-neck cocktail dress that skimmed my knees and strappy black heels with an elegant gold brocade all from an upscale boutique Celia had recommended. I'd twisted my hair back into a chignon, borrowing some dangling silver earrings and a simple black clutch from Celia. I took a deep breath and stepped from my Uber as the valet opened the door for me.

"*Buenas noches, señorita,*" he said, splaying his hands toward the entry.

The façade of Casa Batlló was a riot of color and form. In order to sound intelligent, I'd Googled details about the venue last night over some cava and chocolate truffles. Gaudí used a mix of different architectural techniques and materials to create a wave-like structure, with a facade adorned with a colorful mosaic made from broken ceramic tiles, a technique known as "trencadís." The roof, resembling a dragon's back with large, iridescent scales, has an arched shape, which many interpret as the dragon slain by Sant Jordi, the patron saint of Catalonia. The balconies resembled skeletal structures, often likened to masks or skulls, while the supporting pillars in the lower floors had bone-like qualities. Gaudí's love for nature was evident in every curve and color of the building, as he shunned straight lines for their absence in nature.

I stepped forward, smoothing out any minor creases in my dress, already hearing the muted strains of music and conversation from within. This was the place to be, an exclusive culinary party where the crème de la crème of the food world came to mingle. And somehow, I was on that guest list.

From the entrance, I could see the grandeur only continued inside. Crystal chandeliers hung overhead, reflecting their brilliance onto the attendees below. Men in sharp sports coats and trim slacks and women in elegant dresses of every shape and color animatedly chatted, their laughter punctuating the ambient hum of voices.

Inside, the design was just as innovative. Light wells welcomed in the moonlight. The central well was covered in blue tiles, with the tiles getting lighter the higher they were to ensure an even distribution of light. Gaudí's ergonomic designs, such as handrails carved to fit the human grip and mushroom-shaped fireplaces designed to sit by, showcased his consideration for the building's inhabitants.

I was handed a glass of Cava by a passing waiter. Its bubbles tickled my nose as I took a sip, letting the familiar effervescence calm my nerves. Even in New York, I wasn't used to such glamorous events.

As I made my way through the crowds of people, I felt the weight of gazes on me. Perhaps it was curiosity, or perhaps recognition from my blog, but I tried to maintain an air of confidence. I belonged there, too.

The atmosphere was intoxicating. Everywhere I looked, there were familiar faces, renowned chefs, infamous critics, and celebrities of the culinary world. Even a famous Food Network cooking competition host. The excitement in the air was palpable.

As I wound my way through clusters of chatting elites, a commanding presence drew my attention. She was an elegant, statuesque woman with platinum blonde hair slicked back into a tight bun. Her sharp, intelligent eyes scanned the room, missing nothing. She stood with an air of confidence, her posture upright, shoulders squared. She wore a tailored, dark blue pantsuit that contrasted strikingly with her fair skin. I recognized her, but I couldn't place her.

A whisper from a group beside me caught my ear. "That's Greta Wolf. Have you met her yet? Big-time restaurant investor. She's tall anyone is talking about right now," Someone with an American accent said.

"I've heard she's the reason why half the people are here," another woman responded.

Drawn in by curiosity, I made my way closer, just in time to hear her begin a conversation with a French chef I recognized from a *New York Times* article.

"Barcelona is ripe for change," Greta said, her German accent crisp. Her voice had a melodic but assertive tone. "There's so much potential here, but it needs... refining."

The chef nodded, clearly hanging on to every word. "And you believe you're the one to bring about that change?"

Greta took a sip from her glass, looking the chef directly in the eyes. "I've done it in Berlin, Paris, and Milan. Why not here? With the right investments and partnerships," her gaze briefly flicked toward me—did I imagine that?—before returning to the chef, "Barcelona could become the next global culinary hotspot."

"I think it already is," a woman said beside them. "It's one of the hottest destinations in the West."

Greta pursed her cherry-red lips, clearly not keen on being countered. "There is always room for improvement."

I felt a sudden chill as something stirred in me. Was Greta the reason Joanne was so keen on me attending tonight? Was I one of those 'partnerships' she was referring to? The idea felt a little disconcerting. Before I could dwell on it further, Greta had gracefully moved onto another group, leaving a trail of hanging jaws and whispered conversations in her wake.

I retreated a bit, trying to process the implications. Everything about Greta screamed power and influence, and from the snippets I caught, it seemed she had big plans for Barcelona. There was no way it had anything to do with my presence, though. I was overthinking things.

* * *

Nature called, and I headed toward the restrooms. On the way back, I passed by a slightly ajar door leading to a smaller, more intimate room. It looked like a private lounge. The dim lighting and the hushed voices from within piqued my curiosity. I stopped briefly to peek in, curious about every aspect of this building, but then thought better. Don't be nosy, Vera. But then I caught Greta's distinct voice, and my curiosity was stronger than my common sense. I stood close to the door and leaned in to hear.

"Barcelona is a gold mine, Greta. With the right moves, we can redefine its culinary scene. How are the preparations for *Santos California?*" A male voice said.

Santos California? Rafa's restaurant?

"Mmm. All is going as expected. Santos is wound up like a jack-in-the-box, but he's very talented. We just need to make sure the opening is a hit," Greta said. I heard the clink of ice that indicated she was pouring a drink.

"That's where Vera Stone comes in?" the man said.

I stiffened. What? I couldn't resist, and I peered through the slit in the door. Greta stood like an elegant gazelle, clutching a crystal low-ball. She was talking to a middle-aged man a good few inches shorter than she was, with red cheeks and a head of salty hair.

"Yes," Greta's voice interjected smoothly, "Her reviews have sway. Her glowing write-up in the magazine's feature will ensure our success."

"How did you manage the timing of this?" The man asked, an amused incredulity spreading across his face.

Greta smirked with an expression that said, *wouldn't you like to know my secrets?*

"What have I told you, Lyle? When you know what people want, you can give it to them. And then they can give you what you need in return. Everyone knows journalism is a struggling business right now. Readerships are down. Editorial

strikes. Blah blah. Even the top circulations like *Travel Luxe &*
Leisure are suffering. A nice little contribution goes a long way.
And it worked out that this city happened to be Vera's culi-
nary crush. Really, I did her a favor."

The man—Lyle—raised his glass. "If there is a string, you
know the right way to pull it."

Greta's chuckle sent shivers down my spine. "You don't
get to where I am without that skill, my friend. Research and
connections are your best friends."

"And she is good to write a glowing feature?" Lyle asked.

I sucked in a breath.

Greta waved away the question. "Of course she is. It is the
exact kind of restaurant concept she adores. And the food is
brilliant. I would not be the key investor otherwise. Besides,
have you seen Rafa Santos? He could probably even turn your
straight white arse his way. His Instagram borders on
obscene."

Lyle chuckled and said something in response, but my
mind was whirling too fast to comprehend the subsequent
words.

I leaned back against the wall and breathed. I wasn't here
on a writing assignment. I'd been turned into an unwitting
public relations agent. And Rafa—did he know? Did he know
my presence was bought and paid for? Was all his charm and
attention at the direction of Greta Wolf? And the kiss—I
closed my eyes and shook my head. I always knew he must
have ulterior motives, I just didn't realize it could be quite this
convoluted.

My mind went to my editor. Sure, Joanne was my boss,
but I'd always felt like we had a solid, trusting relationship. But
she had lied to me. Worse, she'd pimped me out against my
knowledge or consent.

I felt the weight of the information pressing down on me,
making the air in the corridor seem stifling. It was as if I had

stumbled upon a secret meeting of puppet masters pulling strings behind the scenes.

Taking a deep breath, I forced myself to move silently away from the door. I needed to think, to process, and, most importantly, decide what to do next.

* * *

I navigated my way back to the main party, my steps on autopilot. My mind was racing, tangled with thoughts of what I'd just overheard. The loud chatter and clinking glasses now felt jarring, each sound amplified by the turmoil inside me.

Finding a vacant balcony, I stepped outside, welcoming the cool Barcelona air on my face. The twinkling city lights offered a stark contrast to the dark thoughts clouding my mind.

As I leaned on the railing, I felt a hand on my shoulder. I turned to see a familiar face—Daniela, a French girl who had interned at our magazine's marketing department the previous summer.

"Vera?"

"Oh my God! Daniela, I didn't expect to see you here." I leaned in for a cheek kiss.

"Oui. I am here with my publicity firm. I am doing marketing and PR for the hospitality industry now."

"Oh, that's wonderful. And perfect for you. Do you live in Barcelona now?"

"Oui! For a year, anyway. I don't know if I'll stay, but she has my heart more every day. And you? Are you here with the magazine?" She purred in her Parisian accent.

I nodded. "Yes, I'm doing a piece on a few of the up-and-coming places. It's been so much fun."

"You looked like you'd seen a ghost when I walked up. Everything is ok?"

I hesitated, twirling my glass. "What do you know about Greta Wolf?" I said, feeling the abruptness.

Daniela's mouth fell slightly as she mulled over my question. "She's, uh, a major player on the culinary scene. She invests in turning old neighborhoods into culinary hotspots in cities all over the world. And from what I understand, she doesn't fail. Her eye is on the mark."

I sipped my wine and considered. "And does she—can she be trusted? Does she play fair?"

Daniela's expression scrunched. "I really don't know. I haven't worked with her. I just know her by her reputation, is all. She's a shark, but that doesn't mean she's not fair. I don't know. Is anything ever fair in the restaurant business? It's shady by design."

I sighed. Daniela wasn't wrong. There was something about this industry that constantly operated on a thin gray line.

I nodded. "Right. Of course."

"Hey! Since you're in Barcelona for a bit longer, you must come to this wine-tasting event in a couple of days. My company is hosting. Top winemakers in the area. Many restaurant owners. It's like speed dating, pairing people up," Daniela said.

My mind was so clouded with racing thoughts, it took me a moment to process what she'd said.

"Oh. Yes, that would be great. Do you have the details?"

"*Oui*. Is your number the same? I will WhatsApp the details."

"Yes, it is." I forced a smile that I hoped looked grateful.

"*Bien*. Ah, I must go. I see my boss waving at me. It was lovely to see you, Vera. Hope to see you in a few days?"

"Definitely."

She leaned in for a cheek kiss and scampered off, leaving me to my whirling thoughts.

Chapter Twenty-Seven

The sultry rumble of Flamenco music filled the intimate tapas bar. The soulful guitar and soft wail brought him back to an old album his father listened to after a long night at the restaurant. Rafa closed his eyes and let the haunting lament lull him into a sense of peace. He breathed in the smell of spices and fermenting grapes, mixed with the subtle body odor of people cooling down from the sweltering Spanish October heat. He opened his eyes and took a long sip of his cold beer, feeling the heat of the day wash away. Summer did not seem to want to die this year. It had been a brutal season—very little rain, fires everywhere. Some days it felt like all of Europe was melting into a lava pit. But, he was lucky enough to live near a bar that had air conditioning.

Rafa was feeling a little lighter lately. As the grand opening grew closer, he knew he probably should feel more anxious. But as he felt more and more ready, his anxiety was melting away. Maybe it was that he had a feeling Vera was going to give him a rave review. He thought he'd earned it. He was damn proud of what he had built. Everything was falling into place. It was the right location. He had a great staff. A new and innovative concept that worked. He had sourced the best ingredients. And he was passionate about every detail. He knew the grand opening was going to be a smash success.

At least, he hoped so.

At least right then and there, surrounded by the heart and pulsing vibe of Barcelona, he had to believe that what he was doing was going to work. Because if it didn't—well, he couldn't even think about it. He didn't have a backup plan.

He polished off his beer and set it on the counter, contemplating whether or not he was going to dig into a tin of salty sardines and some *tortilla*.

"Get you another, amigo?" A voice said.

Rafa turned to see Martí Gonzalez standing beside him. Rafa worked his jaw and said nothing. Aside from their brief encounter at the Rival club the other night, he hadn't talked to Martí in a while, and he wasn't exactly thrilled to be making small talk with him now. Tonight was a solace, a time to unwind from all the hard work he'd been putting in. He didn't want to sully that with Martí's snarkiness or negativity. Because Martí never had anything good to say. He hadn't in a long time.

Martí was looking smug as ever with his golden hair slicked back and his shirt buttons undone one too many.

"Sure, why not?" Rafa said anyway. He might not be in the mood for Martí, but he was never one to turn down a free beer.

Martí signaled the barman for two more Estrellas.

"What do I owe the honor?" Rafa asked as he took a long swig of his fresh frosty beer.

Martí shrugged, eyes trailing out over the crowded room. "I just saw you from across the way and thought I'd say hello. It's been a while since we properly chatted."

Rafa half-laughed. "And who's fault is that? You're the one

who doesn't want be around me. Holding on to old grudges and all that."

Martí sighed dramatically. "Si, I know. I have been bitter. You can understand, can't you? You cut my family deeply."

Rafa shook his head, so tired of paying for the sins of the past. "What happened between me and Elena is our business. It has nothing to do with you or your family. And it was a long time ago. Life gets in the way sometimes. You should know that. You run a successful business. You know what this career means for personal relationships."

"It just could've gone so differently between you two," Martí said like he even cared. Rafa was certain that his old friend and often rival was just holding onto his grudge like a safety blanket. He hadn't spoken to Martí's fiery-eyed younger sister in years, but he'd heard she'd long moved on.

Martí went on. "But, alas, like you said. It's none of my business, and it is many years past now. So," he raised his beer. "Let bygones be bygones, or whatever they say."

Rafa cocked a skeptical eyebrow, but nonetheless, he clinked his bottle against Martí's.

"So the big day is coming, si?" Martí asked. It was a subtly sly shift in topic, but Rafa wasn't surprised. Of course, that's why Martí was over here. He wasn't there to make small talk or reminisce about the past. He wanted to talk about Rafa's new restaurant. Probably wanted to sniff out the competition.

Rafa and Martí had been rivals as long as Rafa could remember, going back to childhood playgrounds. Back then, they had been something of best friend rivals. Even though they had been inseparable, there was always a level of playful competition between them, from playground games, football, and girls. As they grew older, however, the competition had shifted from a playful rivalry to something a little more menacing. After Rafa started dating Elena, Martí's younger sister by two years, things intensified. They stayed friends, but

Martí grew more bitter. His playful jokes became sharp jobs. What's the word the girls use? Frenemy? After Rafa broke things off with Elena to go to culinary school in the United States, Martí dropped all pretense of friendship. And when they both landed on the Barcelona culinary scene a few years back, their bitter standoff turned into a fierce rivalry. Martí had been the first to open his restaurant, of course. And it has been a smash hit right out of the gate. He'd been the golden boy of the culinary scene for years now. Rafa had still been learning the ropes as a sous chef, and then a head chef, and then finally an executive chef at one of the top places in the city. But when he decided and announced he would be opening his own concept, that's when Martí's claws came back out.

They had barely spoken in the last couple of years, except for a few events here and there. They ran in the same circles on the periphery, though they no longer shared any close friends. The culinary world was small, and it was hard to avoid tripping over each other, but they did their very best.

Until now, apparently.

Rafa had heard a rumor that Martí was gossiping about him like a schoolgirl.

"Yes, we open in two weeks. Very exciting." Rafa, said, not wanting to give much more information than that.

"Rafa, amigo. I owe you an apology for the way I've acted. I'm proud of you for what you've accomplished. As someone who's done it myself, I know it's no small feat. It's a harsh business. And we should stand by each other's side. We're on the same block, no? We should be allies, not enemies."

"I appreciate the sentiment, although I'm not sure, I believe you," Rafa said, eyeing him suspiciously.

Martí shook his head bashfully. "I know, I deserve it. And you don't have to be my friend, and you don't have to believe me. But just know that what I say is true. I'm happy for you, my friend. I'm happy for you, and I wish you all the success. There's room in the city for everyone. People can't get enough food, that's one thing I know. And I know you have talent. I've had your paella. You're going to do great." He raised his beer.

Rafa studied him for a moment, this former friend turned enemy, turned—now what? Professional ally? Rafa had to admit, he liked the idea of that. There were times he missed Martí. Sure, their relationship had always been a bit acerbic, but they'd been buddies. They spent many years fighting off bigger enemies, swooning over girls in their neighborhood. Roughhousing, playing football. He had hated the idea that they were never going to talk again.

Rafa raised his beer too. "Gracias. Means a lot to me coming from you. You've been a pillar of success. A true inspiration for all of us. So I appreciate the kind words."

"Salud," Martí said, clinking his glass.

They stood in silence for a moment, the hum of the tapas bar buzzing about them. The music had kicked up a beat to a more dance-worthy melody. Rafa felt his feet instinctively tapping. Laughter rose above the din. The clink of plates and wine glasses.

Finally, Martí spoke again, "So, you and that food critic are getting close."

Rafa stiffened and flashed him another look. "Which food critic?" He said, playing dumb.

Martí flashed him a knowing look. "Right. Definitely not the one you were all over at Rival the other night."

"We're friends. I was showing her some local places. So?"

"She's a bit famous, or so I hear. And I guess her reviews can make or break a place."

Rafa worked his jaw again, the incredulity seeping back in. Why was Martí bringing this up? It all seemed too well-scripted.

"*Sí*. I guess a lot of restaurants are itching to get her stamp of approval. Including you, I guess. She came to your place, did she not?" Rafa asked.

Martí sipped his beer and looked quite pleased with himself. "Sí. She came in and tried out some of my dishes a couple of nights ago."

Rafa felt his whole body light up with irritation. "To review?"

"No, not officially. More personal. We had a good time. Drank some good wine. Maybe a little too much, you know? I should be more careful around a journalist."

Rafa now wanted to smash his bottle over Martí's head like an ape. But he breathed and just nodded nonchalantly.

"Ah, I see."

Martí did not let up. "I don't know if she's going to write anything about the place, not that I really need it. I mean, not to sound arrogant, it's just we've had a lot of really good press already. Then again, it's always important to stay relevant. I hear she's got quite the following on Instagram, too. Big influencer in the food scene."

"So I hear," Rafa said, trying to hold back saying more. The last thing he wanted was for Martí to know how well he actually knew Vera. Or that he cared about any of this. He wasn't going to let him get under his skin. Not now when so much was on the line.

Martí leaned in conspiratorially. "I'd be careful, though."

"Oh, yeah? Why? She's dangerous?" Rafa said with a smirk.

"Maybe, in a matter of speaking. I hear she's got the sharpest tongue in the industry. That she wiggles her way in and gets close to people under the pretense of flirting or being friendly. She gets people to drop their guard and do something embarrassing or show her behind the scenes in a way that affects people negatively. Then she writes about it and blasts you in front of the whole world."

Rafa processed what Martí was saying. That just didn't mesh with what he knew about Vera. She seemed so transparent, so brutally honest. She was the one intrepidly putting herself out there on Flamenco stages. And yeah, he'd read a couple of her reviews and knew she could be a little harsh, but her words seemed honest and not duplicitous. But then again, what did he really know about her? Apparently, she'd been having dinner with Martí one minute, then dancing and kissing him under lamppoles the next. Talk about operating in gray areas.

And apparently, Rafa was a petty little boy. Grow up, he chided himself.

"Well, I'll be sure to keep my guard up, then."

"I actually read this review that she wrote recently," Martí pulled out his phone and opened up an app. He shook his head. "Absolutely brutal. Pretty much destroyed the place before it even got going." He slid the phone toward Rafa. He glanced down at the screen. It was an opinion piece on another blog talking about how Vera had come in under false pretenses, pretending to love the place, flirting with the chef, sharing after-dinner drinks with him and everything. Got the chef to share some personal backstory, which she then printed in her article. The chef was mortified and said it severely damaged his business. He warns anyone to be wary of Vera Stone.

Rafa let his eyes run over the words multiple times. That couldn't be right. Not Vera. She—then again he went back to, what did he actually know about her? He handed the phone back to Martí. "Well, that doesn't bode well, does it? Next time I see her, I'll be sure to be careful. Guard my secrets."

Martí nodded curtly and took his phone, slipping it back into his pocket. "That's good, my friend. I would hate to see you damage your business before you even got it off the ground."

"I'm sure you wouldn't."

"How about another? With this hot weather, these are going down just a little too fast," Martí said.

Rafa smiled thinly, studying Martí. What was he playing at here?

"Sure thing."

Chapter Twenty-Eight

I woke at the crack of dawn the next morning with a splitting headache, and I thought it had less to do with the wine and more to do with the bomb drop I'd received and the fitful night of sleep that followed.

I didn't know what to think exactly. I had always trusted Joanne, my editor, to have my back, despite her reputation for being self-serving. She could be ruthless, no doubt. It was a hard industry for women, and she'd fought hard to climb the ladder. But she was ethical. So I thought. This whole situation just felt wrong.

I pulled up my phone to check for alerts. I groggily opened Instagram and scrolled through my notifications. Lots of likes and generic comments. Plenty of DMs asking me to be a jewelry ambassador or a sugar baby. Nothing of too much interest. I hesitated, then navigated over to @ChefRafa.

He'd posted a new reel the previous afternoon. He stood

at the commercial stove in a tight, white button-up shirt with the sleeves rolled up to the elbows. There were those forearms again. Corded muscles and a faded tattoo. I took a long drink of water. He was demonstrating a traditional *tortilla* recipe. So simple—eggs, potato, and seasoning—but God, did he make it sensual. I clicked off. What was I doing Instagram stalking like a teenager?

I shook my head. I would deal with Rafa later. Right then, I needed to hear this from Joanne's mouth. I glanced at the clock. I doubted a 1 a.m. phone call would be welcomed. Grr. Coffee. I needed coffee. I popped one of my daily allotted espresso pods into the machine and waited.

Finally, at 1 p.m. Barcelona time, I nervously sipped another coffee from the lobby while I waited for Joanne to pick up my FaceTime call.

"Vera, so nice to hear from you. Especially at 7 a.m.," she said dryly. She was already dressed in a light-knit beige sweater with her cropped blonde hair pushed back in a headband, giving her 40-something age a youthful look.

I didn't care it was so early.

"Yeah, hi. Sorry for the early hour, but this is important. Do you have a second?"

"A second. I wouldn't answer the phone otherwise. Fortunately, you've caught me over my latte."

"Right," I said, my voice quivering.

"Out with it, Vera. What's going on? Problem with the article?"

"No, the article is going fine. The problem is that I learned a little something at the industry party last night."

"Oh? How was the party? Everything you'd hoped?" She sipped from an oversized ceramic mug.

"Yeah, it was fine. Fun. But, like I said, I learned some very interesting information."

I waited a moment to gauge her reaction. Would she offer up the truth freely? I doubted it. As expected, her face remained expressionless.

"Ok. Were you going to delight me with any details, or is that the extent of your engaging story?"

I resisted the urge to roll my eyes at her sour sarcasm. I wasn't in the mood. I also stayed emotionless.

"I learned that I'm here at the request of Greta Wolf."

There was a long, pregnant pause. She stiffened, and it looked like she was holding her breath. She looked down as though she was distracting herself with something on the table. Finally, she turned back to the screen with a bright expression. "Yes, and?"

"Well, is that true? Did I get put on this assignment because of Greta?"

Joanne shrugged. "And if you did? What's the problem with that?"

"Because—well," I faltered. "Well, don't you think that's something I should've known?"

Joanne stared into the screen—hard, blue eyes studying me.

Finally, she spoke. "Vera, I don't understand what you're upset about right now. Yes, Greta came to me wanting my help. She likes your work and your ability to sniff out the up-and-coming, the quality. And you've been bugging me to go to Spain for years. This just seemed like serendipity. So here we are."

I shook my head. Just like Joanne to gloss over some key details.

"Are you forgetting the part where she is paying you—a

magazine—for an *unbiased* feature review of a new restaurant *she invested in."*

Again, Joanne's face was stony, her natural defense against revealing too much.

Finally, she sighed. "Vera. Again, why does it matter? Do you hate the restaurant?"

"What? No. It's very good. Fantastic, actually."

She threw up her hands. "Then who cares who's paying you? You're not being asked to lie. You'd be giving this place a five-star review anyway."

"Yes, but it doesn't feel authentic now. It feels like I'm doing somebody's dirty work. Like I'm just some PR puppet."

"Dirty, how? You're getting to write a feature article in our quarterly magazine—a huge win—on a place that you love. Case closed."

"How much is she paying for this?"

Joanne laughed incredulously. "You know I can't discuss company finances with you."

"All my expenses, I assume. What else? Lining your pocket with a little something extra?" My cheeks were feeling a rush of heat as my anger mounted.

Her eyes narrowed into small beads of ice. "Watch yourself, Vera. You are playing out of your league now."

"What about the other restaurants on my list? Does she have a vested interest in those, too?"

Joanne fiddled with her tennis bracelet. "No. Those were selected by our scouts. We needed to have an appropriate number of places on the list."

"To hide the insider job. Keep any suspicions at Bay.

This time, Joanne rolled her eyes. "Vera, I admire your integrity. I really do. I went to journalism school, too. But you have to get over your naive sensibilities. Everything you learned in *Reporter Ethics: 101*? The world doesn't work like that anymore. Frankly, the world never worked like that. So just forget all the things you learned in a textbook case study, and start paying attention to the real world. Yes, sometimes people are on other people's payroll. Everything from start-ups to business to government. We all have outside investors. It's the way the world works." I started to argue, but she held up her hand. "Think of it this way, Vera. We found a way to make your dreams come true. End of story. Just be happy and do your job. You like this restaurant and the Barcelona food scene? Great. Write the best damn review you can and do it justice. Who cares who paid for the plane ticket."

I tried to take what she was saying to heart. And I tried to believe that we weren't actually crossing any ethical lines. I guess at the end of the day, she didn't actually tell me what to write. Or did she?

I sighed. "Ok. I guess." I shook my head.

"Take this all as a compliment, Vera. Greta hand-picked you. She likes your editorial style. She respects what you've built. She knew you had the ability to bring light to her vision. That's a huge professional compliment."

I wanted to push back—Joanne was always very good at playing to people's egos. But I had to admit I was starting to see her point. Maybe I needed to just get off my high horse and accept the win.

"It just feels sort of, I don't know. A little bit dirty?" My words were starting to feel thin.

Joanne chuckled. "You're a journalist, Vera. Your life is dirty. Try working the Capitol Hill beat. Or Wall Street insider trading. You'd see what dirty really is. So, go eat some paella with sexy chefs and write about it. OK? I have a meeting, so I have to go." She hung up the phone before I could retort.

Chapter Twenty-Nine

The bright afternoon light slipped through the windows of *Pintxos Celia*, casting an inviting glow across the intricate tiles and rustic wooden tables. The sounds of a working kitchen combined with the muted chatter of early patrons to create a homey soundtrack. I felt the weight of expectation—when I announced this Instagram Live session, the excited feedback had been overwhelming. Now I felt like I'd better deliver. I had managed to set my iPhone on a tripod on a cleared section of the bar, aiming it to capture the vibrant tapas spread that Celia had meticulously laid out.

Taking a deep breath, I tapped the 'Go Live' button. "*Buenos Dias* everyone from the heart of Barcelona! I'm here in the Barri Gòtic at Pintxos Celia, a fantastic hidden spot that I'm guessing won't stay hidden for long."

As viewers started joining, their wave emojis and greetings floated up my screen. I panned the camera over the display Celia had laid out. "Look at this spread! Who's drooling already?"

Celia, looking every part the confident Barcelona local

with her flowing dark hair and mysterious smile, stepped into the frame and sat next to me.

"And here she is, Celia herself."

"¡Hola! Welcome to my little slice of Barcelona," Celia said in a chipper tone.

"Celia, thank you for letting me and all of my viewers have a look into your world. Maybe you could start by telling us about the history of tapas?"

She nodded, her face lighting up as she started in her smooth accent. "*Si, claro*. The name 'tapas', means 'covers' or 'lids' in Spanish. There are a few tales of how this little finger food became such a staple of our culture. My favorite story features King Alfonso X, known as Alfonso the Wise He was gallivanting around his kingdom many moons ago, when he decided to visit an inn and duly ordered a beer. The innkeeper served this ale with a small complimentary dish of food on top of the glass. The King thought it was such a good idea that he decreed all inns throughout Spain to serve food with any alcoholic drink." She grinned. "A great legend, although perhaps a more probable origin, is that these little 'lids' were a custom used to keep the flies off the sweet sherry. But, as with many things in Spain, we turned this utility into a rich culinary tradition."

Picking up a plate with finely sliced jamón and crusty bread, she continued, "It's not just about the food. It's about community. Tapas are shared, they encourage conversation. In one sitting, you can taste a myriad of flavors."

"But these are not really *tapas,* per se, right?" I asked, waving my hand over the treats on display.

"Not exactly. We call them *pintxos*. They are a style of tapa that originated in the Basque Country, in San Sebastian. Some of the bars created a method where patrons can help themselves to these mini bites. You will find this trend in all of Spain now, but it is very popular here in Barcelona."

I picked up a small slice of bread topped with goat cheese and caramelized onions, skewered with a toothpick. I removed the toothpick and popped it in my mouth and closed my eyes in pure bliss.

I swallowed it down with a sip of wine and continued.

"I could eat that all day. Is there anything unique about pintxos or tapas in general here in Barcelona that you won't find anywhere else?"

Celia paused and also sipped her wine before continuing. "Si, Barcelona's tapas are unique. We have the sea, so there's always fresh seafood on our menu, but because we are also close to the mountains, you will find dishes that mix seafood and meat, which is not common elsewhere. And fresh vegetables are a staple too. We're fortunate to have access to so many wonderful ingredients. We also have this constant desire to innovate. We are not afraid to try new flavors or incorporate global flavors."

"Would you say food is an important part of Spanish culture?" I asked.

Celia let out a deep gut laugh. "That's the understatement of the century."

I grinned. "Can you elaborate?"

She wiped away a laughter tear. "Food is the very essence of our identity. It's how we connect with our families, communities, the environment. It's our history. We have a strange and unique cultural makeup here. Romans to Christian conquerors to the Arab rule. All of them left a mark on our culinary influences. Did you know that the first cookbook in Spain was written in Barcelona?"

I raised my brow. "Really?"

She nodded. "In 1477 by Ruperto de Nola."

I flashed the camera an amused look. "Did you know you were tuning in for a history lesson?" I turned back to the food.

"Ok, so tell me more. What is this drizzle here? I noticed you have a lot of different sauces."

Celia laughed lightly. "Ah, si. We love our sauces here. That is a *remesco*. A garlicky sauce made from peppers and nuts. Sauces can really spice up a very simple snack."

"Can you tell us about your personal story? How did you get started here? What made you want to open a tapas bar?"

She took a deep breath. "My brother and I started this place. I always wanted to own something of my own, something I can pass down to my daughter. As a single mama, it's not been easy, but this place, these little tapas, they're my heart. They connect me to my past while letting me craft the future."

Comments were flooding in, questions ranging from cooking tips to how Celia managed her work-life balance.

"Running a business with a small child isn't easy, but I am so lucky that I have my family close. In Barcelona, we are a giant community. We welcome children in all aspects of our lives and help each other with the burden."

I thought of my friends with small children in New York —how they were constantly stressed about the cost of child-care. How they complained they got dirty looks every time they brought their kids to a restaurant or a movie.

Celia went on, "And from the beginning, I just took her to work with me. Now that she is a little older, she helps me make the food!"

Celia went on to field each question with grace and charm. She even spontaneously showed us how to prepare a simple pintxo using a tin of anchovies.

"Thank you, Celia, for sharing a piece of your world with us," I said.

Celia smiled warmly. "Si, it was my pleasure. If you ever

find yourself in Barcelona, you know where to find the heart of the city."

With a final wave, I ended the live session.

She flashed me an exaggerated look of exhaustion. "My television debut."

I laughed and tossed the anchovy-pepper treat into my mouth.

"I never knew how much I needed canned fish in my life," I said.

"You will never be the same. How did it go? I did ok?"

I shook my head slowly. "You were fantastic. A natural. You should consider doing that regularly to promote the restaurant. You could have your own little cooking show!"

Celia looked pleased with herself. She shimmied her shoulders. "Maybe I have a backup career if the pintxos business doesn't work out."

I started wrapping up my recording equipment and put it into my duffel bag. "Well, I don't know about you, but all those descriptions of food made me absolutely ravenous. Should we go get something? Maybe a little something strong to wash it all down?"

"You read my mind. But I don't want to be here. As much as I love her, I spend entirely too much time in here."

"I'm open to any and all suggestions."

"I know a place just up the street. They have some more innovative creations. I really like what the owner does with flavors. We like to visit each other's places from time to time."

"Lead the way!"

We finished packing up and lazily meandered through the

winding corridors until we came to a little bar tucked into a corner.

The inside was eclectic, with local modern art and a full wall mural in a lovely Picasso tribute. Funky low-vibe music played in the background.

La Vaca Bonita was mostly empty, but for a few locals starting to trickle in and search of sustenance. It didn't seem like a tourist spot but rather the kind of place that the local scene would know about.

"I love the interior vibe," I said, glancing around.

"The owner has a real passion for art. He's always trying to find the next up-and-comer."

I took a couple of snapshots with my phone.

We sauntered up to the barstools, and I instantly started to take inventory of the selection of tapas behind the little glass partition.

"Hola, CeCe," the barman sauntered over, smiling at Celia. He was young with suspenders and a thin hipster mustache. His jet-black hair was tied back into a small knot at the nape of his neck.

"*Hola, Diego. Como estas?*"

"*Bien, bien. E tu?*"

"Bien. This is my friend, Vera. She's from New York."

His expression lit up. "New York? Fabulous city. Mucho gusto, vera. What are we drinking?"

"Vino tino? Dos," Celia said.

"Si, bueno." Diego popped the cork on a bottle of red wine and poured two very full glasses.

"Hungry?" Diego asked.

I nodded. "Very. Can you—how about a selection of your favorites?"

He gave a surprised expression and flashed Celia a look.

Celia smirked. "She's adventurous."

Diego looked quite pleased as he gathered up a selection of tapas and laid them out in front of us.

I eyed the spread greedily, which looked to be a bowl of fresh ceviche, a mound of fried squid, and a collection of small, breaded croquettes.

"Well, well. I seem to keep running into you everywhere."

Celia and I turned toward the confident male voice to see Martí standing beside us. He was with a couple of other men, all clutching bottles of beer. They all had a sun-kissed nonchalance about them.

"We sure do. Are you sure you're not stalking me?" I said teasingly.

He smirked, but I thought I saw a glint of something in his eye. Maybe annoyance? I was starting to get the impression that while he could definitely throw around the banter, Martí didn't like being on the receiving end of jokes.

"Tired of your own food, CeCe?"

Celia flashed him an annoyed look, then a tight smile.

"Just spreading the love around."

There was definitely some kind of history between them. I wondered if maybe they used to date. If the culinary scene here was anything like back home, it was a small, tight-knit world. Paths crossed all the time, and it could be somewhat incestuous. Dating outside the industry was challenging, given the demands and the hours, and dating within the industry came with its own complications. I was starting to see why everyone was single.

"What are you having?" Martí said, eyeing my small collection of tapas.

"House favorites," I said. "I was feeling adventurous."

A wicked little smile danced across his face. "Are you now? This place is known for more adventurous things than *calamares fritos*, you know?"

I defiantly tossed a little squid in my mouth and looked him in the eye. "Do you have some suggestions?"

Martí pointed toward a plate on display with what looked like small, breaded morsels. "Ever tried these? They're a delicacy here."

I looked over, intrigued. "What are they?" I asked with a healthy dose of incredulity.

Martí smirked, that mischievous twinkle appearing in his eye that might be considered endearing, but I found it suspicious. "They're called *Criadillas*. Very traditional, especially in some parts of Spain. Give it a try. If you're feeling adventurous, that is."

"Martí," Celia said with a warning tone.

I was never one to turn down a unique food, but Celia looked downright nervous.

"What exactly is it?" I asked.

"Does it matter? Are you afraid?" Martí said. I glared.

"Never. Fine, I'll have one."

He grinned and signaled Diego for an order. When Diego looked amused, I knew I was in trouble. But in for a penny, and all. Diego set three small, breaded mounds in front of me.

I picked one up with my fork and, with a breath, took a tentative bite. The taste was unique, crispy on the outside and tender inside. It was a bit gamey but not off-putting.

"You like?" Martí asked.

"It's...different. Not bad, I guess," I began, attempting to pin down the familiar taste. "Kind of reminds me of... something I can't quite place."

Martí seemed to be holding back a chuckle. "Maybe you have had—"

"Martí!" Celia snapped.

I took a moment to chew, then swallowed. I wouldn't say

it was good, but it wasn't gross by any means. "Some type of offal? Liver? Kidney? Heart?"

Martí's laughter spit out like a schoolboy. "Not quite. Let's say it's... a very specific part of a bull."

My eyes must've looked like saucers as it registered. Ok, I was brave, but I hadn't been expecting *that*. I felt a heat rise to my cheeks and grabbed my water glass, gulping down to swallow both my shock and the remaining bite.

I flashed Celia a look. "You could have warned me!" I said, half-laughing and half-indignant.

She held up her hands in mock surrender. "You were hell-bent on showing off how adventurous you are, so who was I to get in the way?"

Martí's grin was unapologetic. "Ahh, come on. Where's your sense of fun? Besides, you said they were good!"

"I said they weren't *bad*. Big difference."

Rolling my eyes, but with the ghost of a smile forming on my lips, I shot back, "I guess that's one more thing to tick off my culinary bucket list."

Martí plucked one up and tossed it into his mouth with a daring smirk.

I rolled my eyes and pulled out my phone.

"What are you doing?" Celia asked.

I snickered. "Do you really think I would miss the chance to post about eating bull testicles?"

"That's not a sentence you expect to hear every day."

I snapped up and there was Rafa in all his intense glory.

I felt a wide smile spread across my face then reined it in. Everything that had transpired between us and everything I'd found about Greta flooded my brain.

"Rafa. Hi."

His eyes darted from me to Celia, then narrowed in on Martí.

"Hola," he said, but there was a note of suspicion in his

tone, as though he'd caught us smoking behind the school gym.

"Amigo! Glad you could come down to our little boys' night," Martí said. He patted Rafa on the back in that way men do.

"I didn't know *las damas* would be here," Rafa said.

"Ah, neither did I. Happy coincidence," Martí said.

"Martí here was just teaching me about the joys of *Criadillas.*"

"How kind of him. And what did you think?" Rafa asked.

"Chewy."

There was a moment of pause and then everyone burst into laughter. Even Rafa visibly unwound.

With an uneasy alliance of laughter and levity, I tried to navigate the remainder of the evening without things diving into completely awkward territory. After a few glasses of wine, Celia was getting a little closer to Martí, and their long, knowing gazes for getting longer. Yeah, they had history, all right. And clearly some unresolved chemistry.

Rafa's demeanor was an unspoken riddle. Every glance and half-smile seemed to be soaked in a quiet turmoil. I guess I couldn't blame his surly demeanor. All my talk of professional boundaries, and here I am eating cow genitalia with his rival. Ok, yeah, we had firmly taken up residence in awkward territory.

But part of me desperately wanted to ask him about Greta. It wouldn't change the trajectory of our non-existent relationship, but I guess I just wanted to know.

But every time I tried to bridge the conversational gap with Rafa, I was met with restrained responses. And as the wine loosened my common sense, I had the desire to reach out, to peel away the layers Rafa had cocooned himself in, even if it was all my fault.

Unable to take any more of his brooding silence and thousand-yard stares, I excused myself to the bathroom to collect myself. I needed to just let this whole thing go. I'd made my choices. There was no fixing this.

I stepped out of the bathroom, and Rafa was standing there. I yelped in shock.

"Sorry, you scared me."

"*Lo siento*. I didn't mean to. I just—I thought I should clear the air. Things are—charged."

I exhaled. "Yeah, a little. Look, I'm sorry if I've made things awkward."

His gaze flitted away, seemingly engrossed in the intricate patterns of the cobblestone beneath our feet.

Finally, he looked back up at me. "Esta bien. There are no hard feelings. Seeing you with Martí—it was a little triggering. The way he looks at you—then at me." He shook his head. "It doesn't matter. We are all just professional friends, now, si?"

I smiled, but the muscles wouldn't fully engage. "Si."

The tension between us started to melt. "Let's go have some fun. Forget the tension."

"Yeah. I'd like that."

We returned to the lively atmosphere of the bar, walking a little too closely than we should as though invisible magnets were pulling us close.

Martí's eyes flickered over us as we returned, an unreadable expression dancing across his face. Annoyance? Jealousy? Suspicion? I shook it off. I wasn't playing Martí's game.

The night wore on, and as the crowd thinned, signaling the approach of the late hour, we collectively decided to bring the evening to a close.

"This was fun," I said. "Thank you for introducing me to such fine delicacies," I teased Martí.

He bowed. "Here to serve."

My eyes met Rafa's, but we said nothing. There was nothing left to say.

"I'll see you at our next meeting," I finally offered.

He offered a perfunctory nod. "Have a good night, Vera."

Celia and I left the bar and with a soft, introspective smile, I began my solitary walk through the cobblestone streets back to my hotel, the events of the evening playing like a gentle melody in the recesses of my mind.

Chapter Thirty

Rafa felt a knot of dread twist tighter in his stomach as he re-read the words, the glow of his phone casting a harsh light in the shadowed confines of his soon-to-open restaurant. The space felt colder, unfriendlier with the ghost of this goblin of a review lingering in the air, an unwanted guest in a place built on his dreams and hard work. His normally steady hands shook slightly, the screen blurring for a moment before he forced himself to ease his breath.

A loud click resounded, breaking the eerie silence as Lorna entered, her face illuminated by the soft foyer lights set to welcome their first customers in just a few days. The expression on her face, a mix of horror and disbelief, echoed his internal turmoil. He knew instantly she'd also read the anonymous vendetta.

"It's bad, isn't it?" Rafa asked, his voice breaking the charged silence. The physicality of his vocalized fear hung heavily in the room.

Lorna bit her lower lip and stared at him before finally nodding. She struggled for words, her normally articulate self clearly wrestling to make sense of it. She eyed the screen again with a detective's scrutiny.

"It's just one person's opinion, a coward hiding behind anonymity. And obviously, it's all lies. We haven't even done our soft opening yet. There's no way anyone could have eaten here."

Rafa felt a swell of anger overtake the initial shock, his mind racing through potential suspects. His heart pounded heavily, each beat like a war drum calling him to defend what was his.

"Who wants us to fail so desperately they'd do this?"

When he got the Google alert that morning and clicked through to a local community blog, he couldn't believe what he was seeing. A full-page review of Santos California absolutely slamming the concept. Everything from the decor to the food. He had reread it a hundred times, trying to make sense of the anonymous words.

"It's just internet trolls, Rafa. Some people just hate themselves so much they'll do anything they can to tear someone down. It's anonymous, you can't take it seriously."

Lorna paced, the soft sound of her shoes against the wooden floor echoed in the quiet space.

"Could it be a competitor? We've been getting a lot of attention in the press lately, maybe someone feels threatened?" she suggested. He could visibly see her mind working a mile a minute trying to bring logic to a situation that felt anything but logical.

Rafa found himself sinking into one of the dining chairs, the elegant piece of furniture offering no comfort as he massaged his forehead.

"I—I don't know. Si, I suppose."

She went on. "And here, what they say about your Huevos a la Flamenca. *Huevos a la Flamenco with a twist—more like a twist of trying too hard. Adding serranos to the dish? That's bold. Maybe too bold.'* Rafa, That's not even on the proposed menu. They're just making things up."

Something clicked. "Huevos a la Flamenca," he said quietly.

"Huh?"

He shook his head slowly. No, it couldn't be. "I did make *Huevos a la Flamenca* for Vera the other night when she stopped by. I mentioned I was debating putting it on the menu and wanted her opinion."

Lorna stared at him with an unknowable expression for a minute. Then she shook her head. "No. She wouldn't do this. Why would she do this? That makes zero sense."

Rafa sighed. "Si, I know. She wouldn't. That wouldn't serve her purpose. It's just a coincidence."

Lorna walked over and rested a hand on his shoulder. "We'll figure out who did this. And even if we don't, it will wash over. It's just a dumb community blog. Who even reads it? You're going to get a feature in *Travel Luxe & Leisure*. Remember that. That will blow all of this nonsense into the ether."

He flashed her a phantom smile. "I hope you're right."

She patted his back. "I'm always right, Rafa. That's why you keep me around."

"It's definitely not for your humility."

She winked "Come on. Chin up. Let's focus on what we can control, the food, the service, the experience we are going to offer. We'll let our work speak for itself, louder than any false review ever could."

Chapter Thirty-One

I was nestled in a quiet corner of a cozy, old-world cafe in the heart of the Barri Gòtic. An untouched *cafe doble* and a croissant lay next to my notepad. The cobbled alley was alive with the soft chatter of locals and the distant, melodious tendrils of a busker's guitar. I could almost taste the aroma of freshly brewed coffee in the air as I scribbled down notes from the morning's escapades.

My posts and Lives from this trip were turning into the most successful of my career. Apparently, the whole American-in-Spain thing was extra romantic to my followers, and I'd gained thousands more just in the past week.

That morning I had wandered down to the Gracia neighborhood in search of the outside-the-box. With local design workshops, vegan restaurants, and even Japanese patisseries, the neighborhood was an absolute tick-list of trendy spots, a place where tradition met with contemporary flair in a seamless dance. The squares were filled with market stalls that I was told disappeared around seven so the locals could gather in the streets and drink. I made a note to return after dark one of these days.

Sitting now in this age-old place, the modernity of Gracia seemed like a distant dream. I finished editing the video reel I'd taken and uploaded it. I leaned back in my chair and tucked into my croissant.

Out of nowhere, a voice that was a portal to my past reached my ears.

"Vera? Is that really you?"

I looked up, my heart skipping a beat. Those familiar big honey eyes, the boyish grin... it was Alex, my college boyfriend. The memories of those passionate yet tumultuous days washed over me, feeling like another life.

"My God, it is you. How random," Alex said with an edge of surprise.

"Alex!" I said with a half-laugh.

"Wow. I can't believe it's you. It's been—what, like ten years?"

I shook my head slowly. "Something like that." *Since I broke your heart*, I thought. "What are you doing in Barcelona?"

"Here for work, actually."

"Really? Which is?" I asked.

"Oh, I ended up in healthcare tech. We just launched an app that's getting global traction. Here to do a presentation to a hospital group." Wow. He sounded like such a grownup.

"Wow. That's really impressive."

He shrugged humbly. "It's been a good gig. And you— maybe I shouldn't admit it, but I've followed your career. Your reviews crack me up. Every restaurant in New York gets jittery at the mention of your name."

I laughed. "I doubt that, but I appreciate it. I always wanted to inspire fear. Hey, do you want to sit for a minute?"

Alex glanced around as though checking we weren't being

watched but then complied and slipped into the chair opposite me.

"It's great to see you, Vera. It's kinda surreal."

"You too. Feels like another life."

"It kinda was. So you're here for work, too, then?" he asked, eyeing my notebook. A server came around, and Alex ordered a *cafe solo*.

"Thought you were stalking my Insta?" I teased.

He held up his hands. "Sorry, I'm a little behind. Been busy."

I grinned. "Yeah, I'm here writing a feature on the Barcelona food scene. Old vs. new type thing. Looking at some of the really innovative concepts and how they compare to the traditions."

He smiled. "You always had a vision. It's awesome to see you doing what you love."

My cheeks warmed. Alex was always the thoughtful type, quick with a compliment and kind words. He was always *nice*. Too bad I had never been very good with nice.

"So how have you been, other than revolutionizing health care worldwide?" I asked.

He chuckled. "Good, good. We moved out of the city a couple of years ago. Have a big old country house now with trees and a tire swing. Total American dream, right?"

I raised my brow. "We?"

"Oh, right. My wife Chelsea and I. And our two kids. Oliver and Mia." He swiped his phone screen and flashed me a professionally taken portrait of a smiling family in matching blue and khaki attire in springtime New England. "Ollie is five now. Mia three."

"They're beautiful," I said. But as I said the words, I felt a pang of... something. Jealousy? Regret? I couldn't quite place it. Here was the guy I'd run away from, fearing commitment, now with a picture-perfect family. The contrast between our lives was unsettling.

"What about you?" Alex asked. "Married? Kids?"

I shook my head, feeling heat climb up my neck. I don't know why I was feeling ashamed—I loved my life. But so many people had this ridiculous notion that women in their 30s without those life milestones must be lacking in some way.

"No, still operating solo. Which works for me."

He smiled and nodded, but I swear I caught a look of pity in his eyes. Grr. I did *not* need to be pitied for my singlehood.

"It does. Works for you, I mean. You look great. And you're living the dream!"

Was I living the dream? I was living my dream, that was for sure. And that's what mattered.

A moment of silence took over. I wasn't exactly sure what to say to him. Back in college, he had wanted so badly to settle down with me. Get married right after college, jump right into domestic bliss. Do all the normal American life things. And I had run away like I was a spark and he was gasoline. Looking at him now, though, with his successful career and beautiful family, I couldn't help but feel like I had done him a solid favor. A girl like me never would have satisfied his sensibilities in the end.

Finally, he filled the void. "Remember that time we snuck into the university's kitchen at 2 a.m. just because you wanted to prove you could make a better dessert than the cafeteria?"

The randomness of the story shook me from my reverie. It took me a moment to conjure the memory, and then I laughed. "Oh, the infamous tiramisu heist. How could I forget? We got caught by that security guard, and you tried to bribe him with a piece of the tiramisu."

He laughed heartily. "And he actually took it! Gave us a warning and said if the tiramisu was as good as it looked, he'd forget he ever saw us."

I smirked. "That was the day I realized the true power of good food. God, how much vodka had we actually had?"

"Probably way more than was reasonable even for twenty-one-year-olds. We'd been at that art student mixer that night with your roommate."

"Ah, that's right. With the nude paintings that had pig heads? Still gives me nightmares." I laughed at the memories rushing back to me.

Alex sipped down his espresso, his smile lingering. "We had some wild times, didn't we? That time we went on that disastrous camping trip? You were so adamant about cooking fish over an open fire, and it rained the entire weekend."

I groaned. "Oh, don't remind me. I mean, really, have I ever been the outdoorsy type?"

He chuckled. "Hey, the fish was your idea. I was perfectly content with a can of beans."

I sighed playfully. "See? And that was why we were never meant to be. Fish girls and canned bean boys never mix."

I regretted the words instantly, seeing a flash of regret in Alex's eyes. But his expression quickly faded, and he nodded.

"Turns out, sometimes the universe knows what it's doing," he said.

"It does. I think it worked out for you."

There was a comfortable pause, both of us lost in memories of days gone by.

"You know, Vera, as much as things have changed, some things remain constant. Your passion for food, your drive... it was always there. And I'm genuinely happy to see where it's taken you."

I nodded, feeling a mix of nostalgia and gratitude. "Thanks, Alex. I'm happy for you too. It looks like you have the life you always wanted."

"I always did have a more vanilla palate than you. It's still my favorite ice cream flavor."

I half-laughed and finished my coffee. "The world needs vanilla bean. It complements devil's food chocolate perfectly."

He raised his empty espresso cup. "To the vanilla beans among us."

I clinked my glass with his. "To the paths we choose."

"How long are you here?" he asked.

"Another two weeks, actually. I'm so lucky. This was a total dream assignment."

As I said it, I thought about how I got there. I thought about Greta Wolf and Joanne's deal with her. Joanne's words rang in my ear. Did it really matter how or why I was there?

"That's awesome. Hey, if you get a chance and want some really authentic food, check out this place." He pulled a business card from his wallet and slipped it to me. I stifled a laugh seeing the name.

Martí Gonzales, head chef and owner
Vila Cocina

"I will, thanks."

Alex stood. "I better get going. Actually have a meeting soon. God, it was good to see you. I, uh, hey I'd love to say let's grab dinner or drinks or something while we're here, but I'm not sure Chelsea would like that. She has a little jealous streak when it comes to you."

I raised my brow, genuinely shocked. I was surprised Chelsea even knew who I was. "Me? Why?"

He shrugged. "Well, I mean, look at you. You're kinda famous. And, well, there's our history, you know? I made the mistake of telling her how many pieces you left my heart in. I was still kinda cleaning up the mess when I met her." He flashed me a bashful smile. I tried not to blush.

"That's all very—well, I guess it's flattering. And surprising. But hey, it's ok, I understand. I would never want to cause an issue."

"*Annnd*, she'd never admit it, but she totally follows you on Instagram."

I laughed incredulously. "Not awkward." Alex shrugged.

"You're—Alex, you're a really good guy. Chelsea is a lucky woman."

He chuckled lightly. "She'd be over the moon hearing that from you. If I dared tell her. Take care of yourself, Vera."

"You too, Alex."

As I watched Alex and my past meld with the Barcelona crowds, a sense of contemplative solitude enveloped me. I contemplated what future lay ahead. Would I ever share a similar fate of domestic bliss? I wasn't sure I was cut out for that.

Chapter Thirty-Two

I leaned against the wooden bar in Celia's place, the dim lighting casting a golden hue on the old terracotta tiles. The evening crowd was starting to trickle in, filling the small space with the sound of chattering voices and clinking glasses.

Aitana stood behind the counter, her tiny nimble fingers artfully arranging a vibrant mosaic of ingredients into edible delights. She was magical, truly, with an essence that seemed to literally sparkle. She was still cherub-faced and wide-eyed but with a seriousness and determination you didn't often see in kids so young. I couldn't help but grin as I watched her work.

Celia came around the back, wiping her hands on a towel. She eyed her daughter's handiwork with appreciation.

"*Perfecto, mija.* Ay, but make sure you add the caviar like this." She started to demonstrate the technique, but Aitana swatted her hand away.

"I have it, mama. Go away. Let me work."

Celia flashed me an exaggerated look.

. . .

"She'll be the death of me, I think. I don't know where she gets that spirit. Or maybe I do, *Dios mío*. But she is my great joy in life."

My heart warmed at the sentiment. What must that kind of love feel like?

"Where is—" I started to ask but then shut my mouth. Her personal life was none of my business.

"Where is her father?" Celia finished for me with a knowing side smile.

I grimaced. "Sorry, that's none of my business. I didn't mean to pry."

Celia shrugged. "Está bien. He's probably in Seville at the moment."

I waited for her to continue. She plucked a bottle of open red wine from the counter and filled up two small tumblers. She took a sip, her eyes glossing over with a sheen of nostalgia.

"He is a professional flamenco guitarist if you can believe it. We had a little fling one week when he was here in Barcelona, and Aitana here was the result. It wasn't exactly my intention, but that's life sometimes. Sometimes we're not as careful as we should be. But every day, I am grateful for that mistake." She spared her daughter a glance. "I cannot imagine my life without her."

"Life is funny like that," I said. My thoughts drifted to Alex and how his heartbreak led him to the perfect life.

"She has his eyes," Celia murmured a hint of wistfulness in her tone. "And his spirit."

I sipped my wine. "What was he like?"

She took a deep breath, her gaze lost in the distance. Then she exhaled a light, breathy laugh. "His name is Javier. Like I said, he is a Flamenco guitarist from Seville. I met him during *La Mercè* festival years ago."

"Here in Barcelona?" I asked.

She nodded. "Si. It's an annual festival. The whole city was alive with music, dance, and fireworks. You actually just missed it. It's a magical time. I had set up a small food stall, right there on the *Passeig de Gràcia*. One evening, as I was packing up, I heard the most enchanting guitar playing. I followed the sound and found him just playing on the corner, surrounded by a captivated audience."

I could picture the scene in my mind, the seductive melody punctuating the sultry Spanish night. Who wouldn't be seduced?

"He had this intense, passionate look in his eyes as his fingers flew over the strings." Celia's hands demonstrated the movements absentmindedly as she spoke. "I must have been feeling pretty bold because, after his performance, I went right up to him and asked him to join me for a drink. From the moment we locked eyes, though, there was this... undeniable connection. Maybe it was just the magic of Flamenco music, but we spent that entire week together, wandering the streets of Barcelona."

"That all sounds wildly romantic," I said, picturing the affair unfolding beneath the sultry Barcelona nights.

She sighed again, her smile fading. "It was. But the week ended, and so did our time together. He was headed back to Seville, and I had my life here. We said our goodbyes, promising to keep in touch, but life got in the way. As it goes, you know? A few months later, I found out I was pregnant with Aitana. I tried reaching out to him, but his number had changed. I never saw him again."

I felt a crack run through my heart of the romantic tragedy of it all.

"He never came back to the festival or anything?"

Celia shrugged. "Honestly, I don't know. I didn't want to look for him. After I couldn't reach him and never heard from him, I figured he didn't want to see me again. And while part of me thought he deserved to know about Aitana, I didn't want him to feel trapped. He was a wandering musician, not a papa."

I placed a comforting hand on her arm. "Celia, I'm so sorry."

She gave me a small smile and waved away the words. "It's okay. Aitana is the best thing that ever happened to me. But sometimes, when she strums on that little toy guitar of hers, I can't help but wonder—" She trailed off, lost in thought. After a moment, she cleared her throat, her tone shifting. She stood straight and threw back her wine. "But enough about my old love story. What about you? Any romantic tales from New York?"

I laughed, the tension in the air dissipating. "Nothing even remotely as romantic as that. My terrible Tinder coffee dates couldn't possibly compete."

"Not even one little juicy story? I lay my heart bare for you, and you give me nothing?" She *tsked* teasingly.

I laughed. "I had a couple of boyfriends in college. One broke my heart by scooping my very first big assignment for the school paper."

"Ouch."

"Right? Taught me not to trust a man with my work. The other was—well, he was a great guy, just not my type. And I haven't really had anyone serious since." I shrugged. "To be honest, my life in New York is... chaotic. Between trying to climb the ladder at work and hopping from one restaurant to another, there's hardly any room for romance."

She raised a playful eyebrow. "Really? The city that never sleeps doesn't have room for a little love?"

"It's not that. New York is filled with opportunities to meet people – dates arranged by friends, dating apps, events, you name it. But I've always been more... focused on my career, I guess. Dating just feels like a distraction. I mean, I've seen so many of my friends lose themselves in relationships, forgetting their own ambitions."

She seemed genuinely surprised. "Ay, Vera! How can you not believe in love? That's such a foreign concept to me, especially in Spain where every corner, every song, every dance, speaks of *el amor.*"

I offered a subdued laugh. "It's just...I guess if I'm honest. I've always felt that if I let love in, it'd consume me, you know? There's so much I want to achieve, and I can't let anything divert my focus. Marriage and kids and all that—I just don't see it for me."

Celia's next words came out almost in a shout, her melodic voice drawing glances from a few patrons. "*Ay Dios mío!* Trust a New Yorker to turn love into a calculated risk." Celia spoke with directiveness. "*Mi amiga*, love isn't a diversion. It's fuel. It's what gives life its flavor, its zest. Imagine a paella without saffron or tapas without olive oil. That's life without love."

"You have a very poetic notion of it all."

She smirked. "Spaniards are just not afraid to experience passion." She pointed to an elderly couple sitting in a corner, lost in each other's eyes, sharing a plate of patatas bravas. "You see them? Look how happy they are. Love adds a sparkle to life!"

I pressed my lips together and glared playfully.

Celia shook her head and refilled my wine glass. "Don't worry, Barcelona has a way of teaching people about the beauty of unpredictability. Just you wait."

I raised my glass. "I won't hold my breath."

She leaned forward, resting her elbows on the table. "And what about Rafa?"

I stiffened, my glass pausing mid-sip. "What about him?"

"Ah, I see we are still denying our attraction. Sounds healthy."

"Are you just trying your hand at matchmaker or what? I came here to eat and drink, not be set up." I mock glared.

Celia smirked. "Then I guess you need some food."

* * *

As the clock ticked past 9 p.m., the tapas bar started to fill up, and Celia was now fully engrossed with her patrons. I figured it was time for me to head home. I was feeling sleep knock at my door. Even though New York had a reputation for late nights, it was nothing compared to the Spanish tradition of eating dinner at 11 p.m.

I stepped out into the crisp Spanish night, enjoying how the weather had turned just slightly, taking the edge of the hot days. Ok, maybe I wasn't quite ready for sleep.

I breathed in and decided what I wanted was a hot chocolate to end the night. I pulled up my phone to Google a place.

"Are you Vera?"

I looked up from my phone to see a middle-aged man staring down at me with cold, dark eyes. A little chill went through me. I instinctively took a step back.

"Are you Vera Stone?" He said again, a little more forcefully.

I swallowed a lump. "Um, who's asking?"

"Are you @VeraStoneEats, responsible for this?" He held up a phone screen where I saw a screenshot of one of my Instagram posts. I narrowed my gaze and saw it was my not-so-favorable review of *El Rincón de la Abuela*—the first restaurant I'd visited when I got to Barcelona strung out on jetlag. Oh, crap.

My lips instinctively formed an O shape, then I pressed them together. "Oh. Um, yes. That would be me. And you are?" I looked up with a forced, friendly expression.

"The owner of this restaurant." He pointed angrily at the screen.

Oh, double crap.

I shifted uncomfortably. "Oh, I see. Well, I imagine you're not too thrilled with my post then." I tried to smile, but the muscles contorted into a grimace.

"You think this is funny?" He asked.

I shook my head. "No, I —"

"Do you know the damage this has done?" His voice started to rise, and he moved toward me. My panic instinct flared to life.

He went on. "We rely on our local clientele. They trust us. They've been coming to us for years. And this stupid post goes viral talking about how horrible our customer service is. Railing about the lackluster food and how we do not embody the Spanish tradition. We've had negative reviews and cancellations. Business is down!"

My lip quivered as I opened my mouth to speak. I nervously scratched at my arm.

"I can't imagine that my little Instagram post has hurt your business if you have such a loyal clientele. Who am I to any of them?"

He lowered the phone. His nostrils were flaring like a bull. "Well, I asked myself the same thing. I think, why should it matter? Then I look you up and realized who you are. You are some famous food critic. And apparently, people take what you say seriously. Very seriously. And you have hundreds of thousands of followers. When someone with almost a million followers posts something, people listen. So again, do you know the damage done?"

My whole body shook at the angry man's words. I had written negative reviews before. I'd posted plenty of less-than-favorable opinions. But I never had somebody come at me like this in person. I had had people try to get me to reconsider. Offers to revisit the restaurant. But never this level of anger and vitriol. And something more—something like hurt. I had wounded this man.

"I—I'm very sorry. But maybe you should take what I said to heart. I had a terrible experience at your restaurant. And as the owner, maybe you'd want to hear about that."

"Si, that is when you send me an email. You don't put it online."

I sighed. "I'm sorry for any fallout, truly. But I don't know what to tell you. It's my job. And that's part of being in customer service, you know? You have to make sure that your staff isn't rude. And frankly, your staff was really rude."

I felt my defenses going up as I fell under attack. He had some nerve to assault me like this in public. But maybe I also felt a little guilty. If I was honest, I wasn't exactly in my right state of mind when I was there. And yes, the service had been terrible and the food lackluster, but maybe my sour mood added a layer to it. Maybe it wasn't nearly as bad as I made it out to be. A feeling of shame suddenly washed over me.

His face was tight, veins pulsing.

"Look, I—"

He threw up his hands. "No. Don't bother. There is nothing you can say now. The damage is done. Good luck with your little reviews. God help any other restaurants you visit."

The angry man shoved his phone back in his pocket and stormed off. I stood there, feeling like a guppy with my mouth gaping open. I glanced around. Had anyone else witnessed that?

"I am sorry for that. That was uncalled for," a softer voice said. A woman who had been hanging in the wings approached. "My husband takes the restaurant very seriously. We have owned it for thirty years, and it means everything to him. I'm not sure anyone has ever said anything quite so negative about it. I think he's just hurt."

I swallowed. "I'm sorry. Really. I was probably harsher than I needed to be. I'm only human, you know? I make mistakes."

She smiled softly, and I thought she was being just a little too understanding.

"It's hard to run a family business. It's all a part of you. It's easy to take everything personally, and it can be difficult to see our own failures. While I won't say that I'm happy about your post—it definitely did do some damage—it's probably time that my husband paid attention to some of our faults. He's been resistant to hiring extra staff, and I think the quality is suffering for it. We knew we were going to have a booming tourism this year, but he still insisted we weren't going to over-staff the place." She shrugged. "And I guess our mistake is showing. I think once he cools off, he'll take what you said to heart."

I tried to smile, but my lips felt weak. "I appreciate how understanding you are. I hope you know it's never my intention to ruin anybody's reputation or damage a family business."

"I know. You're just doing your job. The way we all are. Enjoy your time in Barcelona, Vera. I hope you find better experiences in our city."

She offered me a weak smile and then turned and joined her husband, who had made it down the block and was still shooting daggers at me through the night.

I stood stationary, processing the whole thing. My heart was pounding as I replayed the words.

"What was that all about?" Celia said, stepping from the restaurant. "I was about ready to call *La Policia*."

"I reviewed his restaurant recently."

"Ah. And you were not a fan."

"I was not. And he was not a fan of my negative feedback." I shook my head slowly. "I might've made a mistake. Said some harsh things I shouldn't have." A lump was forming in my throat.

"It's your job, Vera. It's going to happen. Anyone who puts their work out there will face this. He knows that. You just wounded his pride."

I flubbed my lips. "I've never had someone so upset with me."

Celia wrapped an arm around me, steering me away from the spot, her grip both comforting and grounding. "Then it's a rite of passage for you too. Don't worry about it. He will get over it."

I sighed. "Do you have any hot chocolate?"

Chapter Thirty-Three

I stepped into the opulent ballroom where Daniela's wine-tasting event was in full swing. A gleaming chandelier hung from the high ceiling, casting a warm glow over attendees who looked like they'd just stepped out of a Wall Street boardroom or a fashion magazine. It was a sea of glamour and capital, and even in my slinky Hervé Léger cocktail dress (courtesy of *couturerental.com),* I still felt like a fish out of water.

The gentle hum of excited murmurs filled the ornate room, with fragrant notes of different wines wafting through the air, creating a lively yet sophisticated atmosphere. My attention was momentarily captivated by the meticulous arrangement of wine glasses set out on tables in front of various winemakers, each filled with a varying shade of ambers, reds, and glistening golds, a visual promise of what was to come.

As I glanced around, the mixture of restaurateurs, chefs, and wine enthusiasts conversed energetically, the vibrant exchanges underscored by genuine smiles and gentle clinks of wine glasses.

"Vera! Wow, you look *très fabuleux.*" Daniela rushed over to me, leaning in for a cheek kiss.

"Merci," I said. "As do you." I eyed her curve-hugging canary yellow tee-length number and admired her ability to pull it off.

"Merci for coming. I wasn't sure what to expect, but this is quite the turnout," Daniela said. "Better than we even hoped. Love matches will be made tonight." She wiggled her thick, painted-on eyebrows.

I chuckled. Her animated Parisian accent made everything sound delightfully wicked.

"Thank you for the invitation. Obviously, this is a foodie's dream," I said.

"Don't go slamming me on your Instagram, ok? Only nice words." She flashed me a playful glare.

I feigned insult. "Do I really have that bad of a reputation?"

Daniela grinned and slipped her arm through mine. She tugged me along. "Come, let me introduce you to some of the winemakers. Sample their wares and get a little tipsy."

We approached a large display in the back of the room where a man stood proudly behind a table draped in black with the logo reading *Bodega Dos Patitos*.

"Buenas Noches, *damas*," the winemaker said.

"*Buenas Noches*," Daniela said.

"Bienvenida. I am Esteban." Esteban held a bottle of white in his hand like a precious artifact, his eyes glinting with a mix of mischief and passion. "Por favor, help yourself to a first glass." He gestured toward the row of glasses on the table. Daniela and I each selected one, and he splashed some white wine in each.

"You seem like someone who enjoys a good glass, si?" Esteban asked. I wasn't sure if it was just a weak sales tactic or if I had the air of a lush. Either way, he wasn't wrong.

"Si. Mucho. However, I must confess I'm no connoisseur."

Esteban flashed a crooked smile. He mindlessly stroked a full beard that managed to remain immaculate despite his enthusiastic sips of wine.

Esteban's chuckle was hearty and warm. "Worry not. Wine, like life, is to be enjoyed first and understood gradually over time, sí? This one is a story of risk and reward. It is a love letter from the vine to the bottle." He gestured to the pale liquid in my glass. "The Xarel·lo grape. Resilient, adaptable, and with an undeniable character, just like the Catalan spirit itself."

"Coming from the Penedès region, just a short journey from where we stand, is a land of vibrant contrasts, offering us a symphony of wines that embody both modernity and tradition." As he spoke, I found myself transported to sun-drenched vineyards and timeless landscapes.

The wine was a pleasant burst of crisp apples and gentle floral notes, a vibrant yet unassuming cascade of flavors.

My surprise must have been evident as Esteban continued, "You didn't expect such a bouquet of flavors, si?"

I shook my head, trying to frame my impression into words. "No. Or, si. It's unexpectedly complex and... bright?"

"How does it manage to be so layered and yet so refreshingly simple at the same time?" Daniela asked. She was always the eager intern.

A knowing smile played on Esteban's lips. "Ah, it is the dance, señorita. The dance of the sun, the soil, the rain, and the vine. They move together, sometimes in harmony and sometimes in passionate disagreement. But every year, a new dance, a new story to tell."

Then, with a playful glint in his eye, he leaned slightly forward, "And between you and me, a small secret – the vines, they whisper to one another when no one is watching. About the weather, the soil, the caretakers... and they decide what story they will tell for the next year. At least, this is what I choose to believe."

I couldn't help but be enticed by the fantastical imagery his words had painted.

"I wonder what they would say about you," a familiar voice said a little too close to my ear. I felt a chill nip the base of my spine and slowly crawl its way up each vertebra.

I slowly turned and looked up into Rafa's dark eyes.

His expression mirrored my curiosity, lips curving into a delighted smile that crinkled his eyes, causing my heart to flutter unexpectedly.

Without a word, he took the glass offered to him, and our glasses met in a quiet, but intentional toast, both of us mindful of the charged undercurrent threading through the simplicity of the action.

"I didn't expect to see you here," I said. I felt the tremble in my voice and pressed the glass to my lips to hide it.

"I could say the same. Although I should not be surprised, no? If there is a prestigious food event in Barcelona, you find a way to arrive."

"And are you?" Daniela was beside me then, extending her delicate hand toward Rafa.

"Oh, sorry," I said. "Rafa this is my friend Daniela from Paris. Daniela, this is Rafa. He's a chef—"

"*Mon Dieu*! Rafa Santos," Daniela said with delight.

Rafa had the decency to look bashful at his newfound fame.

"Afraid I am he. Mucho Gusto." He took her hand and then leaned in for a cheek kiss.

"And for the next!" Esteban practically shouted, pulling us back into his court. We all extended our glasses, and he splashed a light garnet wine in each glass. As we explored more wines, Esteban comically offered tales and theories of spirited vines and their whispered secrets. He imbued us with facts about of soil, vine, and climate, underscoring the symbiotic relationship between the earth and the grape, and how each bottle was a time capsule of the conditions from which it was birthed.

He was a born showman this one. And the wine was fabulous. Although I basically thought all Spanish wine was fabulous, so I'm not sure I was the most discerning client. But his enthusiasm for his craft went a long way in my book. I made a point of taking a few key photos of the bottle for my post.

Every few moments, I felt Rafa's eyes on me, and I would spare him a look only to see his gaze lingering. I snapped away. What was he doing, leering like that as though we had an intimate shared secret dying to break out? Maybe we did. The wines flowed, and between the notes of crisp whites and robust reds, I found myself ensnared by the complexity and simplicity entwined in both the wines and the man beside me.

We concluded the tasting lineup and another small group took our place.

"He was really something," Daniela said with a laugh.

"A flair for the dramatic. I appreciated it," Rafa said. "I might have to have him into the restaurant for a private tasting. I could probably sell tickets to that show."

Daniela clapped her hands together with delight. "That is exactly what we hope for! Culinary romance."

Rafa chuckled.

"Oh! I have to talk to Ricardo over there. Please excuse me for a moment," Daniela said and rushed off.

"She's charming," Rafa said.

"She is. She interned for us in New York last summer. Now she's doing the PR for food and wine events like this one. She has the right energy for it."

Rafa smiled, but his gaze lingered on me long enough to make me squirm. Finally, he broke the tension.

"So, you think the vines really talk to each other?" He swirled his glass thoughtfully, the liquid catching the light in a lazy, languid dance.

I played along, grateful for the silly banter. Adopting a mock-serious tone, I said, "Absolutely. And I think they gossip horrendously. The Albariño," I motioned to my glass with a grin, "was probably the vineyard drama queen. Far too popular for her own good."

"Oh, and what do you think they say about us, then?"

I pretended to ponder, taking a small, thoughtful sip. "Hmm, they're probably scandalized. 'Look at those two humans, sharing wine and exchanging glances. Disgraceful!'"

Rafa's jaw worked like he was trying not to laugh. "And what if they secretly approve?" The tone of his voice made my stomach flutter in the most delightful way.

I tilted my head. I was starting to feel light and airy from the wine, my flirtation finding footing. My voice dropped to a conspiratorial whisper, "Then they'd conspire, ensuring each grape holds a note that tells a fraction of our tale, turning each bottle into a chapter of our story."

Rafa's brow went up. "Quite poetic. Is that a line from your blog?"

I shrugged cavalierly. "No. I just made it up. I'm basically Shakespeare."

Rafa didn't hold back his laughter this time. "I'll drink to that." He clinked his glass against mine.

We sipped, and for a moment, the world fell away, leaving just the two of us, suspended in a strange slice of time where it seemed only we existed.

"Vera!"

The moment shattered. I jumped and spun around.

Daniela had reappeared at our side. She looked out of breath, probably exhausted from fluttering around like a hummingbird in heels. "Vera! Ok, remember when you asked me about that investor, Greta Wolf?"

I stiffened. I felt Rafa's presence do the same.

I swallowed. "Yes. Why?" My voice wobbled.

"She's here. I guess I'm not surprised. It's a small little world we have."

My head swiveled slowly, and I subtly scanned the room. My eyes landed on her. Greta Wolf stood near a lavish display of wine bottles, her platinum blonde hair shimmering under an overhead light. She was engaged in conversation with a group of people who looked as influential as they did wealthy. Even from a distance, she exuded a sense of control and authority, clearly in her element among the movers and shakers of the culinary world.

"She's downright intimidating, no?" Daniela said.

"Mmm. She does have that air," I said. My eyes drifted to Rafa. He was starting at Greta, too, with a tight expression, as though he was trying to unravel something.

"Do you know her?" I asked Rafa.

He took a moment to respond. "Yes. Actually, I do." I sucked in a breath, awaiting his response. Would he confess that he knew all about her plans to buy my words? "She invested in my restaurant. Quite a bit, actually."

I exhaled. Ok, at least he was telling the partial truth. "Oh, wow. That's incredible for you. I hear she's very influential and knows what she's doing. If she invested in you, then she believes you have something special. Which you do." I felt my cheeks flush with the last words. Rafa stared down at me—still inches above me, even in my towering heels. His eyes locked on me, peeling away layers with his gaze.

"Gracias," he said, almost in a whisper. "If you'll excuse me, I need to speak with someone."

He smiled thinly and turned abruptly before I could say anything. As though sensing the tension, Greta's gaze turned in my direction. Her eyes followed Rafa, then back to me. She said something to her circle of admirers and then, to my shock, started walking toward me. I instinctively took a step back. I pressed my wine glass to my mouth as though I could hide behind it.

She stopped in front of me with a scrutinizing expression. Her eyes flicked over me, sizing me up in an instant. Then she offered me a calculating smile, one that was more icy than welcoming.

"Vera Stone. We meet finally," Great said, making it sound like she was meeting an interesting but ultimately inconsequential curiosity. "Your reputation precedes you. Revolutionizing how we understand Spanish cuisine, one Instagram post at a time."

"Greta Wolf. Are you mocking me?" I asked.

She chuckled lightly. "Of course not. I very much admire you."

"So I've been told."

Her lips turned up with a tinge of bemusement. "I am guessing Joanne explained our...arrangement."

"Arrangement. Interesting word choice. You hired me to be your publicist. All without me knowing. I should congratulate you on your stellar business skills."

"Now who's mocking?" Greta tipped her own glass of wine to her lips. "I would think you'd be thanking me. An all-expense paid trip to your dream city?"

I pressed my mouth together, choosing my words wisely. "Thank you for the lovely trip, Greta. But maybe next time, don't lie to me. I don't appreciate being a pawn."

She rolled her eyes, and I noted the muscles in her face made no movement. She'd had some good work done.

"You are a very talented writer, Vera. And you have a wonderful presence that people find quite charming. Can you blame me for wanting to work with you? But you are naive."

"Having integrity doesn't make me naive."

She smirked. "Doesn't it?" She set her empty glass on a nearby side table. "Let me ask you, do you like Rafa Santos' new restaurant?"

I opened my mouth to respond that, of course, it was incredible. But I stopped short. I felt so used.

"And if I do?"

She smirked again. "I thought so. So just eat your fill of *tortilla* and write the article and enjoy your rise in fame."

My mind bounced back and forth like a tennis match. Did she have a point? Was I being ridiculous by standing on such grounded principles?

A conspiratorial look flashed in her eyes. "I saw you talking to Rafa earlier."

Heat flooded my cheeks. "So?"

She tilted her head. "Looks like you two are rather friendly."

I nervously finished my wine. "We are friendly *professional* acquaintances."

She now looked infuriatingly amused. "Mmm, I'm sure. And I'm sure you would love this opportunity to help a friendly acquaintance get all the publicity he can. The next time you're feeling mired in a moral crisis over this assignment, just think of Rafa."

"Does Rafa know?" I asked meekly. "Does he know you paid the magazine for this?"

She let out the shadow of a laugh. "Rafa doesn't know a whole lot, my dear. And it's probably better that way. Chefs have fragile egos." She glanced around the room. "Ah, I must go. It was lovely to finally meet you in person, Vera. I trust you will write a beautiful piece that will fuel your career greater than you'd ever dreamed." She leaned in and kissed my cheek before sauntering off.

Rafa was at my side then. "What was that about? You two seemed—intimate."

My whole body was trembling as I spoke. "Greta was just asking me about my time here. She wanted my opinion on the food scene."

"Did she ask you about me?"

I turned to him nervously. "Why would she?"

"Because she's an investor. Like I said. Figured she'd be trying to get your ear."

He grinned.

His tone was so earnest, I had to believe Greta was telling the truth when she said Rafa knew nothing about any of this.

I smiled. "Well, yeah, she did. Wanted to know what I thought. I was honest. Absolutely horrendous food." I shuddered playfully.

Rafa chuckled. "She's a shark. Intimidates the hell out of me."

My eyes wandered back toward her, where she was now holding court over a group of winemakers. As though sensing me, she looked up, and our eyes locked for a prolonged moment.

"Yeah. Same," I said.

Chapter Thirty-Four

The evening had descended into a gentle hush. Rafa was at my side as we left the event and stepped into the quiet evening. The night sky was a glittering blanket of navy and diamonds.

My heels clicked lightly against the cobblestone, echoing slightly in the serenity of the night. The air, cooler now, whispered against my skin as we walked in stillness.

"That was fun," I said.

"It was. I don't usually enjoy industry events, but the company was much improved tonight."

My cheeks warmed and I looked down. Rafa's presence was like this unspoken question lingering in the quiet space between us. I didn't know what to make of it. I could just ask, but maybe I also didn't want to know the answer.

There was a palpable hum of energy radiating in the air between us, an undercurrent of something unsaid that danced on the periphery of our earlier interactions. He lingered a step behind. I stopped and turned back toward him.

He seemed to be wrestling with a hesitation.

"Is everything ok?" I asked.

He stared at me for a long beat. "I know I should just flag a taxi, usher you home and call it a night, but I find myself unwilling to let this night end."

I tilted my head slightly, my senses delightfully dulled and sharpened all at once by the wine and atmosphere.

"If you're suggesting Flamenco dancing, I'm out."

He smirked. "Fair enough. But how about one more drink? At my place."

No, no, no. Every synapse in my brain fired with warning bells. Go home, Vera. Go to bed. Unfollow him on Instagram. Forget Barcelona exists.

But I was always a terrible listener.

My head involuntarily nodded. "One more drink. Just one."

Rafa's eyes lit with a subtle, restrained joy. We navigated the next few winding streets in silence. The faint buzz of some late-night-goers echoed around the corners. The sound of whizzing cars and the occasional ambulance with its distinct whirring sirens.

He walked a little closer to me now. His proximity was both a comfort and a danger—a dichotomy that thrilled and terrified in equal measure.

In almost near silence, Rafa flagged down a taxi. We climbed in and drove into the night. My heart pounded along with the soft hum of the taxi's radio.

We reached Rafa's apartment and caught the lift of the ancient building. I took a breath as I stepped into the tiny carriage.

"Don't like elevators?" He asked.

I exhaled and shook my head. "Not a big fan of small, confined spaces. Especially not ones older than my home country. But I'll be fine. Just press the button."

As the carriage ascended, the anticipation hung around us like a fragrant perfume, intoxicating and ever-present. My heart thrummed a steady beat, its rhythm betraying the calm I tried to project.

We reached his apartment unscathed and stepped inside. As he took my jacket, his fingers lightly brushed against mine, sending a jolt of awareness through me. My senses, already heightened, pulsed at the contact.

"Make yourself at home," he said. "Wine or digestivo?"

I nervously smoothed my hair as I stood in the living room. "Oh, um. Digestivo, I suppose. Seems fitting."

He nodded and opened some cupboards. He returned a moment later with two brandies.

"From Madrid. Perfect way to end the night." He gently pressed his glass to mine. "To unexpected evenings and new beginnings."

"To the unexpected," I echoed back, the clink of our glasses sealing the sentiment.

We both took a moment, sipping in synchronized harmony. The sharpness of the brandy burned a trail down my throat, but he was right that it was the perfect ending.

"How about some music?" Rafa finally said.

"Sure." My glass felt like a brick as I clutched it with both hands. Rafa walked over to a compact speaker on a shelf, and soon the room was filled with the soft hum of folky guitar.

I strode over to the window, which boasted an expansive view of the city. The twinkling of the night lights transported me to a different world.

"It's why I rented this apartment. The view," Rafa said, coming to stand beside me. I felt the warmth radiating from his skin, creating a magnetic field.

"It's stunning. I think I'd stare out the window all day and night if I lived here. I live on a high floor in New York, but I stare out at a brick wall." I laughed thinking about my tiny studio on W 97th.

I felt his gaze lingering and I turned toward him. He was

staring at my hands. He looked up at me. "I was admiring your fingers."

"As far as compliments go, that one is strange," I said.

He laughed lightly. "A chef notices people's hands. Ours are destroyed. See?" He held out his hands, which boasted long, strong fingers and a collection of scars. "Cuts, burns, bruises. Can't avoid it."

I instinctively reached out and touched a particularly menacing scar along the left thumb. I asked the question with my eyes.

"Grabbed a boiling pot without a mitt. Wasn't thinking."

I winced. "Ouch."

He bobbed his head. "Wasn't my favorite feeling."

Without warning, his hand traced the exposed skin of my shoulder, the calloused trace sending rivulets of electric energy down my spine.

I closed my eyes against the sensation. For a moment, time was suspended.

I opened them again and looked at him directly. "What are you doing?"

He sighed. "*Yo no sé.* I don't know. What I want to do, I suppose."

The world around me grew still, as if holding its breath in anticipation of the next move. The gentle melody of the guitar filled the room, each chord a gentle push and pull, accentuating the mounting tension. A solitary bead of condensation from my forgotten drink meandered down the glass to my hand, startling me. I looked down at the amber liquid, then tossed it back.

"That's good brandy," I said dumbly. Not that I would know.

He smirked and tossed back the remainder of his as well. "Life is too short not to drink the good stuff."

Wise words.

I fiddled with my empty glass. His hand reached out and took it from me, his fingers brushing mine. He set them down and turned back to me. He was so close I could smell the brandy on his breath.

"Rafa, what's happening? What is this?"

His voice was breathy, charged with an intensity that made my heart race. "Why does it have to be anything? Why can't it just *be*?"

"Because—because we have our jobs to think about. We don't want to complicate things."

"Vera," God, my name sounded so much sexier on his tongue, an elixir headier than any stiff drink. "You complicated things the moment you bumped into me at *el mercado*. We are so far beyond complicated."

His thumb traced the outline of my lips, sending a jolt through me. His eyes, dark and unfathomably deep, offered a silent question, one to which my heart already knew the answer.

"Rafa—"

"Stop thinking, Vera."

Then his lips were on mine again. This time, there was nothing soft, nothing tentative. He came at me full force, on fire. I stumbled back, but he slipped his arms around me and pulled me upright.

The world, with its logic and rules and professional boundaries, fell away, leaving only the pulsing of want and need. His hand cradled my face, fingers lost in strands of my hair, while my hand found a home on the curve of his neck, feeling the pulse of his heartbeat through my fingertips.

He pulled away slightly, leaving a pulsing vacancy where his lips had been.

"Stay with me," he said, low and raspy. "Stay the night."

I no longer cared what uncertainties the dawn would

bring. In that moment, I knew what I wanted. Life was too short indeed.

"Yes."

He slipped his hand through mine and led me back to the bedroom.

Chapter Thirty-Five

The dawn came too soon, as it always does when the previous night had been perfect. I rolled over sleepily, seeing Rafa was already awake. He was in the kitchen, fussing about. I could smell coffee and something savory I secretly hoped would be something of the fresh pastry variety waiting for me. I sat up and rubbed my eyes. I slept like the absolute dead after our interlude. I looked around for clothes and realized all I had was the cocktail dress from the previous night. That was going to look a little awkward, wandering down the streets of Barcelona in my towering heels. I heard footsteps, and a moment later, Rafa popped his head into the bedroom.

"*Buenos dias, bonita*," he said.

I tilted my head and admired him. He was a little scruffy this morning, a few days' growth dotting his chin. He wore a tight white T-shirt and workout pants.

"Good morning. Is that coffee I smell?"

"Of course. And I made croissant."

"God bless you," I said, pressing my hands to my heart playfully.

"I wasn't sure if you'd want to put your dress back on. So I pulled out a T-shirt. It's right there."

I spotted the fresh shirt folded neatly at the edge of the bed.

"Thank you. I was literally just wondering about that."

"And I can call you a taxi or something, so you don't have to walk home. I'm not sure that your little feet would fit in anything I own shoe-wise."

He did have exceptionally large feet...

I laughed off the embarrassment washing over me. Besides, I haven't had a walk-of-shame situation since college.

"I guess I'll worry about all of that after coffee and croissant."

He flashed me that wicked grin. "Well, get your lazy butt up then."

I smiled, and as soon as he was out of the room, I pulled myself up. I slipped on his T-shirt, which, luckily, given our vertical differences, came nearly to my knees.

Rafa handed me a large espresso and a piping hot pastry as soon as I walked into the main room.

"I could get used to this," I said, then instantly hoping he wouldn't read into it.

To his credit, he only smiled at the comment. "Full service at Casa Rafa. So, what is on your agenda today?"

I sipped my espresso, the bold shot going straight to my blood. I eased into the comfy sofa and admired the view again in the bold light of day.

"I have to start finalizing my article." All the complications of the situation flooded my brain, and I felt my cheeks go hot.

"Everything ok?" Rafa asked.

I tossed some pastry in my mouth to buy time. I knew I

needed to say something, especially after what had transpired last night.

"Rafa, I–I need to tell you something. It's not that big of a deal, but it is a little messy, professionally speaking."

He came around and sat next to me. "We seem to specialize in that."

I sighed. "Greta Wolf."

"What about her?"

"I didn't know this when I took this assignment. But apparently, she basically hired me without me knowing to write a feature on your restaurant."

Rafa's expression was blank, and then, slowly, the muscles furrowed. "What do you mean, hired you without you knowing?"

I sipped down the last drops of espresso. "She paid my editor to give me this assignment. Covered all my expenses. I don't know what exactly she gave the magazine, but we all know she has sway. So essentially, instead of a thoughtful, honest piece on the innovative culinary scene here, it's a paid PR piece." I shrugged, feeling nauseous as I explained it all out loud.

Rafa was quiet, his brain visibly working through everything I'd said.

"I'm not sure what to say about that," he finally said.

"I know. It's weird and unprofessional and not something I would *ever* have agreed to."

"You really didn't know?" He was looking at me with such incredulity I wanted to cry.

I shook my head. "Honestly. I thought I'd gotten lucky and scored my dream assignment. Which I mean, I guess I still did, I just hate that it was all orchestrated by someone with deep pockets."

He leaned back on the couch and rubbed at his neck.

"Huh. So you were going to give me a good review either way?"

"Well, not exactly." His face fell. "No, what I mean is, when I arrived, I had every intention of being honest about what I found here. And what I found was an incredible new concept. But honestly, Rafa, your restaurant, your food. It's amazing. Whether Greta was pulling strings or not, you deserve a glowing feature piece. And you're going to get it."

His lips pulled into a thin smile. "Gracias. That means a lot. Kind of crap to find out you've been a pawn."

I sighed. "Don't I know it? I admit, at first, I thought you knew and that was why you were trying so hard to seduce me."

He flashed me a devilish grin. "Is that what I've been doing? Seducing you?"

I glanced down at my bare legs protruding from a man's tee shirt. "Considering the current circumstances, I'd say yes. I was just minding my own business and there you were with a large *pulpo*."

We both giggled at the innuendo.

"In that case, you must know, my seduction was all my own. Greta never said a word to me about any of it. I thought my PR team just had a really good pitch," Rafa said.

"She played us both. And I imagine we're not the only ones."

"I was warned she was a shark when we first talked investment. But who was I to turn her down? She is a kingmaker," Rafa said.

"I think at the end of the day, we're both getting what we want. It's not how I would have liked it to unfold, but I'm still getting to write the feature pieces, which is great for my career. You're going to get amazing publicity."

"Si, you are right. I guess things in business are never as black and white as we like to think."

"Well, I should probably get going. I have a lot of work to do," I said. "Thank you for the coffee and croissant."

"Si, me too. It was—it was amazing, Vera. Thank you for a beautiful night."

"It was."

I collected my things from the bedroom. I slipped my dress back on, then threw Rafa's shirt over it and tied it at the waist, hoping it would pass for intentional. I rummaged through my bag and found some wet wipes and concealer and went about tidying up my face the best I could, then threw my hair in a messy knot. With great relief, I remembered I'd packed my hand-dandy New York foldable flats in my bag.

"Looks like I won't need that taxi," I said, holding up the little black ballet flats.

"You fit those in that bag?"

"We women are very resourceful when it comes to a night out in heels."

He shook his head. "Your species amazes me."

"If I could maybe just borrow this shirt and a bag of some sort to carry my heels so it's not completely obvious I'm doing a walk of shame."

He chuckled and dug out a paper shopping bag from the closet. "The shirt is yours to keep. A souvenir of your time."

There was a note of finality in his tone that made my stomach flip-flop. This feeling that I would never stand in this apartment again or feel his hands on my skin. I smelled the faint whiff of him on the shirt and thought maybe I'd never wash it.

I reached the door, and Rafa placed his hand on mine. He turned me around and kissed me lightly on the lips.

Chapter Thirty-Six

Rafa felt a gaping hole after the door shut behind Vera. He knew this was how it had to go. Professional complications aside, she lived across a literal ocean. Their lives would never converge.

He set about tidying up his apartment to distract himself. He cleared the glasses and plates and rearranged the pillows. He made his bed, making sure to sniff the pillow where Vera's pile of dark hair had been only hours before. It smelled of blood oranges and amber from her perfume.

He looked down and noticed Vera's leather notebook was on the floor by the bed. It must have fallen out of her bag. With its faded leather and brass buckle, it looked more like a spell book than a journalist's notepad. He reached down to pick it up, but accidentally dropped it. As it hit the bed, it fell open to the latest page, marked by a ribbon. Rafa was not one to pry, but there was no way his eyes could miss his name written at the top of the page with a bubbly heart, like a schoolgirl's diary. He smiled, then saw the words Santos California. He didn't *mean* to read the next words. Honestly, he really didn't, but his eyes scanned the words detailing his Huevos La Flamenca. He smiled at the description, but then his stomach dropped when the familiar words stuck out.

Huevos a la Flamenco with a twist—Adding serranos to the dish? That's bold. Maybe too bold?

No. No, no. It couldn't be. With a trembling hand, he pulled out his phone and pulled up the anonymous review. He had almost forgotten about it after the last few days, pushing it to the recesses of his mind. But there was no denying it—the verbiage was almost identical.

"*Huevos la Flamenco* with a twist—more like a twist of trying too hard. Adding serranos to the dish? That's bold. Maybe too bold."

The words were nearly the same, but Vera's notes were complimentary as they went on.

"*...That's bold. Maybe too bold? Not for this critic. I'm constantly impressed by the way Santos pushes the limits of what we accept.*"

Conversely, the article went on to knock the concept and flavors. But it couldn't be a coincidence that the same words were used to describe the *same* dish. And flashing back to what Lorna had said—"We don't even have Huveos la Flamenca on the menu."

She was right. Vera was the only person he'd run the idea by. He hadn't even told Lorna he was thinking about it.

Rafa stood frozen, the notebook clutched tightly in his hand as a torrent of realization rushed over him. He felt a sting of betrayal that seemed to tighten around his chest, leaving him breathless. His mind raced, grappling with a whirlpool of emotions – hurt, anger, and a staggering sense of loss. The giddy excitement from seeing his name encased in a heart rapidly vanished, replaced by a bitterness that engulfed him.

Rafa blinked and squinted to read more of her notes, then

back to the article. It wasn't word for word, obviously—but some of the same sensory descriptions were there. The same adjectives to describe the restaurant interior and the flavors of the foods. He quickly shut the notebook. He shook his head, his whole body trembling. Had Martí been right? Had she lured him into dropping his guard, to giving away way more than he should have? But why? Why would she give him false hope that she actually liked the place? That she actually liked *him*. Memories of the previous night flooded his mind. The grasping hands and heavy breath. The vibrations of their skin pressing together. And she'd all but said this morning a glowing feature was coming. Was she lying?

Or maybe he'd been telling himself stories. Maybe he had read way more into it than he should have. A part of him wanted to refuse to believe what was glaringly evident. But deep down, a hard knot of truth settled in. He had let himself be duped. And he was an idiot.

He sank into the nearest chair, the notebook lying ominously on the table before him, a Pandora's box of secrets that threatened to spill out. He resisted the urge to read any more. As he sat there, lost in the labyrinth of hurt and emerging truths, the doorbell rang.

He snapped through his haze and came to attention. He opened the door to find Vera standing there in his tee shirt. He sucked in a breath as his sense of betrayal and his longing to kiss her competed like gladiators.

"I think I forgot my notebook!" she said.

Chapter Thirty-Seven

As I stood there in the doorway, Rafa said nothing. He just stared at me like he'd suddenly forgotten English.

"Rafa?"

"Sorry, what?"

I narrowed my eyes curiously. "I said I think I forgot my notebook. The one I carry around for work? It must have fallen out of my bag in the bedroom."

After a split second, he nodded curtly. "Right. I found it."

He opened the door and gestured for me to come in.

The air in Rafa's apartment felt tight, almost suffocating, as I stepped in. It was like there was an unseen yet highly tangible cloud of bad energy that immediately set my heart racing. He pointed to the table where my little baby sat.

I picked it up and slipped it back into my bag, and turned to him. "Is everything ok?"

"Did you write that review?" His voice, usually warm and resonant, had a razor's edge to it.

I blinked. "Um, can you be more specific? I write a lot of reviews."

"The anonymous bad one. About Santos California."

I blinked, trying to decide what Rafa was talking about. "Are you being serious or joking around about something? Sometimes I can't really tell with the cultural humor differences." I tried to lighten the mood, but the words felt fragile, cracking in the thick air.

His eyes narrowed. Ok, no, not joking.

"What review are you talking about, Rafa?"

"Did you write it or not?" He crossed his arms. I said nothing and he laughed incredulously. "You are really going to pretend?"

It took me a moment to process the weight in his words. A deep frown carved lines on his forehead.

"Rafa, what are you talking about? I haven't even finished writing my piece yet."

"Really? You didn't write this." He slid a printed-out article in front of me. It was printed from *Hungry Voice* online magazine, one of those open to anyone publications. My eyes scanned the words, trying to make sense of it all.

"Rafa—I didn't write this."

"Those aren't your words?"

I read the small black print again. The thing was, he was right. They were my words. Sort of. It was like a franken-article of my notes. I recognized some of the descriptions and words I tend to use. I shook my head slowly.

"Rafa, I swear. I didn't write this. I mean, yeah, it's bizarre that they have some of my exact phrasing, but this isn't my voice. As a whole, this isn't how I write."

"Then how are these descriptions the same as your notes?"

I looked up at him. "How do you know they're the same?"

He inhaled and exhaled deeply several times as though reining in his anger.

"It wasn't on purpose. But I saw your notebook on the floor, and it fell open, and I accidentally saw what you had written. I remembered the words from the article. When someone writes something like this, it tends to stick in your mind."

"Whoa, you read my notebook? Haven't you ever heard of a violation of privacy?"

"It was an accident!" he snapped.

I leaned back and glared. "The book falling open might be an accident, but your eyes taking the time to process the words? No, Rafa, that's called intentional."

He folded his arms. "Of the sins committed in this room, I think that's the lesser."

I folded my arms too. "I. Didn't. Write. This."

"Then who did?" He snapped. His jaw was set, his face a canvas of pain, confusion, and betrayal, a storm that threatened to erupt at any moment.

I shook my head slowly. "I—I don't know. Someone who wants to hurt you. Which isn't me. I—Rafa, I—" Words caught in my throat. "I would never want to hurt you." My voice cracked. "Let me see that."

A vein was pulsing in his neck, but he nodded and handed me the paper. My eyes scanned the hateful words. It wasn't even a very well-written article.

"Whoever wrote it has a personal vendetta. Someone who does not appreciate your twist on traditional food."

I looked up at Rafa, and the answer seemed to click for both of us.

"Martí," we said in unison.

Rafa shook his head. "That still makes no sense. How would he know your intimate thoughts on my place?"

As the possibilities swirled in my mind, his eyes narrowed again.

"Of course. He all but told me, didn't he?" Rafa said.

"Told you what?"

He laughed incredulously and shook his head. "I should have put it all together. The private dinner with him at his place. How he was drinking with you when I arrived the other night. Rubbing it in my face that you were seeing him too."

An unexpected laugh burst from me. "*Seeing* him? I'm not seeing him. Yes, I had dinner at his place. One time. But it was nothing. Totally friendly."

"And what, you told him about my place? What you thought of the food? Shared secrets I had told you? Martí warned me you would do that. I was too thick to listen."

"Rafa—that's not true, I—"

"Just go, ok? You've done enough damage. I have work to do."

"Rafa! You're being ridiculous."

His face grew red. "Fine. I'll go!"

"Rafa!" I called after him as he stormed out of his apartment. I shut the door behind us and chased him into the elevator. This was absurd.

"Get out," he snapped.

"No. You're acting like a child. Let's talk about this."

He jabbed his finger into the elevator button, and it clattered to life.

"Nothing to talk about. You betrayed me."

"I didn't! I did not write that article. Will you stop being so thickheaded?"

He fell back against one wall of the elevator, but given the intimate size, we were still barely inches apart. "Ok, fine. Let's say Martí wrote it, but you gave him the ammunition. You described it to him."

I shook my head fervently. "No! I wouldn't do that. I don't know how he—he must have gotten his hands on my notes. But I don't know how or when—"

My words were cut short as the elevator juddered to a halt.

I shrieked, falling forward into Rafa. I quickly righted myself.

"What the hell?" I asked, looking around. "Did it stop?"

Rafa's expression was tight as his eyes darted about the small carriage, blinking rapidly.

"I think we might have broken down," he said calmly.

"What?" My voice came out like a squealing piglet.

As if to answer me, the overhead light gave a final, feeble flicker before plunging us into darkness. The only light left was a weak, eerie glow emanating from the emergency fixture, painting our features in sharp contrasts of light and shadow.

For a moment, we were both stunned into silence. Then the panic swelled in me. My breath came out in sharp, rapid bursts as I felt the walls closing in. I slumped down to the floor and pulled my knees to my chest. *No, no, no.* I did not want to die angry in an elevator.

Rafa was beside me in an instant. "Vera? Vera, look at me."

I forced my head up and squinted through the darkness as my eyes adjusted.

The small space felt smaller with every passing second. My breath came in hurried, shallow gasps, my heart pounding a frantic rhythm in my ears.

"Hey, just breathe. Breathe slowly, ok? In and out?" he demonstrated slow, composed breathwork.

I nodded and tried to follow suit. In spite of the anger that had been so palpable moments before, his hand found mine in the dark, a warm, solid presence in the midst of my spiraling panic. His touch was grounding, pulling me back from the edge of hysteria.

"We're going to be okay, I promise. This elevator is an old piece of junk the supervisor refuses to update. I'll file a serious complaint after this, I promise."

I forced a shaky smile.

A part of me wanted to reject his comfort, to pull away from his touch, but the larger, more terrified part clung to his hand desperately. Tears blurred my vision as I tried to control my breath, each inhale a shaky effort to regain composure.

"You really are scared of small spaces, aren't you?" he said.

"Apparently," I said with a weak laugh.

The blinding panic that had surged within me eased slowly as the moments ticked by until I was finally breathing normally.

And just as I was feeling a sense of calm, a jarring sound echoed around us. My breath caught in my throat as the elevator gave a shuddering jerk before gradually rising. The dim emergency light flickered and gave way to the steadier glow of the main light as the elevator resumed its descent with a whirring sound that seemed too loud in our silence.

The doors finally slid open with a dull metallic creak to reveal a concerned maintenance man standing there in his coveralls, his expression a mix of relief and professional annoyance as he seemed to recognize Rafa.

Rafa helped me to my feet, and we exited the carriage. As we stepped out of the confined space, our hands finally parted, a sudden coldness enveloping my fingers where his warmth had been. Rafa shot the maintenance man an icy glare.

"¿Lo arreglarás ahora, idiota?" Rafa snapped as we pushed by him. The maintenance man muttered something back at him with a less-than-friendly hand gesture to match.

We stood at the entrance to the building, and I suddenly felt like I had run a marathon across coals. The silence stretched on, a chasm growing between us with each passing second, until finally, I found my voice, albeit shaky and uncertain.

"I... I should just go."

Rafa offered a pale imitation of a smile as I fought to hold back the tears threatening to spill over, the emotional turmoil of the last hour crashing against my fragile composure.

I turned and hurried away. Rafa didn't try to stop me. The further I got, the faster I moved with a frantic need to distance myself, to find space to breathe, to think, driving me forward.

Around the block, out of sight of the prying eyes, any remaining facade crumbled. My breath hitched, and unabated sobs broke free, racking my body as I allowed myself to release.

My hands shook as I wiped away the tears. The intensity of our encounter, the fear and vulnerability, the moment of connection, and now the piercing loss of it, echoed in the empty street around me. I leaned against the cold wall of a building, feeling the rough surface against my skin as I tried to ground myself, to find some stability in the storm of emotions that threatened to sweep me away.

What the hell had just happened and what was I going to do next?

Chapter Thirty-Eight

Everything was perfect. Or at least perfect from the outside looking in. The atmosphere was warm. The tables were artfully arranged. The painstakingly selected decor—a meticulous blend of modern sophistication and rustic charm with polished wood and indoor plants—was impeccable. The guest list was even more impeccable. Rafa didn't know how Lorna had done it, but she had brought in some of the top players in the industry as well as some of Barcelona's who's-who with very deep pockets. Tonight's soft launch was going to be a smash hit, he knew it. He checked the bubbling pots on the stove and inspected the kitchen. The appetizer lineup was a painting come to life — a vibrant mosaic of fresh, colorful ingredients. The aroma wafting from the kitchen was an ensemble of delightful fragrances—sharp paprika blending with the yeasty scent of fresh-baked bread and the intricate spices woven into the signature dishes of the evening.

He turned toward the kitchen staff.

"How is everyone feeling?" Rafa asked.

He was met with eager, if not slightly exhausted, faces.

They had been working non-stop the past few days to put the finishing touches on everything.

"Everything's great, chef. Tonight will be smooth. We've got it all covered. You go out there and impress everyone," Juan, the assistant head chef, said.

Rafa nodded curtly. He had put together a stellar team. Everyone worked together like a well-oiled machine. They executed his recipes with meticulous care, and they loved it almost as much as he did. And now all he could do was trust that he had arranged everything perfectly.

He went back out into the dining room and checked in with Lorna.

"Are we set? Reservations look good?"

"Rafa, we're completely booked. Tonight is going to be wonderful. So just take a breath and relax. Pour yourself a glass of wine."

"Are you suggesting I drink on the job?" He grinned.

"I wouldn't even recognize you if you weren't drinking on the job."

As if on cue, the door chime sounded, and the very first guest stepped through with wide-eyed curiosity. Rafa took a breath and stood straight. He watched with a gimlet eye as the hostess greeted them, checked the name in the reservation book, and then led them to their assigned table.

"Alright. It's show time," he said.

Rafa wandered over and greeted the table. Mario and Paulina Ortega, a local quite monied couple known for giving sizable donations to charitable children's causes. They were very well-connected within the community, and they were the exact kind of people Rafa wanted as loyal customers.

"And how is everything tonight?" Rafa asked as he approached the table with a chilled bottle of cava.

"Wonderful. We are absolutely in love with this concept," Paulina said.

"It's just what the neighborhood needed," Mario echoed. "I did my PhD at Santa Barbara, you know."

"Is that right? Muy bien." He held out the bottle. "Compliments of the house. Please let us know if there's anything else you need beyond the prepared menu."

They beamed as he poured them each a glass of the pricy cava and set it in the ice bucket.

Rafa moved with graceful, nervous energy, greeting each guest as they arrived, trying to be personable to each and every one. His heart echoed in the melodious background tune, a classic Spanish song adding a touch of nostalgia to the buzz of conversation and the clinking of glasses. He knew the power of stories, and every element in the room narrated a tale, from the hand-picked paintings gracing the walls to the centerpiece, a delicate vase holding fresh California Irises.

"Rafa," Lorna approached midway through the dinner service. "There's a reporter here that wants to talk to you."

Rafa's heart skipped a beat for a moment. A reporter? Then he shook away the thought. Of course, it wasn't Vera. They were not currently on speaking terms, so he couldn't possibly imagine why she would have the guts to show up here.

As if sensing his thoughts, Lorna filled in the blanks. "She's from the *Barcelona Centennial*. It's the English language newspaper."

Rafa nodded. "Si, of course. Send her to the back booth, and I'll join her."

Rafa walked back toward the booth with a glass of Crianza in hand, a sliver of him still expecting to see Vera's bright blue eyes staring back at him. But, of course, she wasn't there. A woman with olive skin and fiery red hair sat in the booth. She wore red eyeglasses and a black pantsuit. She looked like what he expected a journalist to look like.

"Rafa Santos?" She asked as though he could possibly be anyone else.

"Si, that's me. So nice to meet you. Thank you for coming tonight," he said, trying to muster as much personality as he could. He had definitely drained his well of charm these past few weeks. He was finding it hard to even muster the energy to do those silly Instagram reels his publicist had convinced him to do (which, if he was honest, he secretly enjoyed. As it turned out, the fawning validation of strangers was addictive). After all of this, maybe he would finally take a vacation.

He wondered what New York was like this time of year... he shook his head.

He slipped into the booth opposite her.

"I'm Ella Mora, *Barcelona Centennial*."

"It's nice to meet you, Ella. Can I get you anything? Have you had a chance to have a glass of wine or try some of the food?"

She smiled thinly, and she looked as though she was fighting off a bribe. His thoughts drifted back to Vera. Everything about Vera was fun. She hadn't resisted a glass of wine or a free appetizer. Vera understood this industry.

"No, that's ok. I would love to ask you some questions about the concept, though. It's definitely new and innovative."

"Si, claro. What can I tell you?"

"It is indeed a pleasure to be here on such a pivotal night for you. I have to say, the buzz around this place is already palpable," she said, her eyes scanning the room before settling back on him. Her face was a canvas of professional curiosity.

"Gracias, it means a lot to hear that. We've put heart and soul into every corner of this place," Rafa responded, his voice steady yet with an underlying tremor of nerves. His hands instinctively reached for his wine, taking a sip before continuing, "This place is not just a restaurant, it's a canvas of memories, stories, and traditions that have nurtured me since childhood," he continued with the press-approved story of his restaurant and his inspiration. The story he'd been practicing and tailoring in the press release for the past few weeks. She listened eagerly, keen eyes fixed on him, and recorded everything.

"Your choice of fusing modern California-inspired culinary arts with traditional Catalan cuisine is indeed ambitious. What sparked this vision, and how have you managed to steer clear of becoming just another themed restaurant in a city that has seen it all?"

"It's not a theme. It's a living, breathing entity that celebrates the warmth of Catalan culture while embracing the exciting innovations modern cooking offers."

She seemed satisfied with the answer, jotting down notes before her gaze fixed on him again, more piercing this time.

"It seems your journey hasn't been all smooth sailing. Just last week, a scathing anonymous review was posted about this place. Many speculate that this might have a personal vendetta behind it. How did you pick yourself up from that devastating blow, and how has it shaped your approach towards this launch?"

A knot formed in Rafa's stomach, memories of betrayal and hurt surged, but he fought them down, forcing a smile that held a tinge of sadness. "I would not call it a devastating blow in the least. Whoever wrote that was a jealous troll simply out to cause problems. The author had clearly never even set foot in my restaurant, and I won't give it any more energy. We have elevated every aspect of our offering, ensuring that every guest leaves with not just a meal, but a memorable experience."

Ella gave a small, appreciative nod, her next question softened, yet with an undercurrent of curiosity that sought more. "Your family is steeped in culinary traditions, yet you chose to step away to carve out your path, even pursuing culinary training abroad. Was there resistance from your family in breaking away from tradition, and how have they influenced the person and the chef you are today?"

The questions continued, and he offered his well-practiced responses until Ella seemed satisfied. She clicked off her recorder and leaned back.

"Thank you. Your passion for this place shines through. Here's to new beginnings and to a place that seems ready to carve out its narrative in the heart of Barcelona."

"Gracias. I do hope you'll stay for dinner."

He excused himself and then made his way to a group of influential figures within the culinary world, recognizable faces from television and print graced the space. And right in the center was Greta Wolf. He hadn't expected her to grace him with her presence.

The group had an air of casual elegance, but he knew this was a group that carried weight in their words, and whose approval could pave golden roads for the restaurant's future.

Taking a deep breath to contain his rising nervousness, he approached with a genuine smile that crinkled his eyes.

"Buenas Noches. I am delighted to have you all here. Señora Wolf." He nodded toward her.

"It's all smashing, Rafa, really. The paella was exceptional, don't you think everyone?" Greta said to the group. They all nodded enthusiastically. Rafa smiled humbly.

"Muchas gracias."

"Where is Vera?" Greta asked. "I was certain she'd be here to witness your triumph. Has she finagled her way into the kitchen?"

Rafa kept his expression tight as he forced the words out. "Unfortunately, she could not be here tonight. But I assure you she has experienced all that Santos California has to offer. Her article will not disappoint." He met her eyes with a look that unveiled it all. He knew what Greta had done, and he wasn't happy about it.

Greta pursed her lips and nodded. "Well, then. I look forward to reading it." She raised her wine glass. "Salud to a successful opening." The rest of the table raised their glasses as well and shouted, "Salud," in unison.

Chapter Thirty-Nine

"I just... it's so confusing, you know? I can't make heads or tails of what happened," I said, tearing my bread into increasingly smaller pieces, my appetite vanishing with the swirl of questions churning in my mind. How had things gone so horribly wrong?

Celia moved her fork around the plate. The clamor of the small outdoor cafe echoed around us—chatter and glassware and passing street musicians serenading for a euro.

"I don't know Rafa well, but I know chefs like him. They are proud and short-tempered. Sounds like he was blinded by hurt and anger and didn't want to see reason."

I sighed. "I know it sounds crazy, but do you really think Martí could have written it? Would he do something like that?"

Celia bit her bottom lip and her brows knit together.

"We'd like to think we all stand united, especially in tough times. But let's be real—this industry can be brutal," she sighed, her eyes drifting as if tracing the histories written in invisible ink in the air. "They were once close as brothers, but you can see how that unraveled. Martí is—he is ruled by his ego. And like a lot of proud, powerful men, his ego is actually quite fragile. It's why he dates so many women and inevitably treats them terribly. It's why his friendship with Rafa turned so bitter."

"What exactly happened between them?"

Celia popped a bite of tortilla in her mouth and slowly chewed as though trying to recall the details.

"I don't know the whole story, but Martí told me some of it when we were...involved. They were thick as thieves growing up. But I get the impression that there was always this kind of rivalry, you know? Then Rafa started dating Martí's sister, which never goes well, let's be honest. He broke up with her to go to culinary school in America. Broke her heart I guess. And Martí never forgave him. It turned into a rivalry after that. But *no sé*, I sometimes think Martí is the kind of man who's just looking for an excuse to make enemies. I mean Elena is married now. I doubt she still pines for Rafa, but Martí can't let it go." Celia shook her head. "Martí tries to maintain a professional front, but spend some time with him, and his bitterness seeps through."

Memories of Martí warning me off Rafa began to play in my mind, followed by the realization that he might have been working his angles to get close, not necessarily for a positive review but possibly something darker. Was it jealousy steering his actions, aiming to strike at Rafa through me the entire time?

I felt a cold hand grip my stomach at the possibility.

"I still don't know how he captured my words like that. It's so strange. It was like he took it right from my notebook. But I don't see how that's possible."

Suddenly Celia's face went a shade whiter as though something was clicking.

"What?" I asked.

She bit her lip again. "When we were at *La Vaca Bonita*. The night we ran into Martí and he tricked you into eating—"

"Yeah, I remember." I shuddered at the memory.

"When you and Rafa went to the bathroom. You left your work bag at the counter."

"Right," I said with uncertainty.

"I got up to get another glass and when I got back to the table, Martí was moving your stuff around. It just looked like he was rearranging things. But what if he had sneaked a look at your notebook? Taken a picture of the pages or something?"

My stomach roiled, then I snapped. "That ass!"

Celia half giggled at my outburst.

"It's something he might do. I wouldn't bet against it."

A heavy sigh escaped me as I leaned back, feeling the weight of the complexity of human emotions — jealousy, rivalry, and perhaps even vengeance. I then wondered if he could have even had something to do with my hacked Instagram account. Could he have been trying to distract me? Or even discredit me?

I knew I had to find out, for my own peace of mind, and maybe for a little vindication. I couldn't stand the fact that Rafa thought I would betray him.

"Maybe confronting him would bring some clarity?" Celia said.

"If he's duplicitous enough to do all this, then I doubt he's just going to admit it."

Celia pursed her lips and shrugged. "Doubtful. But don't underestimate his pride. Maybe you can use that to your advantage."

Chapter Forty

I chose a quaint little café situated in a calm street—a place where the noise level was subdued and yet public enough to keep Martí from causing a scene. The pretext was innocent — a casual chat about a potential collaboration. I could feel my heart pounding in my chest as I waited, my hands wrapped around the warm ceramic mug of tea, waiting for him to arrive.

Martí was bordering on unfashionably late when he finally strolled through the front door, a confident smile gracing his face—a face I at first found handsome but now just sleazy.

"Vera. A vision as always," he said, slipping into the seat opposite me. He wore tight blue pants with an even tighter white polo with the buttons undone. His sandy hair was tousled in a *just got off my yacht* kind of way, but I guessed was meticulously styled to appear so.

I forced a smile. "Thanks for meeting me."

A server came around and he ordered himself a beer. "So what is this endeavor you wanted to talk about?"

I sipped my spicy chai tea with honey.

"I have to confess that I wasn't entirely honest about why I wanted to meet."

His brow went up, looking amused. "I'm so intrigued now."

I took a breath and slid the printed-out review toward him. I watched his expression carefully as his eyes scanned the paper.

"What's this?"

"I think you know."

The server delivered his beer and he paused to take a long sip.

"This is a pretty harsh review. Your doing?"

"Coyness doesn't suit you, Martí."

He bobbed his head. "I've been told otherwise."

"They lied."

He chuckled. "You really are a firecracker, Vera Stone."

"The criticism is harsh, almost intimately so. It feels so... familiar, don't you think? The depth of knowledge about the private aspects of the menu... it got me thinking."

Martí blinked, the smile vanishing from his face as he leaned back, suddenly looking like a cornered animal.

"Thinking is a dangerous pastime," he teased. But I saw the nerves mounting. His foot bobbed. His hand clenched tighter around his bottle.

"It's normal for critiques to sound similar, Vera, there are only so many ways you can describe food."

I sipped my tea, taking my time with this. "Hmm. The description of the Huevos—don't you think it's inaccurate?"

He worked his jaw. "It's his fault for mucking up a classic recipe with serranos." He took a thoughtful pull from his beer and continued. "Vera, you're overthinking it. People speculate, they make educated guesses. And honestly, that recipe is a disaster. You wouldn't have to taste it to know it would be terrible."

"The thing is, that recipe isn't actually on his publicized menu, you know? So the person either made that up completely...or knows something the public doesn't."

The café fell silent as his words hung heavily in the air, an inadvertent admission that left a bitter taste in my mouth. I could feel my heartbeat in my throat as I pressed on, the depth of his betrayal becoming painfully clear.

His eyes narrowed at me. "I know what you're implying. But why would Rafa tell me anything proprietary? As close as you two have gotten, I'm guessing you know we're not exactly *besties.*" He said the last word with a mocking feminine uptick.

Screw this. I was tired of playing games.

"Did you steal my notebook?" I asked bluntly.

The confident demeanor he carried crumbled, and a flash of guilt washed over his features.

"What?" He said with a nervous laugh.

"Celia saw you. No sense in denying it. Look what's done is done, and it's not like I can have you arrested for looking at my notes. But I just want to hear it from you. Admit you're so insecure you were threatened by Rafa."

He guffawed, but I saw a sheen of sweat on his brow. "Threatened by that *artist?* You know nothing. Mind your own business."

"This is my business. Literally."

His expression was steely. "Don't be so naive as to fall for him. He'll abandon you, too."

There it was.

"I hear Elena is married now. Do you think she cares nearly as much as you do?"

He slammed his palm on the table. "Leave my sister out of this."

I smiled placidly and took back the printed-out review.

"You know what, Martí? I don't need you to admit it. It doesn't matter. Your petty, childish attempts at sabotage will be forgotten by next week. Desperately cling to relevancy if it gives you a false sense of agency. But the rest of us will move on."

I stood abruptly and picked up my bag.

"Vera—don't be so idealistic. It's business. And this is a hard business—"

"Good luck, Martí. You'll probably need it."

I walked away, leaving behind a man hopefully haunted by the gravity of his own actions. Or maybe not. Maybe I was just walking away from a narcissist who would never really see his own actions. But either way, I was walking away. And that's what mattered.

A flicker of resolve ignited in me as I stepped out into the bright sunlight, the cold air hit my face, a stark contrast to the heated confrontation. I had work to do.

Chapter Forty-One

I settled down at the little desk in my hotel room, the familiar hum of my laptop greeting me as I opened it. The glow of the screen illuminated the surrounding darkness, casting shadows that danced gently with every flicker.

A swirling maelstrom of emotions coursed through me as I thought about the levels of duplicity I'd faced in the past few weeks. But I was also fueled by a new energy pulsing through me. My fingers hovered over the keys, and I allowed myself a moment to close my eyes, to delve deep into the trove of experiences I'd had here in this culinary haven of a city.

I thought of every bite of food Rafa had thrown my way. A ballet of traditional and modern. But it was more than just the food that made it all special. It was the passion he breathed into his work, into the pulse of the restaurant.

Every meticulously crafted creation was imprinted with his energy, his love.

I started to write:

"My time in Barcelona has been a whirlwind of experiences, a journey that ventured beyond the realms of mere dining, transcending into an experience that catered not just to the body but

to the soul. Every intricate detail, from the fervent discussions over the quality of ingredients to the orchestrated harmony in the kitchen that bore witness to a team united in purpose, every aspect drew me in, compelling, inviting me to be a part of something beautiful, something pure and unapologetically real."

My fingers raced over the keyboard as I found my rhythm and the words flowed out, immersing myself in the narrative that celebrated the vibrant canvas of Barcelona.

As the sentences unfurled, I found myself writing more than just a review of Santos California. It was a narrative, a heartfelt homage to the essence of culinary artistry that flowed from Rafa's creative fountain.

By the time I finished, and my eyes were too bleary to type another coherent word, it was nearly 3 a.m. Whoops.

I forced myself to stay awake and re-read my words:

"In the vibrant heart of Barcelona, nestled amidst cobbled streets and echoing with the whispers of the past, you'll find Santos California restaurant—a harmonious fusion of Catalonian roots and Californian flair, embodying the soul of two worlds from opposite sides of the globe.

From the moment you step through its doors, there's an energy that captures you—a pulsating rhythm reminiscent of Barcelona's dynamic spirit. This is not just a restaurant—it's an experience, an intimate dialogue between the chef and the diner, a narrative woven with flavors and memories.

Rafa Santos, the brainchild, head chef, and proprietor, shows palpable dedication. Every dish, while exuding innovation, pays homage to tradition. The menu, a symphony of fresh produce and age-old recipes, carries the essence of Catalonian streets, while the fresh Californian influence introduces a refreshing, vibrant twist complete with a plethora of avocados and fever-inducing peppers. It's a gastronomic journey where the classic and contemporary dance in delightful harmony.

But it's not just the food that leaves an indelible mark. The atmosphere is an artful blend of rustic charm and modern elegance. Walls adorned with family heirlooms contrast beautifully with contemporary furnishings, creating a cozy embrace that makes you feel both at home and on a gastro-adventure.

However, the true magic lies in witnessing Rafa's passion. In every simmering pot and meticulously plated dish, you see a story, a legacy, a dream. This isn't just about cooking—it's about preserving a heritage while fearlessly charting into new territories.

Visiting Santos California is akin to taking a deep dive into Rafa's creative mind and getting a front-row ticket to his experience and upbringing—his culture, history, and unyielding spirit. It's a place where every bite tells a story, where every meal is a celebration, and where, as a diner, you're not just a spectator but an integral part of a beautiful culinary narrative.

In a world where authenticity often takes a backseat to commercial demands, Santos California stands as a beacon of genuine passion and dedication. A visit here is not just recommended—it's essential for anyone seeking to understand the true essence of Barcelona's gastronomic brilliance."

My heart hammered wildly as I uploaded it to my Instagram along with a series of artful photos. I scheduled the post to go live in the morning and closed my laptop. I closed my eyes and smiled as I passed out.

Chapter Forty-Two

I woke the next morning to my phone buzzing incessantly like a heartbeat.

I groggily threw my hand out and flailed about the side table for my phone. I squinted at the screen to see an excess of message banners. My breath caught in my throat as I opened the first of the messages, my heart swelling with a mixture of pride and anxiety as I navigated the labyrinth of reactions, comments, and shares that were quickly ballooning out from my post.

I sat upright with a start. Oh my God. The post had already gone viral.

There was an electric energy all around me as I watched in real-time as my post swirled in a cyclone of instant virality, its tendrils reaching into the far corners of the online space, grabbing hold of hearts and sparking spirited discussions in its wake.

I threw my hand over my mouth to contain my excitement. Then a sense of dread knocked. Oh hell. What was Joanne going to say? Had I, in my slightly buzzed, vigilante state, jeopardized the quarterly feature?

My mind spiraled with sudden thoughts of repercussions, fear mingled with excitement, forming a potent cocktail that surged through my veins. The potential backlash loomed ominously like storm clouds on the horizon, threatening to eclipse my thrill at my success.

I forced myself to breathe. Surely, this could only be a good thing for the magazine. Coffee. I needed coffee to think clearly.

I popped in an espresso pod then sipped slowly as I monitored the post. I jumped when my phone rang suddenly, snapping me out of my introspective reverie. I glanced down. Joanne was FaceTiming me.

Ohhhhh hell. I closed my eyes and took a deep breath, then clicked answer.

"And what do you have to say for yourself?"

"Hiiiii," I said with a playful wobble.

"Vera Stone. What were you *thinking?* Like seriously. That was something an intern would do. You literally *scooped yourself.*"

I winced. "Um, yeah, I know. Jo, I am *so sorry*. It was a strange situation, and there was this other chef, Martí and—"

"Vera? Be quiet."

I sighed and closed my eyes. "Am I fired like yesterday?"

She started laughing then. My eyes shot open. "Well, geez, don't take too much pleasure in it," I said.

"Will you relax? You're not fired. Yeah, I'm not thrilled you went AWOL and scooped your own story. But," she paused and typed something. She looked back at me. "Have you seen the numbers?"

I sipped my coffee. "Um. Yeah. I have. It's incredible."

"Damn right, it's incredible! The board is thrilled. They feel like they have a celebrity on staff now. I mean, this is real influencer territory, Vera. So as much as I wanted to be pissed at you, you basically deserve a raise."

My stomach fluttered. I almost couldn't believe what I was hearing.

"Joanne, I—I don't know what to say."

"Say nothing. Just nurture this thing, ok? Respond to comments, keep promoting it. Keep the momentum going. Internal Marketing is going to repurpose it, ok? You're the face of *Travel Luxe & Leisure* at the moment. Don't waste this."

"I won't. I promise."

"Good. Ok, well, I wish I was there to toast you, but make sure you go out and expense a very nice bottle of champagne today, ok?"

I nodded. "Yeah, ok. I will."

"Ok, it's late here. Gotta crash. Keep it up, Vera. You're going places."

She clicked off. I fell back onto the sofa as my head spun.

My phone buzzed again. It was a WhatsApp from Daniela.

"Whoa! Just saw the post. *Incroyable!*"

I smiled and wrote back a thank you.

A few similar notes popped up on my messages over the next hour as I pulled myself together.

I might never truly mend things with Rafa, but I hoped he would at least reap the immediate benefits of this. The grand opening was only days away now. I smiled nostalgically, thinking of missing out.

But it was what it was. I had gotten myself into this, and it was my bed to get cozy in.

I slipped on a pair of high-waisted black pants and my favorite Italian walking sneakers and packed up my bag for my final Barcelona adventure. I couldn't believe that my whirlwind adventure here was coming to an end. But I guess all experiences have a shelf life. The famous fall Mercat de Mercats kicked off today— a celebration of local markets, sustainable and proximity food, and general gastronomy.

I really did come to Barcelona at the right time of year.

Today's market marked not only the end of my tenure here but also the end of the true summer season for locals. I eyed the weather—despite the fact that the dial was still set to reach mid-80s today. Despite being mid-October.

I would do one final Instagram Live from the festival to say my goodbyes. And hopefully, eat my weight in paella just once more.

* * *

I stepped out of the cab, immediately swallowed by the exuberant vitality of Mercat de Mercats beautifully unfurling under the architectural magnificence of the nearby Barcelona Cathedral. I made my way to the front of the Cathedral of Barcelona, where the surrounding areas and streets were bursting with vendors from various markets across the city showcasing their goods. I was assaulted by mountains of fresh products, including fruits, vegetables, cheeses, meats, and seafood. Not to mention, I immediately spotted ready-to-taste foods sizzling on every corner.

I inhaled, letting the myriad scents envelop me—sweet ripeness from one booth, the robust earthiness of truffles from another, all underlined by the comforting, homely aroma of freshly baked bread.

I spotted some wine booths setting up as well and checked the clock—I'd give in an hour.

More *cafe* first.

Patches of late morning sunlight peeked through the lush foliage above, playfully dappling the cobblestones beneath my feet with patterns of light and shadow.

I pulled out my phone and started filming some B-roll. The rhythmic beats of traditional music reverberated through the air, and children giggled as they darted between adults, chasing after gigantic soap bubbles created by street vendors.

A gentle ache twinged within me as I took it all in. I was already feeling a sense of grief at the thought of having to leave this all behind. But the city seemed determined to make sure I absorbed every last ounce of the present, to relish the remaining moments, and to commit every sensation to memory.

Positioning myself for the live segment, I chose a spot with a panoramic view of the festivities. Behind us, the iconic 'castells', or human towers, started forming. The local teams, clad in their vibrant team colors, meticulously built their towers, each level supported by the strong backs of those below. Street performers dazzled their audiences with daring acrobatics and mesmerizing fire dances, providing the perfect backdrop for my broadcast.

Lost in thought, I rehearsed my opening lines, feeling the weight of what I wanted to convey. My journey in Barcelona had been nothing short of transformative, and much of it had to do with Rafa. I needed to find the perfect words. The right sentiment. Taking a deep breath to steady my nerves, I clicked the timer on my phone and sat back.

"We're live in three, two, one..." I playfully said to myself.

With a bright smile, I began, "Hola everyone! Joining you live from the heart of Barcelona's *Mercat de Mercats* festival. For those unfamiliar, this vibrant festival celebrates the city's farm-to-table gastronomy—in other words, all things local food. So basically, my dream come true."

I paused for a flood of likes and emojis to come through.

"In the past few weeks, I've delved deep into Barcelona's

culinary treasures. From hole-in-the-wall eateries in the Barri Gòtic to bustling markets like La Boqueria, every taste told a story." I felt myself getting unexpectedly emotional as I spoke. I swallowed a lump and tried to keep my usual dry humor about me.

"But," I hesitated for a heartbeat, gathering my thoughts, "Barcelona has been more than just about the food. It's been about the passion, the dedication, and the love that goes into every plate. I met chefs who put their entire heart into their creations. But one chef... one particular chef, truly epitomized the soul of this city for me."

Rafa permeated my mind — his fire, his broody eyes, the touch of his hands. The feel of his lips. I willed my cheeks not to turn candy apple red on camera.

"I'm sure you all saw my post this morning. And can you believe it, it went viral. So thank you all of my loyal followers and readers who shared it! Rafa Santos, who I wrote about, showed me a unique culinary approach marrying tradition to innovation. It's breathtaking, it's memorable, and it's frankly freaking delicious. Everyone, hear me. If you are ever in Barcelona do not, as though your life depends on it, miss Santos California."

I took a moment, letting the ambient sounds of the festival fill the short pause, the merry laughter and distant melodies giving a voice to my silent reminiscences.

"From the vibrant streets of Barcelona, amidst its biggest celebration, this is Vera signing off. Always remember — food is not just about flavors—it's about the stories, the histories, and the connections. Until next time!"

I cut the feed and was left with the sounds of the festival dancing around me. But in that fleeting moment, amidst the cacophony, I found some long-eluded peace.

I spotted Celia coming toward me just then looking amused. She had braided her long dark hair down her back and wore a colorful scarf wrapped around her head, giving her the appearance of an exotic fortune teller.

"Well, that was touching," Celia said.

"I aim to pull on the heartstrings," I said, folding my tripod up and slipping it into my bag.

"Cómo estás?" she asked.

I sighed. "I'll be better with a glass of wine. But I'm ok. I'm sad to be leaving tomorrow. But incredibly grateful for these past few weeks. Not to sound dramatic, but I really think this experience has changed me."

She smiled. "That's not dramatic. That's what experience does—it changes us. We are never the same people we were yesterday."

"Now who's being touching?"

She snorted a low laugh. "Have you spoken to him?"

I lowered my eyes and fiddled with the clasp of my bag. "No. I didn't expect to. He's really angry, and I get that. I don't blame him."

Celia sighed. "Men and their pride. It's a costly combination to the world." She slipped her arm through mine. "Come. Forget Rafa and Martí and all that drama. Let's pump you full of Spanish wine one last day so you leave on a high note."

"Or a very drunk note."

She chirped a little noise. "I don't see the problem."

Chapter Forty-Three

Rafa wandered amidst the lively festivities, his mood heavier than it should have been on a typically jubilant day. Everywhere around him, the air buzzed with energy, yet, in spite of the infectious joy that surrounded him, morose shadow draped over him, effectively dimming the brilliance of everything around him. He hadn't been this down in a long while. And this was why he didn't date, why he didn't get involved in love garbage. It never ended well for anyone.

"Well aren't you an Eeyore today," Lorna said, saddling up to him with a cup of take-away wine. He took it gratefully.

"Gracias. What's an—Eee-ore?"

She laughed. "Eeyore. The cranky donkey from Winnie the Pooh?"

He furrowed his brow, then shook his head. "If you say so. I'm just pensive."

"Mmm. Did you see her Instagram this morning?" Lorna pressed her wine to her lips, hiding a smirk.

He stopped and stared at her with annoyance. "And why would I have? I don't need to be reminded of her."

She bobbed her head. "You might want to take a look at the latest post."

He shook his head. "Pass."

"Stop being so stubborn and just look at the damn post, Rafa."

He sighed with annoyance and pulled out his phone. He opened the app and navigated to her profile. It took him a moment to process what he was seeing on the screen. His eyes flicked to Lorna.

Laughter and chatter filled his ears, yet it sounded distant, detached from his reality as he processed.

On Lorna's screen was a glowing review that sang praises of Rafa's culinary artistry, showering his restaurant with accolades and tenderly crafted phrases of appreciation. *Dios Mio*, she could really write something beautiful. She deserved a much bigger platform than this tiny screen, he thought. But then he saw that post had gone viral and his stomach flip-flopped. Millions of people had read these intimate accolades about his life's work.

"I don't know what to think," Rafa said dumbly.

Lorna snickered. "I think, dear boss, she just put Santos California on the map. And I am pretty certain that's not the work of someone who would try to anonymously sabotage you."

Rafa wiped sweaty hair from his brow. "But Martí—she must have—"

Lorna held up her hand. "Rafa, stop. You're just using this all as an excuse to run away from something that might actually bring you some happiness. You know in your gut—in your heart—she didn't tell Martí anything. He is a sneaky bastard, and I can guarantee he looked at her notes when she wasn't looking."

He said nothing as they walked through the crowds. He

silently sipped the crisp white wine from his plastic cup and pretended that nothing Lorna was saying made any sense.

Then a sudden notification chimed on his phone, piercing through the somber cloud encompassing him. It was an Instagram notice with a link to Vera's live stream.

"Well, speak of the American devil," Lorna said, holding up her own phone. "Let's watch."

Rafa shook his head and slipped his phone back into his pocket. "I don't think so."

Lorna rolled her eyes and opened the livestream anyway. She all but forced it in front of his face. "Watch."

He wanted to resist, but as soon as he heard her voice, Rafa's world momentarily silenced, the festival's noisy backdrop fading.

Rafa stood still as Vera went on about her experience and then—him.

"She is still talking about you," Lorna said, elbowing him.

Rafa couldn't pull his gaze from the beautiful face coming through the screen.

The sounds around him were swallowed by the sincere timbre of her voice, which gushed with genuine affection for his city, his food. Him. He couldn't read that post and watch this feed and ignore it.

Her eyes focused on the screen as she bid her farewell to the viewers and clicked off. But in that split second, he could swear she was smiling at him.

His breath caught in his throat as he processed what he had to do. Hesitation rooted him in place. Lorna elbowed him again playfully.

"Stop torturing everyone around you and go show her how romantic you Spaniards can really be."

He spared Lorna a glance then a curt nod.

* * *

With the buzz of Mercat de Mercats in full swing, Rafa powered through the lively crowds, a one-man mission amidst the whirlwind of vibrant colors and lilting laughter. Sounds of vendors haggling and glasses clinking formed a melodic backdrop to his determined steps, every beat amplifying his pounding heart.

Finally, he spotted her. She was packing up her recording equipment and chatting with Celia. She was stunning in the midday sun, the rays catching the slight gilt to her dark hair. She wore the same red dress she'd been wearing when they went to the Flamenco club. He stared, admiring the way it hugged all her curves and edges.

Rafa approached, suddenly enveloped in an unexpected peace amidst the chaos.

As though sensing him, she looked over and froze. Time, and the festival around them, blurred, distilling the moment to just the two of them in a shared, silent exchange.

"Rafa," she said. Celia followed her gaze and had a momentarily shocked expression, then she grinned devilishly as though she'd somehow orchestrated everything.

"Vera. I—I saw the post. And the Live just now. I don't know what—" he shook his head. "Thank you. It means everything to me."

Her surprised expression melted, and she did that lowering her gaze thing she did when she was being shy.

"You're welcome," she said. "I meant it. I meant every word."

Rafa stepped toward her. "I—I couldn't let you leave without saying *adios*."

"I think I need to...do something else for a minute," Celia said, tossing Rafa a pleased look as she wandered off to the side to likely do absolutely nothing but gawk.

Vera turned back to Rafa. He started to step closer. Just then, a flash of black and white caught his eye, and a mime approached them, pressing his hands to an imaginary box in front of them. For a second, Vera looked horrified, then they both nearly collapsed into laughter. Without thinking it through another second, Rafa pulled her to him and smashed his lips into hers.

Chapter Forty-Four

Six months later

The hazy twilight of the early evening streamed through the tall windows of Santos California, painting delicate patterns on the vintage wooden floor. The soft clinking of cutlery, the hum of conversations, and the tantalizing aroma of authentic Spanish flavors mingled with avant-garde gastronomy gave the spacious establishment a cozy ambiance.

I stood by the entrance, watching as the host warmly greeted a British couple celebrating their anniversary. It was early so the place was mostly empty, but the reservation book was packed to the brim tonight as it was every night. The host reported turning away multiple bribes to squeeze people in. Anyone in Manhattan would kill for that kind of buzz. And I doubt there was a host in Manhattan who'd turn away the bribes.

I was starting to miss my home just a little now that I'd been gone half a year. I missed my friends and I hadn't gone this long without seeing my parents in a while, but honestly,

I'd been so busy with work, that I hadn't had much time to think about it. I was planning a trip this summer, hoping to drag Rafa away for a much-needed vacation. A little birdie named Lorna told me he hadn't been on holiday in years.

"Vera! I didn't know you were coming in tonight," Lorna rushed over and kissed my cheek. Her blonde hair had grown out past her shoulders and she'd dyed the tips pink. She sported a black jumpsuit with bright red chunky heels and long cherry red nails with sparkly tips.

"I finished my interview early and wanted to stop by before the rush got too crazy."

"Did you get everything sorted out with the Visa?"

"Yes, thankfully. Believe it or not, my viral post about this place went a long way with the ministry. They appreciated my dedication to the Spanish culinary scene, and my self-employment visa should be good for a year."

Lorna grinned. "Good. Otherwise, I'd have to marry you to keep you here. Although, a certain broody chef might take up complaint with that."

"Is said broody chef here?"

Lorna nodded her head toward the back of the house. "In the kitchen, putting the fear of god in the newbies."

I grinned. They'd been so busy, Rafa had taken on half a dozen new prep cooks.

"But you know he'll be thrilled to see you."

I made my way through the restaurant, waving to a few regulars who somehow managed to always get a reservation. Maybe our hosts were taking bribes after all.

I slipped behind the back curtain and found myself in the heart of the place—the clanging of pots and pans, the clink of china, sizzling dishes, shouts, and the faint hum of Spanish music bringing it all together in harmony.

I spotted Rafa in the prep station, lecturing some poor young woman in a prep uniform.

"You never slice the *pulpo* like this!" Rafa was shouting in Spanish, holding up a poor mangled baby octopus. The intern chef looked like she was about to cry.

"His bark is way worse than his bite," I said in Spanish, creeping up behind them.

Rafa spun around, red-faced, then lit up when he saw it was me. I wanted to bottle up that look, that feeling, and savor it forever. I hoped he always looked at me like that.

"Vera, I didn't expect to see you tonight. This is Marta. She's new."

"Mucho gusto, Marta. I promise he gets better." I winked at her, and she smiled bashfully. Rafa rolled his eyes at me.

"Will you ever stop undermining me?"

I shrugged. "Only when you stop acting like a prima donna chef."

He glared at me playfully, then leaned down to kiss me. "Come. There is something I want you to taste." He turned back to poor Marta. "I—*lo siento*. You're doing great."

He took my hand and pulled me over to a staging area with a collection of plated tapas-sized dishes.

He spooned up a small slice of pastry and slipped it to me. A burst of tart, sweet, and buttery erupted in my mouth. I groaned with pleasure.

He leaned into my ear with a raspy whisper. "I love when you make that sound."

With a bashful smile, I swallowed. "What heavenly nectar of the Gods was that?"

He chuckled. "Cherry Gâteau Basque. Basically, it's a cherry pie. Inspired by our weekend up to the Basque country. I added a little brandy to the cherry preserves. In honor of... our first night. What do you think?"

"Who knew you were such a romantic?"

He shrugged. "I am Spanish, after all."

"It's perfect. I love it. And I expect you to stock our freezer full of it."

I might have given Santos California a platform, but it was Rafa's spirit of innovation and reverence for tradition that had made the restaurant the talk of the town, drawing in both locals and tourists alike.

"Chef! You're needed!" a voice called from the kitchen cockpit.

Rafa gave me an apologetic look. "See you at home?"

I nodded. "I'll be waiting. Don't forget the cherry pie."

Epilogue

I shifted on my seat on the small stage, subtly smoothing down my navy floral patterned dress and tucking an errant piece of hair behind my ear. I took a sip of the water next to me.

"So, Vera, tell us all about your new website, *Tasting the World*," Elodie Brandywine, the host of the local English language television station in Barcelona started with a bright smile. She was British and svelte with huge, white, bright teeth that would rival any American actress.

"First, let me just thank you so much for having me on today. Thank you for allowing me to share my story and my business with your viewers," I said.

"We just absolutely love what you're doing. So tell us all about it. How did you get started?"

"Well, to put it simply, I recently launched my own website dedicated to my favorite subject. Food."

Elodie chuckled softly. "And you have a history of being a food critic, right? That's how you got your start?"

I nodded. "Yes, I was a food critic in New York for many

years. I worked for *Travel Luxe & Leisure*—which is an online magazine."

"I think we all know it. It's the bible for those loving *luxe* travel."

I smiled. "It's a great publication. And happy happenstance, an assignment brought me here to Barcelona. And I fell in love. In more ways than one."

"But your site now, it's about more than just reviewing restaurants, isn't it?"

I cleared my throat and sat up straighter. "Yes. That's what I love about it. I loved critiquing food and giving you my opinion, don't get me wrong. It was a lot of fun and I got to eat at some world-class restaurants. But what I found myself really drawn to, was the stories behind the food. The stories of the chefs and the restaurant's history. The inspiration. The innovation and how foods both define and defy cultural norms. Or how it protects them. What I really wanted was more than what one blog post or magazine review could really offer. And that's how my website was born."

Elodie beamed, flashing her audience a blinding smile before turning back to me.

"So let me ask you the elephant in the room question. You have been romantically linked to hotshot chef, Rafa Santos, the brainchild behind the wildly popular Santos California restaurant. Is that right?"

I waited a bit before answering, knowing this question would be coming. Rafa's local celebrity had indeed skyrocketed, and he was all anyone was talking about. His shirtless Instagrams still helped. And sure, it's not like we were Hollywood A-Listers, but people who cared about the food scene did want a little peak behind the curtain.

"Yes, I'm afraid the rumors are true. We met last year while I was here on assignment, and well, you could say we hit it off."

"And is the real reason you stayed here in Barcelona, abdicating your glamorous Manhattan life?"

I laughed at her over-the-top melodrama. I bobbed my head. "It might have been a deciding factor."

"And does that create any biased opinions on the features that you do? I mean, when you're linked to a very prominent chef, I imagine it shapes the kinds of food and chefs and restaurants you talk about," Elodie asked.

"That's a very fair question, and I will say that I started out as a journalist. And because of that, I hold my integrity on the matter close to heart. I always took my ability to have an objective, unbiased opinion very seriously. And I still do. But that's sort of the glory of what I'm doing now. I can tell people's stories and it doesn't mean they are competition. I don't believe that one restaurant's success takes away from another's. I honestly think there are more than enough hungry bellies in Barcelona for everyone."

Elodie beamed into the camera.

"That's wonderful. Thank you, Vera. Well, everyone, thanks for joining me with Vera Stone, the brainchild and founder of Tasting the World.com. World-class food critic, and known associate of sexy celebrity chef, Rafa Santos. Next week we're going to be talking about how a local fisherman is doing his part for endangered tuna."

"They give me way too much credit," Rafa said as we sipped some Spanish cava in the aftermath of my interview.

"I think you don't give yourself enough credit. Have you seen the reservation book? You can't even get into Santos California right now. Lorna is literally turning down bribes."

"Why is she turning them down?" Rafa said playfully.

I rolled my eyes. "I think you need to lean into your

moment. Hey, the golden light might not last forever, so just enjoy it. You've built something incredible, and people love you. Who knows, the food channel might come knocking any day."

He leaned in and kissed my cheek. "I think people love you too. I heard the data on your website is out of control. And not just because your boyfriend is a celebrity chef."

I raised my eyebrows. "Boyfriend? Are we teenagers?"

He shrugged. "Sometimes I feel like one. Especially around you." He squeezed my side. "What would you prefer to call me?"

I tilted my head. "I don't know. Paramour, illicit lover. Has a nicer ring to it."

He nodded thoughtfully. "All those things sound very good indeed. I have a better idea, though. ¿Qué pasa *Esposa*?"

I furrowed my brow for a moment before his words clicked.

"Rafa," I started. A thousand images flashed before me. His apartment off Las Ramblas. Promenades on sultry Spanish nights. Growing the restaurant, my website. Building a life on the Iberian Peninsula.

He reached into his pocket and pulled out a small wooden box with tiny carvings. With a shaking hand, I opened it and stared down at a shiny platinum ring with a sparkling sapphire as blue as the Med.

"Marry me, amor."

I extended my hand, and he slipped the ring on my finger. I threw myself at him, lips first. He did not have to ask twice.

***

Ever dreamed of a real European Christmas Market? Experience the magic of Old-World Christmas in *A Prague Noel!*

Thank you!

Thank you so much for spending the last few hours in my world. It means so much to me that you trusted me with your time and imagination. You are the reason I do what I do!

If you enjoyed *Tasting Barcelona*, please tell your friends so they can fall in love with Vera, Rafa and Barcelona too!

About June

June Patrick writes cozy, escapist romance set in swoony far away places. She is obsessed with all things European and dreams of moving to the Riviera where she can run around all day like Grace Kelly.

A Northern California native, she now moves around the country like a nomad with her real-life hero of a husband and their toddler daughter. They currently call Colorado home, where they live in a giant country house and begrudgingly battle snow.

Let's connect! Find me on Instagram and TikTok at @junepatrickauthor and follow me on Amazon.

Also by June Patrick

Italian Rendezvous

Monte Carlo Mistake

Tasting Barcelona

A Prague Noel

She also writes thrillers under Amanda Traylor.

Printed in Great Britain
by Amazon

36772388R00182